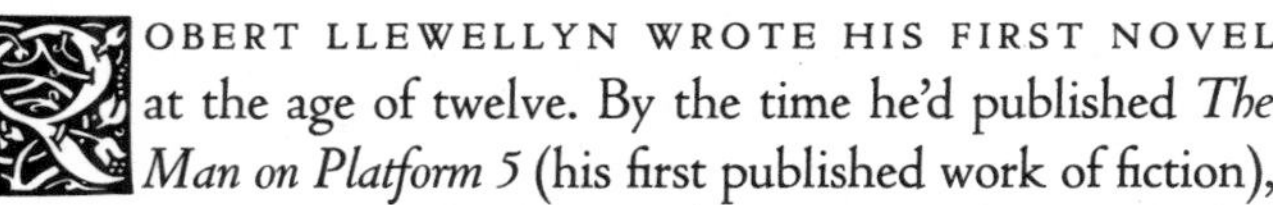

ROBERT LLEWELLYN WROTE HIS FIRST NOVEL at the age of twelve. By the time he'd published *The Man on Platform 5* (his first published work of fiction), thirty years had passed. In the intervening period he'd worked as an artist's model, a bespoke shoemaker, a tree surgeon, a screenwriter, a comedian, actor and TV presenter.

He has appeared regularly on British television since 1987 in various guises including under quite absurd amounts of rubber in *Red Dwarf*; covered in grease and dust in *Scrapheap Challenge*; in terrifying machines on *How Do They Do It?* and sitting in a car chatting in *Carpool*.

Robert Llewellyn writes under a rack of solar panels in Gloucestershire; *News from the Clouds* is the final book in a trilogy. The other titles are *News from Gardenia* and *News from the Squares*.

News from the Clouds

Also by Robert Llewellyn

FICTION

News from the Squares

News from Gardenia

The Man on Platform 5

Punchbag

Sudden Wealth

Brother Nature

NON-FICTION

The Man in the Rubber Mask

Thin He Was and Filthy-haired: Memoirs of a Bad Boy

Therapy and How to Avoid It *(with Nigel Planer)*

The Reconstructed Heart: How to Spot the Difference Between a Normal Man and One Who Does the Housework, is Great in Bed and Doesn't Get All Iffy When You Mention Words Like Love and Commitment

Behind the Scenes at Scrapheap Challenge

Sold Out! How I Survived a Year of Not Shopping

News from the Clouds

Robert Llewellyn

unbound

This edition first published in 2015

Unbound
4–7 Manchester Street Marylebone London W1U 2AE
www.unbound.co.uk

Typeset by Bracketpress
Art direction by Mecob

A CIP record for this book is available from the British Library

ISBN 978-1-7835-20572 (trade hbk)
ISBN 978-1-78352-150-0 (ebook)
ISBN 978-1-7835-20589 (limited edition)

Printed in England by Clays Ltd,
Bungay, Suffolk

This book is dedicated to all the people whose names appear at the back of the book, for one very simple reason, if they hadn't supported the book, it wouldn't exist.

Preface

Global climate change is the greatest threat the United States faces – more dangerous than terrorism, Chinese hackers and North Korean nuclear missiles. Upheaval from increased temperatures, rising seas and radical destabilisation is probably the most likely thing that is going to happen … that will cripple the security environment, probably more likely than the other scenarios we all often talk about.

Admiral Samuel J. Locklear III,
Commander of the United States Pacific Command, 2007

Extreme weather events (floods, droughts, heat waves) will increasingly disrupt food and energy markets, exacerbating state weakness, forcing human migrations, and triggering riots, civil disobedience, and vandalism.

James Clapper,
US Director of National Intelligence, 2010

The first decade of the 21st century saw 3,496 natural disasters from floods, storms, droughts and heat waves. That was nearly five times as many disasters as the 743 catastrophes reported during the 1970s.

World Meteorological Organization, 2014

WHEN CONFRONTED WITH STATEMENTS SUCH as these, the easiest thing to do is get depressed and give up, hide in our safe little world for as long as we can and try not to think about what is really happening to the planet we live on.

Like many fairly well informed people I try to do this every day, because the torrent of anxiety-inducing reports from every corner of the globe could easily drive you to despair.

In the same way, the barking but well-funded loons who trumpet their denials that the way we are treating the small planet we inhabit will make no difference are light relief. I always cheer up when I hear them prattle on.

It's so much easier to deny the 'doom merchants', but if history has taught us anything, every now and then, especially if their predictions are backed by enormous amounts of data collected over decades, it might be worth giving them a listen.

An extraordinary American called Bill McKibben has been hammering on about the issues the entire human race faces since 1989, when he wrote a book called *The End of Nature*.

The now much-maligned term 'global warming' was coined around the time this book was published.

McKibben is the founder of 350.org, named after the number of parts per million (ppm) of carbon in the atmosphere that is considered safe for the continuation of civilised life on Earth.

To explain in simple terms even I can understand, scientists from all over the world, from all manner of organisations, universities, research laboratories and NASA have agreed that if we go above 350 ppm we are going to face serious trouble.

At the time of writing, mid-2014, the latest figure gathered at Mauna Loa Observatory in Hawaii is 401.36 ppm.

I just want to underline where this data comes from – not downtown Los Angeles or London, not the smog-choked streets of Beijing or Mumbai, but from the top of a mountain on an island in the middle of the Pacific Ocean.

Another aspect of human activity making a huge difference to our planet is the use of nitrogen fertilisers. It's what has saved us from mass starvation in the last 100 years, but there is a bit of a downside.

Less than half of the nitrogen that we gleefully sprinkle on fields gets used by the crops; the rest is washed away into streams and rivers and eventually into the sea. As it breaks down it not only kills fish by the shipload, it also releases gasses with a 300 times greater climate changing impact than CO_2.

Bit of a downer.

In the past I have made jokes about global warming along with most of the world's population. Living in a cool, moist island off the coast of Europe, it's a common thing to hear a red-faced yeoman leaning on a bar in a country pub saying, 'A bit of jolly old global warming wouldn't go amiss around here.'

It was only the slow realisation that the results of warming up the global atmosphere would lead to all manner of 'climate change' – again a term much denigrated by a few bitter and increasingly downright evil detractors – that I actually started to worry for my children.

As I have tried to suggest in the previous two books, *News from Gardenia* and *News from the Squares*, the notion of long-term planning is beyond the grasp of most of the world's authorities and particularly our most powerful political elites: the corporations.

What we are facing isn't one sudden storm, one violent change to our world, but a slowly increasing build-up of damaging and increasingly dangerous events. Extreme weather, not a pleasant term no matter how you view it, seems to be the prevailing prediction.

No one knows what is going to happen. I would be the first out on the streets cheering if the whole concept of climate change was proven utterly incorrect; if all the scientists who've been warning about it for donkey's years came out of their research labs and shrugged in embarrassment saying, 'Sorry folks, got the maths a bit cock-eyed, everything is fine, the climate is 100 per cent stable for the next four million years, carry on as you were.'

So *News from the Clouds* could be seen as going against my initial intention with these books which was to try and imagine future worlds where things are better, not worse.

There is no doubt that there are apocalyptic elements in *News from the Clouds* and this may indeed be as a result of the reports, books, studies I've read and people I have spoken with in the last three years. However, I would defend this by suggesting that the power of the human spirit, collectively, to overcome adversity is very much to the fore in the story.

Again and again we have witnessed the collapse of civilisations through history, but not the end of the human race. Something new, sometimes something better, grows from the rubble, and the lessons we can learn from looking at that rubble are invaluable.

I'd put my money on the sun and solar energy. What a source of power! I hope we don't have to wait until oil and coal run out before we tackle that.

Thomas Edison (1847–1931)

A good science fiction story should be able to predict not the automobile but the traffic jam.

Frederik Pohl (1919–2013)

It must be considered that there is nothing more difficult to carry out nor more doubtful of success nor more dangerous to handle that to initiate a new order of things; for the reformer has enemies in all those who profit by the old order and only lukewarm defenders in all those who would profit from the new order; this lukewarmness arising partly from the incredulity of mankind who does not truly believe in anything new until they actually have experience of it.

Niccolò Machiavelli (1469–1527)

You want a future where you're expecting things to get better, not a future where you're expecting things to get worse.

Elon Musk (1971– present)

1

HY I WAS SURPRISED TO SEE A LOAD OF white doughnuts floating around the Yuneec as I came out of the cloud is easy to understand.

Why I wasn't alarmed that I might run into them or be destroyed by them is, on reflection, harder to grasp. I was flying along at a speed the Yuneec had never previously achieved. I remember glancing down at the data screen: 482 kilometres an hour.

Up until the moment the crowd of doughnuts appeared in the clear blue sky I could see nothing, I was totally blind; the cloud was a thick mass of grey nothingness and I had no idea where I was or what was happening.

It stopped as suddenly as it started. I just burst out into bright sunlight surrounded by a load of floating white doughnuts that scattered and formed a little ring around the Yuneec. Maybe a more accurate description of them would be as floating padded toilet seat covers you sometimes see in a disabled loo as I suspected they were much larger than actual doughnuts, maybe even a couple of metres across.

The sun was low and in front of me, just as it had been in London, but I didn't need to blink and rub my eyes to know this was somewhere very different.

The sky above me was beautifully clear, the deep blue of an early autumn morning, in the distance a few low cumulonimbus clouds, but other than the doughnuts, nothing.

I did burst into tears. I'm not proud, but it did happen and it happened suddenly. I suppose the overriding motivation was that it was immediately bloody obvious I wasn't flying over Didcot in 2011. I was somewhere else, somewhere completely new and weird and exhausting. However confused I was at that moment, however tired and wired, I was fairly confident that flying doughnuts had not been around in 2011 or I think I might have read about them on TechCrunch.

I'll tell you now, it's quite hard to fly a plane you're not used to when you're sobbing, but although I'm sure I wobbled a bit, I managed not to lose it completely and dive the damn Yuneec into the ground to get the whole nightmare over with, though it crossed my mind more than once. I had to accept I was perpetually trapped in a bizarre vortex of peculiar worlds, none of which felt like home. I don't know if I gave up at that point, I don't know if I just shrugged off the ache for home and accepted I was doomed to be stuck in bonkers realities 200 years in the future, but whatever it was, I didn't kill myself.

The Yuneec flew true, straight and at great speed yet it felt like I was gliding along an invisible silk ribbon.

The doughnuts travelled alongside me and for some odd reason I found this mildly reassuring – there is something completely un-alarming about a flock of floating white doughnuts. It is hard to explain why, as it's not something anyone from 2011 is likely to have witnessed. It was their shape and manner that reassured me, they were utterly non-threatening, it was as if they were expecting me.

The experience of flying through a small gathering of these things was akin to being met at an airport by friendly people you've never met before but who know who you are. Like a smiling Japanese woman holding a small sign with a friendly kitten illustration at the top and your name written on it at Tokyo Airport. This happened to me once in 2009 and it was very reassuring. It was my first visit to Japan and I was confused about where I should go until I saw this sign.

The white doughnuts weren't carrying signs with 'Mr Gavin Meckler' written on them but they may as well have been. I was smiling as I looked out at them, for some reason they made me want to chuckle.

This mood turned to alarm as I felt something make contact with the Yuneec that was nothing to do with wind turbulence or changes in air pressure. Whatever had made contact felt solid and mechanical.

I peered out of the side window with what I can genuinely describe as mild panic. I couldn't see anything. The second event, which took place mere moments after the first, was the complete cessation of my control over the plane.

I could sense it instantly. For reasons I had no hope of understanding, the joystick was not connected to any of the plane's control surfaces. I wasn't flying the Yuneec, someone else, or as I suspected, *something* else, was.

The plane didn't fall out of the sky like a rock, explode in a ball of flame or start behaving erratically. It continued in the same direction at the same speed and I continued to be surrounded by a load of flying white doughnuts.

After a while, I could sense that we were banking slightly to the left, and it was about this time that I realised the prop was reducing speed and the new electric motor Pete had fixed into the nose cone was slowly spinning down, yet I couldn't sense a drop in speed.

All the data readouts on the smooth screen in front of me were blanks, there was nothing going on, it looked the same as when the plane was switched off.

Was I completely freaked out? To quote a wonderfully amusing Australian colleague I'd worked with in an open cast coal pit in Northern Queensland in 2010, 'How about, yeah!'

I suppose to be fair I was less terrified than I would have been had this happened when I emerged from the cloud over Gardenia. My experiences over the previous months had hardened me to technological, environmental and psychological events over which I had no control.

As the Yuneec slowly banked to the left, something came into view that is once again very difficult to describe. Yes, by this time I'd seen filaments of ridiculously strong thread reaching from the planet's surface into deep space, I'd seen massive ships that moved effortlessly across the top of waves with no moving parts.

Now all I was seeing was a cloud.

Anyone can describe a cloud: it's a white fluffy thing that floats in the sky or a grey low thing sitting above your head for months on end. If like me you grew up in the UK, clouds are very familiar and all I was looking at was a cloud.

The thing that set it apart from its fluffy brethren was primarily the height it was floating along at – it was much lower than I would expect. This cloud was well below me but also on closer inspection its shape and size were unusual.

This was a very big cloud: I would estimate several kilometres long, more than one wide, fairly flat and generally white. That's where its cloud-like appearance ended.

I continued to glide toward this extraordinary vision. I say glide as now all I could hear was the rush of wind over the Yuneec. The motor had stopped and the soft propeller blades were stuck to the nose cone like damp dishcloths.

As I got closer, the inconceivable became concrete. I don't mean I was looking at a cloud made of concrete, I mean I was seeing a human-made construction and not a large formation of water vapour. The floating structure my eyes and brain were struggling with was something more solid and I could clearly see human figures standing among the billowing white shapes. Had I a scintilla of religious sensitivity about me I might have presumed I was seeing angels, but as I got much closer I couldn't spot any wings. I was seeing people, a crowd of people who appeared to be staring up at me.

The cloud did appear mostly white but as I could see more and more detail there was evidently a great many colourful constructions at the centre of this mind-boggling apparition. I could not work out what sort of constructions these were. They were sort of tent-like, vaguely balloon-like, but not quite.

I felt the Yuneec slow down, not violently, more akin to the experience I was familiar with when I throttled back and applied the air brakes when coming into land. The distressing moment came when I could sense no forward movement at all. It seemed I was static in space, hovering above an inhabited cloud that was in turn floating above the ground. By that point I was directly above the crowd of people I had spotted as I approached, and all I could see was the bulbous tops of some bizarre structures surrounding me.

After a few moments of complete stillness I felt the plane descend. I had no control over any of this. As I gently sank down the crowd came into view; I felt utterly helpless. I had been flying free and under my own control, I emerged from the cloud into clear sky, but somehow all control had been taken away from me. Feeling like a fly trapped in a spider's web was one possible analogy; it was creepy.

The Yuneec eventually came to a gentle and slightly bouncy halt, and as I glanced about me I noticed the white doughnuts that had been escorting me had disappeared.

I was stationary, resting on a bouncy cloud surrounded by several hundred people of various races and ages. They didn't look angry or dangerous; in fact they looked quite friendly. Some of them even made little waving gestures.

Two people broke ranks and walked up to the plane: an old man and woman. They were moving toward me in a very peculiar way. I suppose it was a little as if they were walking across a giant mattress.

They both had their palms held up indicating, I hoped, that they meant me no harm. It did cross my mind that they might have been sporting some kind of fearsome body-disintegrating weapon resembling, to the uninitiated, an upheld human palm, but they were smiling.

I opened the cockpit door slowly. I didn't want to make sudden movements that could be misinterpreted so it seemed like the right thing to do.

6 The woman, who was not as tall as the people of London, stood next to the Yuneec's wing and spoke slowly: 'Hallo, Gavin, *es ist eine freude sie zu treffen, willkommen in der anthropocene.*'

2

I WAS KEPT UPRIGHT BY THE TWO OLD German people as I wobbled unsteadily on a white inflatable courtyard. A quilted courtyard made of a cream-coloured material that was definitely inflated in some way. A massive bouncy castle, that was really the only reference point I had. I needed to be held up because when I had climbed out of the Yuneec I had fallen over. It was embarrassing, I had just fallen over like a drunk bloke outside a pub and there were hundreds of people silently watching me.

The two old Germans helped me to my feet with ease and helped me to find my balance. I thanked them, I almost said '*danke schön*' but it came out a bit muffled. I don't speak German but I knew that meant 'thank you'.

By this time in my adventures I had given up all notions of being able to judge people's ages, but the two German people were clearly a lot older than me, let's leave it at that. They both seemed quite agile and strong and weren't gripping my arms as if I was under arrest, they were merely steadying me.

'You will feel much better if you lie down,' said the woman. She had a strong German accent but had somehow already surmised that I spoke English.

I didn't know her name – what I mean is, her name wasn't immediately apparent to me – she was just a German woman who was keeping me upright. I stared in their faces waiting to understand where I was, who they were and where they had come from. Nothing.

I realised with some dismay that even during my short stay in the Squares of London I had become completely used to the ubiquity of the kidonge, the teeny little communication device embedded in the bone marrow of my shinbone. This woman knew my name yet I had no idea of hers. I felt deaf; it was as if a perfectly natural sense had stopped working.

'I am Gertrude,' said the woman. I would guess she was about 60 years old but it was annoying not to know for certain.

'I, um, I don't know where I am.'

'Cloud nine,' said the man beside her. It sounded like 'clout nine' as this man also had a thick German accent. 'Welcome, Gavin, I am Gustav.'

I'd guess this fellow was roughly the same age as the woman. I'd already managed to forget her name which sent me into a right old tizz.

'How do you do, Gustav? Gustav,' I said, shaking his hand and repeating his name in an attempt to memorise it. 'Gustav,' I repeated for good measure.

'And I am Gertrude,' said the woman with a kindly smile.

'Gertrude, right,' I said. 'Hello, Gertrude, Gustav, Gertrude and Gavin, all our names start with a G.'

I smiled at them, I hoped this association would help me remember their names but quickly realised I was giving the impression of being a total nutter.

'I'm Gavin,' I said again. I couldn't help myself.

'Yes, we know who you are,' said Gertrude. 'I hope the life drone did not shock you, we wanted to make sure you were safe.'

'What, the white doughnut things?'

The two people glanced at each other. Gustav held my arm, which was surprisingly reassuring, as I really didn't feel all that stable on my feet.

He pointed downwards behind me. 'That is the life drone,' he said. I turned and looked in the direction he was indicating and saw a large white thing, like a giant mattress, that was slowly shrinking beneath the Yuneec.

'Is that what carried me here?' I asked.

Gertrude nodded and took my other arm. 'It might be best

if you lay down for a while, would you like to come with us?'

I didn't say anything, I just did as I was told. I'd become used to it: emerge from a cloud and have your head done in. By this time it was all part of a day's work for me.

So two people in their sixties guided me across the spongy white quilted courtyard toward what could have been a kind of tent, except it wasn't the shape of any kind of tent I'd ever seen before. It was bulbous and curved and the light reflecting off it was dazzling. In fact I started to wish I had the face-hugging dark glasses that Nkoyo had loaned me in Rio. This whole place was very reflective and I had to half squint my eyes.

As I saw more of it, the thing this weird cloud reminded me of was an annoying 'art installation' that Beth had insisted on going to see in the courtyard of Somerset House back in 2006.

At the time I'd thought the whole thing a huge waste of energy, planning and resources, which Beth said was typical of my narrow worldview.

The 2006 installation was a great big fabric structure you could go inside and experience different colours. It was so mundane and predictable but everyone else inside was walking around as if they were under the influence of psychotropic drugs. 'Oooh, wow, look at the colours.'

Tragic.

But the bulbous structure I was approaching was enormous, more like the size of Somerset House in its entirety and for me at that moment utterly incomprehensible.

The gathering of people that had come to see the Yuneec be landed – after all I certainly didn't land it – stood either side of me and smiled, some even nodding graciously as I passed. It felt like they had come to see some kind of circus freak, and the stares I received seemed to be ones of pity. That flat smile a parent can give you when you've flunked an exam. 'Oh, never mind, darling, at least you tried.'

Once inside the structure the dazzling light was reduced but it was still very bright; clearly what constituted walls in this extraordinary place were semi-porous to sunlight. The scale of the interior was in many ways more impressive than the exterior.

First impressions were of a creamy white mall, a kind of busy emporium with many more people inside. This place was crowded and once again the mixture of ages and races was comprehensive.

'Blimey,' I said, 'what the hell is going on? Where am I?'

Once again I felt unsafe, trapped. I could barely walk, the ground was spongy, I couldn't have made a run for it, it would have been like trying to run across a pile of soft duvets on top of a giant trampoline.

'We will try and explain everything when we get to the sanctuary,' said Gertrude. 'Please don't be alarmed, you are very safe and no one wishes you harm.'

I liked her voice, she was softly spoken and very reassuring so I tried to get control of my anxiety.

We passed through a circular entrance into some kind of inner courtyard. I glanced up and could see blue sky above me. From here we turned through another circular entrance and into a smaller space, a circular room with a kind of raised bench all around the walls. On one side a window, or to describe it a little more accurately maybe it was more a giant porthole or a circular window as you might find in a 1970s 'modern' library building. Through it I could see the cloudscape around us. That is to say they looked like clouds but I was prepared to discover they were constructions similar to the one I was on.

'Rest here,' said Gertrude. They both helped me onto the long bench directly opposite the window and I slowly lay back. I didn't feel too sure I wanted to lie flat but I immediately discovered I wasn't going to. My bottom sank into the bench that at a glance had looked quite solid. My back and head were then supported as my bottom sank, my feet likewise were lifted a little and I became engulfed in surprising comfort.

'Thank you,' I said as I felt my body relax. A massive wave of tiredness overtook me. In the short silence that followed I rushed through a kind of flashback of events that had brought me to this point. The museum, Pete and the team that launched me from the roof, the last glimpse of Nkoyo outside the Institute, flying into the cloud, the violent lurches I felt when I was in the grey dead zone and the sudden burst into bright sunlight and the friendly white doughnuts.

A woman entered the space, she was dressed head to foot in a white body suit. Her gait was unusual: she lifted her long legs slightly more than you would if you were walking on solid ground. She glanced at me and smiled. I smiled back, I couldn't help registering that she was attractive.

'This is Ebrikke,' said Gertrude. 'She is a specialist.'

'Oh, right. A specialist what?' I asked. Ebrikke was staring at me without embarrassment and I did notice her very blue eyes were a little bit odd.

'She will make sure you are comfortable,' said Gertrude.

So I wasn't going to find out what kind of specialist this woman was and I suddenly felt like a dental patient who was being reassured before some major root canal work.

The young woman – once again I had immediately forgotten her name – walked to the far side of the circular space and withdrew a tube, which I hadn't previously noticed, from the wall. It was a white tube on a white wall so I think I could have been forgiven for not spotting it. She seemed to squeeze the end with one hand while holding a small white bag with the other.

The white bag filled. It looked like a mini hot-water bottle. She then did the same peculiar walk toward me and held out the bag.

'Please drink this,' said the young woman.

'Thanks,' I said. The bag had a tube at one end and I put it in my mouth and sucked. It seemed to be cold water and it was just what I needed. 'I'm sorry, I've already forgotten your name,' I said quickly as she was turning away from me.

'Ebrikke, but people call me Bree,' she said sweetly as if she were introducing herself to a toddler.

'Thanks, Bree,' I said.

Bree reached up above me and put her hand on what I took to be a large white cushion attached to the ceiling above me. It glowed a pale green colour and I felt my body tingle slightly. It wasn't unpleasant and I wondered for a moment if what I was feeling was a rather base animal attraction to the young woman whose delightful torso was stretched above me. The light in the white cushion faded and Bree looked down at me and smiled.

She then very gently placed her long forefingers on my temples and closed her eyes. I did feel something at that point, nothing distressing or painful, but something happened. It was a vaguely similar experience to the one I felt when I paid for something in the Squares of London; a kind of physiological wave that ran through my entire body.

When she removed her delicate fingers I felt more relaxed but very aware of what was going on around me. I stared at Bree's almost too beautiful face and tried to understand what the hell was going on.

'Very interesting,' she said after a rather awkward silence. That left me none the wiser. Bree stood up. 'Everything is as expected,' she said with a glance at Gustav and Gertrude. 'Mister Meckler represents no danger. He will now be very tired and should be allowed to rest. I will return to three.'

Gertrude and Gustav nodded and clasped their hands together awkwardly. 'Just so,' said Gustav.

I tried not to turn and look as Bree left the circular room.

'So, Gavin,' said Gustav, who had been watching her leave. 'I am very glad we got to you in time. It's been a bit of a race to get here first.'

'A race?'

'Don't concern yourself with it,' said Gertrude, patting my

arm. She turned to Gustav and shook her head. 'He doesn't need to know details just now.'

'What details?' I asked. This was beginning to sound a bit worrying.

'As Ebrikke just stated, we have anticipated that you will be very tired,' said Gustav. 'I just want to say that you should relax, you can take your time and allow yourself to rest. The stress of coming through the cloud was no doubt an intense exercise and there is no need for you to be anxious. You are very safe and nothing untoward is going to happen. Relax and we will talk later.'

'Am I on a cloud?' I asked.

'Cloud Nine, correct,' said Gustav, and I noticed Gertrude touch his arm again.

'Let's not stress him with confusing information now, he needs to rest.'

'I'm fine,' I said. 'I don't want to be any trouble.'

'You are not trouble,' said Gustav, 'we are very delighted you could join us. Sleep. When you wake we will talk.'

The weird thing was, when I initially arrived on Cloud Nine I didn't feel in the least sleepy, far from it. I was jagged, I was pumped, my brain was running at full pelt, struggling to take in the extraordinary place I'd once again ended up in.

As I lay back on that squashy yet firm bench I was fully alert but I must have fallen asleep at a quite astonishing – and on later reflection possibly narcotic-induced – speed.

3

AKING UP IN GARDENIA WAS, LOOKING BACK on it, no big deal. On that occasion I awoke in an actual bed in an actual room made of stone and wood and some kind of carbon nano-fibre insulation. But the room had walls, a floor, a delightfully carved wooden ceiling, doors, windows and most importantly it was on the ground.

Waking up in the Institute in London was, admittedly, a bit weird but I was still in a room with straight walls in a building in a city. A city that was also connected to the ground.

Waking up on Cloud Nine was a bit more of a challenge.

I was ensconced in a white supportive bench made of an unknown but possibly intelligent material that was in turn encased in a circular, semi-spherical white room with a round window looking out on to totally static clouds. When I say static, they weren't moving across my limited field of vision, I stared for a long time and they didn't seem to budge a millimetre. It was like looking at a well-lit high-definition still image of clouds.

I was alone in this chillingly calm space. I didn't suddenly jump up and run around in a panic, I stayed still simply because I didn't know what to do. I mentally retraced my steps as I tried to get a grip on the situation I found myself in.

Once again the forlorn hope of flying out into the sky above Didcot Power Station in 2011 fell away as this time there was no moment of doubt as to where or indeed when I was.

Coming out of the cloud and seeing blue sky and clouds I could, I reflected, have wondered for a moment if I was over Didcot once again; however, the presence of a couple of dozen white doughnuts flying alongside me soon put paid to that delusion.

I had then been taken over by some sort of flying duvet cover and deposited on an enormous cloud that was floating a few hundred feet above the ground. I had a vague memory of seeing the ground below as we approached the cloud. It appeared to be brown and rocky, not green and lush or even urban and complex. It looked like an expanse of scrubby moorland.

I was comfortable on the bench so I had no great urge to move. I held my breath and stayed motionless in the peculiar white room and concentrated on listening to the sounds around me. I could just hear what I took to be people talking but I couldn't make out anything they were saying. I started to wonder why I could hear no wind noise, no engine noise, no vibration or mechanical sound of any kind. The thing I was in was up in the air and yet it was eerily silent. I could just make out tiny movements, nothing violent, just faint alterations in the supporting pressure on my back.

I slowly moved my body to try and get up. Once again I had no idea how long I'd slept and the light coming through the window was no help, it looked exactly the same as when I'd fallen asleep.

As I shifted my body weight the bench I was lying on reformed itself into a slightly firmer platform supporting my bum. I cannot describe how weird this felt, it was almost as if I was lying on something living; the response was calm but immediate.

I swung my feet onto the odd quilted-looking floor and stood up. I then sat down again rather rapidly because I really couldn't get my balance. The floor was squashy; it gave way under my heels and threw me backwards.

I dropped down on all fours and using hands and knees made my way over to the circular window. It really was like a very big porthole in a ship. There was some kind of transparent material in it to keep the elements out of the room but it wasn't glass. As I touched it I could sense it flexing under the pressure but it wasn't some thin, flimsy material. I couldn't have poked my finger through it, let's put it that way, it had a density and thickness to the touch although I could see through it without distortion.

I managed to get into a standing position by leaning on the slightly flexible side of the room to steady myself. With my hands and feet spread out I could stay relatively stable.

What I saw out of the window was a bit of a shock, in fact two very distinct shocks.

First, the thing I was in was incredibly high up, much higher than when I'd landed on it, and second the view below showed we were above an ocean.

Whatever I was in was above water, and not only that, we seemed to be moving. I could tell by watching the lower clouds pass over the blue expanse of water. Either they were blowing in the other direction or we were moving. It was a very similar view to the one you'd see out of the window of a passenger jet at 35,000 feet. This could only mean one thing: the room I was in was pressurised. It had to be or I'd already have suffocated and frozen to death.

I stared down for a long time trying to make sense of what I was seeing. I was fairly certain when I came out of the cloud and saw the flying doughnuts I had been above land. In both my previous jumps through the cloud I'd ended up in the same place. Well, at the same map coordinates, although it looked very different each time. As far as I could understand, when I came out of the cloud I was still in the vicinity of where the Didcot Power Station had once stood.

However, this time I'd flown through the cloud that was above the Squares of London, and it seemed I had somehow come out above the sea. Had the entire world flooded? Was this cloud really more like a floating Noah's Ark? Would I discover two of every kind of animal stashed in the hold?

I then remembered a graphic representation I had pinned up in my office back in Kingham, which showed the Earth with all the water that exists on the planet gathered into two giant blobs resting above California. The saltwater blob was bigger but still much smaller than you might have guessed; the freshwater blob was terrifyingly teeny. I knew that no matter how much ice melted, how much rain fell, there was just not enough water on the planet for Kevin Costner's second-worst film to have been remotely possible.

So, the question arose in my mind: if I had flown into the cloud over London and flown out of the cloud over the sea, was it possible to fly through space as well as time? A question like that made me feel mildly annoyed, the whole situation was barking mad so why worry about minor details like travelling through space as well as time?

'Ah, you have woken up,' said a voice behind me.

I slid down the wall and sat below the window in order not to fall over as I turned to face the person speaking.

It was the old man who'd greeted me by the plane. I couldn't recall his name, which left me feeling even more annoyed. Why couldn't I remember his name? I felt sure I was better at such basic data storage before the wretched kidonge had wormed its way into my bone marrow.

'Yes, sorry, I'm a bit confused. I'm really sorry, I can't remember your . . . '

'I am Gustav,' he said kindly. 'Don't worry, you are bound to be a bit disorientated. I am, Gustav, and you are Gavin Meckler.'

'I know who I am Gustav,' I said, while repeating his name in my head over and over to try and lodge it in there somehow. 'How do you know who I am? Have you got a different sort of kidonge here?'

'I don't know what a kidonge is but I am sure you will tell me in good time.' His soft German accent was reassuring. 'Please try to relax, you appear to be very anxious. I want to reassure you that you are very safe with us. We are currently 10,000 metres above the surface but there is nothing to be alarmed about, the structure you are on has a 100 per cent safety record.'

'That's very good to hear,' I said, very aware that my face was not showing any signs of reassurance. 'But there are so many things I don't understand and one thing is really disconcerting. Gustav, you knew my name. As soon as the Yuneec, my plane, my drone, I don't know what you'd call it, the thing I came in ...'

'The highly modified Yuneec E430,' said Gustav calmly.

'Yes, yes, well, as soon as it was put down here, on this, on Cloud Nine, as soon as I opened my door you seemed to know who I was.'

'Yes, we know who you are.'

'How do you know who I am?'

'Hopefully all will be revealed to you presently.'

'Hopefully?'

'Yes, we are attempting to navigate our way to the requisite docking point but as you may be able to imagine, navigating a vessel such as Cloud Nine is not an easy matter. We go where the weather goes and while we can predict fairly accurately where that will take us, we have learned that when it comes to weather,' he stopped and smiled, then leant forward and put a hand on my shoulder, 'nothing is certain.'

'Okay, well maybe you can explain that,' I said, gesturing out of the window above my head. 'We seem to be above the sea.'

'That is correct.'

'But when I came out of the cloud, when I was surrounded by those round things, I'm fairly confident I was over land, at least I think I was.'

'Again, correct, however, we have moved a considerable distance since you arrived. We are now over the North Sea, just off the western coast of Norway.'

'What?'

'We are travelling with the jet stream, Gavin, at present taking us on a north-easterly path.'

'So this is sort of like a balloon?' I asked.

'No, it is not sort of like a balloon, Gavin, it is a balloon. Cloud Nine is a very large balloon. It is over five kilometres in length and roughly three kilometres wide. We hope that by this time tomorrow we will be in a calm area over Siberia where we will reconnect with the others.'

'The others?'

'The other clouds. We are one of ten clouds presently although another ten are under construction. When the weather allows we connect with the others and form one super cloud, nearly 50 kilometres across.'

'But why?' I asked, staring at this perfectly sane-looking old bloke. 'Why on earth do you float about on clouds?'

'Remember the moment you got out of the Yuneec E430 this morning, when we met you on the rear court?' Gustav asked.

'Yeah, it's not going to be something I can quickly forget.'

'*Gut*, well, did you feel the wind?'

'Wind?'

'Yes, do you remember as we helped you walk across the court, do you remember feeling moving air, was your hair blown about, did you feel the wind on your skin?'

I thought for a moment. 'No,' I said. 'It seemed very still.'

'Indeed, and yet there was a wind blowing, about 150 kilometres an hour at ground level. Nothing unusual, but we were moving with the wind and hence felt nothing.'

As had been the case in Gardenia and London 2211, every single explanation raised a million new questions.

'So that's why you live on this?' I said, gesturing around me.

'Well, to say we live on the cloud would be a little misleading. We stay on it from time to time, a few months of rest every now and then, plus we get to travel and see the rest of the world. Living in the culverts can be a little claustrophobic.'

'The culverts?'

Gustav smiled at me and with a slow and gentle movement put a bony hand on my shoulder. ‘You will soon see. It is very different here from anything you are used to, but please do not be stressed, you will be fine, we will look after you.’

4

I FOLLOWED GUSTAV OUT OF MY PURE WHITE circular chamber and down a tubular white corridor. The closeness of the walls helped me navigate my way along the windowless but bright tube. I was leaning against one side of the structure as Gustav held my arm firmly, he didn't seem to need any support but he did walk in a peculiar way.

'It's really hard to walk,' I said.

'It takes a little getting used to,' he replied. He didn't glance at me but seemed to be looking toward the end of the long tube we were in.

'You will discover if you accept the floor, it will support you, your body will adjust. Don't try to fight the floor, accept it.'

That comment immediately irked me. It made me think of some of the holier-than-thou mystics that Beth used to get so enthusiastic about, weird old Indian blokes who'd written hokey books or inscrutable Japanese Zen teachers who gave talks in Oxford colleges. 'Allow the floor to support you, do not fight the floor, the floor loves you and will support you.'

Annoying.

We wobbled our way through another circular door to one side of the long tube and I was confronted with a truly massive tubular room that was very full of people. Not dozens, more like hundreds. All ages, races and heights were represented but one thing was certain, they were shorter and thinner than anyone I'd met in either Gardenia or London. I suddenly felt very tall and a bit tubby – everyone was bony thin.

There was an air of the refugee about these people. I don't mean refugees like terrified families fleeing a civil war or drought, they didn't look scared but they did look a bit battered by life.

Most were sitting in long rows eating something out of white bowls. Walking up and down the rows were women dressed in a similar way to the woman who'd furnished me with a drink, again I couldn't recall her name. They had some kind of back-pack strapped to them, a long tube appeared over their shoulders and they were clearly delivering some kind of food to the people sitting on the floor.

The bowls everyone was eating out of were an unusual design, they were all identical and they reminded me of a Danish eggcup my mum had brought back from a weekend trip to Copenhagen when I was a kid. A bright blue plastic moulded unit with a saucer built in. I loved that eggcup; I thought it was very modern.

The all-in-one moulded bowl thing I saw people eating from had a built-in sort of dish at the bottom. I suppose it was in case any of the contents of the bowl spilled as the person holding it tried to walk around.

Most of these people ignored me as I wobbled between two rows of seated diners, all the time being supported by Gustav. Some of them looked up at me and smiled as we passed by, I couldn't help but attract a bit of attention as it was obvious I had no idea how to walk on the absurd flexible floor. However, one thing I noticed as I crashed and wobbled my jumpy way through the crowd was that my movements didn't seem to affect them. It wasn't like I was on a giant trampoline and they were bouncing up and down in response to my ungainliness. They seemed unaffected by my incompetence.

'As you can see, it's supper time,' said Gustav as we continued to make our way through the crowds. 'I imagine you might be hungry.'

'Yes, I am a bit peckish,' I said.

The space we had entered was not silent but the sound was vaguely familiar, not like noisy diners in a giant canteen, more like being at an enormous wedding reception in a massive marquee, only this was a giant pressurised tubular tent. The sound in the cloud was quite unique. There was, I suppose, no echo caused by solid walls but there was a kind of hollow ringing in my ears. I couldn't make out anything anyone was saying but there was a lot of chatter going on.

'Who are all these people?' I asked.

'They are just people,' Gustav answered. 'Some of them work on the cloud, some of them are moving to another area, some are resting.'

'Resting.'

'Yes, a lot of people use the clouds to rest, it's very peaceful. Some of them are sick and attending rehab or injury clinics, I can show you one of the hospices later if you wish.'

None of this information really helped me. It was once again a completely overwhelming experience. Although I'd just woken I already felt frazzled. I hadn't really had time to take in what had happened to me again. I realised that as I flew toward the cloud over the Squares of London, I hadn't been hoping, as I had done in Gardenia, to get back to 2011, I was just eager to get into the cloud in time, as I knew I had a limited window when the anomaly would allow me to pass through.

All my attention and focus had been on flying the Yuneec, on marvelling at the power and aerobatic ability of my new plane, not about getting back home.

But now, in the maelstrom of chaotic people, in this vast, pressurised tubular hall floating above the ground I suddenly felt very lonely and miserable. I wanted something normal, something I understood: a small semi-detached house in Kingham, the smell of burnt toast and coffee. I suddenly wanted to walk in through the door and be greeted by Beth, Beth in a good mood of course, Beth when she was happy to see me.

'You can ask anything you wish,' said Gustav, 'but first, let me introduce you to Hector, he is very keen to meet you and he can explain things a lot better than I. He is a native English speaker.'

We turned left into a long tubular corridor and off that into a small circular room.

'This is the crew space,' said Gustav. We entered through a small circular opening and there, sitting at the far end on a large white cushion thing, sat an enormous bearded figure. It was almost a relief to see someone who was a bit portly. I don't mean fat like the massive people of 2011, just a bit more rotund than anyone I'd seen on the cloud.

'Gavin bloody Meckler, good to see you, my man,' said this big bearded bloke whose name, I wasn't surprised to realise, I'd already forgotten.

'Gavin, this is Hector,' said Gustav helpfully. 'Hector is the captain of Cloud Nine.'

'Hector, of course. Hector, how do you do, Hector?' I said holding out my hand. He reached up to shake it but I'd already lost my balance. Gustav clearly wasn't holding my other arm at that moment and I fell to the floor. It wasn't painful in physical terms, the floor was very soft, but it was deeply embarrassing.

I suppose I wasn't concentrating on what I was doing because I'd been repeating Hector over and over in my head. 'Gustav and Gertrude met me beside the plane, Ebrikke prodded my brain with her weird fingers, this is Hector, Hector, Hector, he's the captain. Captain Hector, Hector.' This was the dirge I was saying to myself.

I heard laughter as I slowly managed to raise myself onto all fours. It became clear that this huge Hector fellow wasn't alone. All around him, and I cannot imagine how I didn't notice them before, were a group of people dressed in a similar kind of uniform as the oversized captain.

'Nice to meet you,' said a young woman in whose lap I had just buried my face.

'I'm so sorry,' I said, trying to gather up what was left of my dignity. 'I'm not used to the floor.'

'He's not used to the floor! Spectacular!' said Hector loudly.

He reminded me a bit of Brian Blessed. He rolled his eyes as he spoke, his mouth was enormous and revealed a great many equally impressive teeth.

'Don't try and get up, man, stay as low down as you bloody can, the rest of us might be able to relax and eat our lunch if you're not falling all over the shop.'

'I'm so sorry,' I said again.

'Don't be sorry, it was very amusing,' Hector bellowed. 'I know I'm an amazing chap, but I don't think I've ever had someone literally fall over when they met me. Must be my charisma.'

Hector followed this statement with a big laugh. I was intrigued to notice he was the only person laughing, the people around him either ignored him or shook their heads and muttered things I couldn't pick up.

As I looked around the faces staring at me I smiled weakly. There was a small boy next to the woman in whose lap I'd just landed, and another group of young children were sitting on the far side of the gathering.

'Would you like something to eat, Gavin?' asked a woman who was to my right. I was still on all fours on the softly undulating floor and really didn't feel I was in a confident position to respond to anyone.

'Hang on,' I said, and slowly manoeuvred myself into a sitting position. I think I said sorry about 15 more times as I tried not to fall on anyone.

'Yes, that would be very nice, thank you,' I said when I finally achieved a static seated position and didn't feel like I was about to topple over.

I watched the woman lean over and reach for one of the white bowls that was placed on what looked like a stable flat surface at the side of the space we were in. I immediately wished I could sit on that, it looked solid. She passed the bowl to me with great care.

'It's noodles today, they're very good,' she said with a kind smile.

I took the bowl and thanked her.

A small plastic spoon was resting on the one-piece drip tray part of the bowl. I started eating. It wasn't bad, a bit like a Pot Noodle, and as a nerdy engineer I was very familiar with Pot Noodle.

The woman watched me as I ate. I looked up and smiled at her. She was possibly in her fifties, with grey streaks of hair leading away from her temples and she was dressed in a kind of quilted dark cream suit which looked like it had seen a lot of use.

Her dress code seemed pretty universal – everyone except the captain seemed to be in a variation of the same outfit. As I glanced at him I noticed he was staring at me with a big grin showing through his impressive dark beard.

'Now you are settled, Mister Meckler, I'd like to welcome you board Cloud Nine.'

'Thanks,' I spluttered through a mouthful of noodles.

'She's a pretty impressive ship, is she not?'

I nodded as my mouth was so full I knew trying to speak would result in showers of half-chewed food flying out. I'd already embarrassed myself enough.

'As you have no doubt been told by my trusty companion and meteorologist Gustav Nussbaum, this particular cloud is 4.7 kilometres long and 2.3 kilometres wide.'

I swallowed. 'I didn't know the exact dimensions,' I said, 'but Gustav gave me a rough estimate.'

'Yes, he's good at giving rough estimates, isn't that right, Gustav?'

Gustav had settled behind me and was already tucking into a bowl of something. He looked up and smiled. 'Wind speeds I can do, estimated times of arrival I can do, exact dimensions of ships . . . ' He waggled his free hand as if to indicate that this area of his knowledge may be hazy.

'Well I'm giving you exact measurements,' said Hector.

‘I’m very impressed with the cloud,’ I said, hoping this was the desired reaction.

‘Jolly good, I like to impress,’ said the captain with a big belly laugh. He turned towards the gathering around him. ‘You see, Mister Meckler is impressed! All I hear from you lot is complaints. Moaning about the food, moaning about the temperature, moaning about the route, always bloody moaning!’

There was a general murmur from the group. It struck me as the slightly suppressed laughter of adults putting up with a rather noisy child.

‘The noodles are very nice, Cap’, I’m not moaning,’ said a teenage girl sitting to my left.

‘Very pleased to hear it,’ said the captain, who passed his presumably empty bowl to a worryingly thin young man sitting next to him.

‘So, Mister Meckler, as you probably know we are currently resting at 10,000 metres and travelling at about 300 kilometres an hour, and yet we have no engines.’

He turned and faced the people gathered around him. ‘You see, in Mister Meckler’s dimension everything had engines, nothing worked without an engine, isn’t that right, Mister Meckler?’

‘Well, we had bicycles,’ I said rather weakly.

‘But you couldn’t transport many thousands of people through the skies without engines.’

‘No, I suppose we couldn’t,’ I confirmed nervously.

‘You couldn’t have schools and hospitals, dormitories, exercise areas, sun lounges, heat, light and food for thousands of people floating gently through the sky.’

‘No, we couldn’t do any of that.’

‘You see, things aren’t so bad here,’ he said to his audience. ‘So no more moaning, alright, chaps? Mister Meckler is very grateful to be here.’

‘I am,’ I said, again hoping this was the right thing to say.

'Now, Mister Meckler, tell me this. Are you aware of your predicament?' Hector raised one of his enormous eyebrows and stared at me intently. It was quite hard not to laugh.

'My predicament? I suppose it depends which one you mean. I seem to have quite a few.'

'I am referring to your predicament here in this lovely dimension. You are quite safe among my crew, we all know your circumstances and hold no resentment against you.'

'Oh, right,' I said, feeling increasingly baffled. 'Thank you.'

The captain stared at me with serious intent. 'Do you know anything about the Original Five?'

'The Original Five?' Just stating that made it fairly plain I didn't have a clue. The captain remained silent so I said, 'No. I don't know anything about, well, about anything. This is all new to me.'

'Excellent, well, let me explain,' he said, leaning forward with his enormous hairy hands resting on his wide splayed knees. I noticed a few of the people sitting around him made no attempt to cover their dismay. It was very like a family gathering where the father of the clan is going to tell one of his stories, the one they'd heard over and over again at every family event.

'The Original Five are the resentful ones. They really won't like you.'

'Oh dear,' I said trying to play along. 'May I ask why?'

For reasons I didn't have a hope of fathoming, this question caused quite raucous laughter among the 15 or so crew members sitting around me.

'The Original Five are a very resentful group of chaps,' said Hector, sitting back against his enormous inflated cushions again. 'They don't like me, oh no. Indeed they do not, they don't like my cloud, they don't seem to like anything that they didn't build.'

'Hector is referring to the first five clouds that were launched more than 50 years ago,' said Gustav. 'They are still flying, not very high, not very comfortably and, possibly now, not very safely. The people who built them have become, how to describe it, renegades.'

'Oh, they're harmless enough, they are just very noisy and can be quite annoying,' said Hector. 'The biggest of the Original Five is a mere kilometre long, it is but a puff of mist, Mister Meckler.'

'But I can't quite understand what they are resentful about,' I said. 'How would they even know about me?'

'Oh, they know everything,' said Hector. 'I believe you've already met one of their number.'

'Ebrikke is from Cloud Five,' said Gustav.

I stared at him.

'Where Ebrikke wants to go, Ebrikke goes,' said Hector. 'She's slung her hook now, she's off back down to Cloud Five which is about 4,000 metres below us, heading away from the pole at a rate of knots, sir!'

I know my mouth was hanging open at that point and I only regret that it may have been full of half-chewed noodles.

'You mean the woman with the cushion that changed colour who put her fingers on my temple is one of these people?'

'That is correct,' said Gustav.

'But if she's one of these resentful people who don't like me, well, you could have told me.'

'There was nothing we could do,' said Gustav quietly.

Hector leaned toward me. 'She's just a little bit difficult to manage,' he said in a tone lower than his normal bellow. 'She's, well, she's very advanced, she understands people more than, well, more than we do. She can do more or less as she wants but it would be wrong to suggest she was dangerous or in any way violent.'

I noticed Gustav nodding in agreement.

'But she seemed perfectly nice,' I said. 'I didn't get the feeling she was resentful about anything.'

'Oh, she is,' said Hector, who then put his enormous fist over his mouth and delivered a substantial belch. 'And they would be resentful about you because they blame the past for the present.'

'They blame the past for the present,' I repeated, although the phrase made no sense.

'The activities of history have taught us nothing, we have become the destroyer of worlds and we must suffer because of it.' Hector glanced at Gustav. 'Or something like that.'

'A fair rendition of their core beliefs,' said Gustav quietly. He turned to me. 'It might be best to think of them as a sect.'

'I see,' I said, not really seeing anything.

'I'm sure you don't see anything,' said Hector with a big grin. 'But worry not, young man, we will look after you.'

I almost jumped off the spongy floor at that moment because Hector clapped his enormous hands together with such force the sound hurt my ears.

'Much as I would love to sit and chat with you lovely people all day,' he bellowed, 'I have a cloud to navigate.'

'Thanks for the update, Captain,' said another young man sitting near him.

'Just doing my job, as I hope in the very near future you will be doing yours. ETA for docking is at zero nine forty,' said Hector as he slowly got to his feet.

He grunted with effort as he stood. He wasn't a small man but as he moved through the crowd toward me I could feel no movement in the bouncy floor.

'Mister Meckler, would you like to accompany me, I'm off to the obs tower to check our progress. I think you'll enjoy having a look at how we do things.'

'Okay, that would be great.'

I stuffed the remainder of my noodles into my mouth and started to try and get up. I suddenly felt an enormous force lift me. Only as I was standing up did I realise it was due to the captain – he had grabbed me under the arms and hoisted me to my feet.

'Come along, I haven't got all day,' he bellowed and started to half hold, half push me along, my feet only occasionally making contact with the springy surface of the floor.

I passed my bowl to a woman who was holding her hand out to take it from me. They did all seem to work together rather well but I was surprised once again to register little interest from the crowd of people that had been surrounding the captain.

'Thanks,' I managed to say as we made our way through the vast crowds of people in this massive tubular tent.

'I'll get one of the young folks to teach you how to walk, it's not that hard, you just have to let the floor support you,' said Hector as he half carried me back into the corridor from the large white bubble we'd been sitting in.

We turned to the right and at the far end we reached a circular doorway where I thought I saw someone sliding down what appeared to be a bright blue wall on the far side of another balloon-shaped space.

Due to the strange way I was being bounced along the floor by the enormous captain, it was hard to know exactly what I'd seen. A woman emerged from the distant room and walked past us.

'Captain,' she said and I saw that Hector nodded at her as she passed. I glanced back at the blue wall as we approached it. Up until that point every part of the structure I had seen appeared to be made of the same off-white material, all except for this blue wall.

It was vertical and set into one of the walls of the smaller spherical atrium we soon arrived in. This was a bizarre enough spectacle, but what was far more disconcerting for my now seriously overloaded twenty-first-century cortex was seeing someone slide up it.

I kid you not, a man just slid up the wall, from what I suppose had to be a lower floor, soundlessly and with no obvious mechanical device holding him there.

'Captain,' he said as he passed. I looked up just in time to see his shoes disappear out of the bubble-like room.

I think I was making sounds, nothing of a comprehensible nature, mostly whimpers of fear.

I was faced with a blue wall which looked a bit like a vertical version of the things passenger jets deploy in an emergency, a kind of inflatable slide. The man who had passed up this vertical blue thing was facing us as he slid up, it was nonsensical.

'You'll have to let me hold onto you until we get you kitted out in a flight suit,' said the captain. 'You may find it a little bit intimate but you'll survive.'

He manoeuvered me toward the inflated blue wall slide then put his two enormous arms around my chest. He leaned against the slide and up we went.

It wasn't particularly shocking at first as the movement wasn't violent. It was just like being in an elevator, except it was nothing like being in an elevator. For a start an elevator has buttons, lights, adverts for the gym and sauna on floor 15, an elevator has sliding doors and most importantly it has a floor.

This vertical journey was not very comfortable. I was being squeezed from behind by an enormous bear of a man and as we went up my head made contact with a soft layer of material.

Initially this was slightly painful because my head was pushed down rather violently as the material flopped back into shape. It didn't cause actual injury or even muscle strain but there's no previous experience I can liken it to so there's no clear way of explaining what it felt like.

'Sorry about that,' said the big captain behind me. 'Just push your head back and you'll be right as rain.'

I soon realised these were floors we were passing, each of these soft floppy layers of quilted material that thwacked my head were floors in an enormous inflatable building.

'Here we are,' said the captain.

He pushed me forward and I half fell onto yet another off-cream padded surface. 'The view is much better from here, you'll be able to see what's going on,' he said as he hoisted me to my feet and we moved along a wide, brightly lit corridor.

We went through a circular opening and into an eye-popping space, a large room with massive windows all around the sides. The view of the cloudscape around us was spectacular.

'Sit there, Mister Meckler,' said the captain, pointing to what I assumed was a raised seating unit along one wall. 'Then you won't be falling all over the place annoying people.'

I clambered up onto the seat. I don't think I've felt so much like a six-year-old visiting daddy's office since I was six and I visited my dad's office.

Once I had settled I tried to take in the vision before me. It's not easy to describe. Obviously being a pilot myself, the vast vision of life above the clouds was no great shock: I could see for literally hundreds of kilometres in every direction through the large windows around me. What was shocking though was my immediate surroundings. I was in a vast floating man-made cloud that, at a glance at least, resembled its water vapour brothers to a baffling extent.

The sun was setting to my right and the light coming through the clouds was breathtaking. Shafts of multi-coloured light bursting forth like some Pink Floyd lighting effect at a 1970s concert. However, my eyes had already grown attuned to the fact that not all the clouds I could see in the vast panorama before me were made of dense collections of water particles. I could spot three that were clearly of a similar construction to the one I was on.

Inside the near-spherical capsule I was seated in were a handful of people in similar garb to the majority of people I'd met. The only one who stood out was the corpulent Captain Hector. I'd remembered his name: Hector.

He had taken up position at a central console and although I couldn't make out what they were saying there was a lot of chatter going on between the various people surrounding him.

As soon as I settled in the seat I was aware of one thing: we were descending. Not at any great speed, but I could sense the movement in my stomach, that slight rise you feel in your gut as you start to drop down.

As we descended I started to notice other cloud formations emerge from the brilliant vista around us.

They started to stand out from the actual water particle clouds around them. These were not clouds, they were constructions like the one I was in. One that was much closer to us than the others looked fairly small, but I suddenly noticed one in the far distance high above us.

It was beyond belief. It was like looking at a storm cloud from 50 miles away, a massive gathering of material that stretched all credibility. It had to be not only miles long, but miles high, it was a full-sized cumulonimbus cloud built by human beings.

Then I noticed another cloud, and another one behind that, one coming in from above and a couple coming up from lower down. Each of them looked large but still we seemed to be slowly circling the truly massive one.

The captain turned to me with a big grin on his bearded face.

'Cloud Ten,' he shouted. 'Pretty impressive, huh? Bet you didn't have them 200 years ago.'

I nodded my agreement as the captain turned back to his work, whatever it was he was doing.

So I was on a cloud that had a captain, a man, a massive bearded man who was clearly in control and very confident of the fact. I felt depressed. Although I'd found the Squares of London a difficult place to understand, there was something hugely relaxing about the women who controlled everything.

This encounter with a large authoritarian male made me feel like I was once again a new boy in a big school and he was the friendly bully.

I had also been told that there were renegade clouds, ones used by people who wouldn't like me, some kind of bonkers religious sect who hated what the human race had done to the planet.

I didn't particularly like any of it.

5

DO CLOUDS COMBINE?

It's not something I've ever considered. I'm no meteorologist and I don't know if naturally formed clouds do actually combine together.

Whether it does or does not happen, what I do know is when huge, inflatable and occasionally frighteningly flexible man-made clouds combine, it's quite an amazing thing to witness.

The docking process took many hours but I didn't miss one minute. From my position in a central inflatable tower formation on Cloud Nine I watched as each part of what was clearly going to be a mega-cloud joined together.

The central cloud pulling every other cloud to its flanks was very obviously Cloud Ten. I had spotted numerous other cloud structures, some seemingly smaller than the one I was on, some larger, but essentially of a similar-looking design.

However, as the really big one lowered down toward us, I think I stopped breathing for a while. The captain called over to me at one point.

'Look up, Mister Meckler, you don't want to miss this.'

As I looked up I admonished myself for not previously noticing the massive window in the roof of the structure. There had been so much going on all around me I had never thought to look up.

There, above me, and much closer than I expected, was the billowing colossus that I knew to be Cloud Ten. It had to be many tens of kilometres across, maybe hundreds. I certainly couldn't see either end as it seemed to fill every window.

It slowly approached us, and when I say slowly I mean really slowly; if you stared at it for a couple of minutes you couldn't see any change, but when you looked at something else and glanced back, suddenly it seemed a lot closer.

It was only after the lower sections of the massive shape came into view through the many side windows that the barely perceptible cloud dance I'd been witnessing started to make sense.

All the other clouds I'd seen had formed a massive circle, a ring of man-made clouds at least 50 kilometres across. Judging distance, size or speed with these floating monoliths was utterly beyond my ability without instruments. Over a couple of hours Cloud Ten slowly descended into this circle and filled it. It was a very different design to the other clouds I'd seen, including the one I was on.

There was something vaguely ship-like in the clouds that had originally joined us. In structure they were long and narrow with high towers and bulbous shapes along the top. The underside seemed almost flat.

Cloud Ten was more like a vast sphere. The lower half of this mind-numbingly huge floating structure passed by us and continued to descend, all the while revealing ever more complex protuberances on its upper surface.

The thing I noticed with a tingle of fear was the rapid drop in light in the cloud I was on. The massive floating hulk of Cloud Ten cast some serious shadows. This was dissipated by the fact that as darkness fell, the white material that made up the majority of the structure I was in started to glow.

I felt a very slight movement as we approached the massive bulk that had now seemingly settled beside us, which then finished with a barely perceptible kind of wobble through the whole cloud.

'We're docked!' shouted the captain. 'Open exterior portals.'

There was suddenly a great deal of movement in the control space. It wasn't like the bridge of a ship or the cockpit of an aircraft. It resembled an inflatable playroom that was safe for little kids, but I could sense that there were controls of a kind that I had no mental tools to understand.

There was a large screen arrangement in front of the captain and I really wanted to get a look at it. It was where most of the crew, if that's what they were, had been concentrating for the previous couple of hours.

'May I join you now?' I asked when the captain's enormous bearded face turned to me.

'Of course you may. Kirubel, give the unstable gentleman a helping hand will you.'

A tall African man who had been standing beside the captain smiled and approached me. He reached out a long arm and steadied me as I attempted to rise to my feet.

'Just pick your feet up very high and lean forward a bit.' He said in accent-less English. I stood up and tried to do as he said. It was easier than I expected. This man was the first person I'd met on the cloud who had bothered to explain how to walk on a soft undulating surface.

I made my way from my raised seat to what I took to be the central control console for the cloud and didn't fall over once. Okay, so a strong African man was holding one arm and keeping me upright, but it was a great improvement on my initial efforts.

'Hold onto that bar,' said Kirubel – I'd remembered his name – he was pointing to a white plastic-looking pole that stood at one side of the console. Finally I was on my feet and standing with other cloud dwellers like a native. As long as I could hold onto something fairly solid I could remain erect.

'That was the most amazing thing I've ever seen,' I said, slightly breathless. 'I thought the lift that brought me up here was the most amazing thing, but this!' I gestured out of the windows. 'This is incredible.'

'Glad you're enjoying it, dear man,' said Hector. 'It doesn't happen that often and it often doesn't happen that smoothly. We have been blessed by the elements today, 30 kilometre wind speeds over northern Norway is not something we often encounter.'

'Okay,' I said. 'Can I ask some dumb questions?'

'Go ahead,' he replied as his hand did something on the screen.

'Well, for starters, what's the screen?'

'The what?'

'The screen,' I gesticulated in the direction of the large flat panel right beside me.

'Oh, the nub, this is the control nub, we just call it the nub.'

'What did he call it?' asked a woman standing the other side of the captain.

'A screen.' I said again, I didn't know why she didn't just ask me directly. 'That's what I would call something like that.'

The woman didn't respond but the captain smiled.

'What we're doing now is just checking weight distribution. You see, dear chap, we have to monitor it all the time. As I'm sure you are aware, this is a lighter-than-air system and so any slight fluctuation in heavier-than-air objects, you and me, particularly me,' he chuckled at this, 'has to be kept in check.'

Kirubel gestured toward the screen. The complexity of the graphics was of course baffling to my simpleton eyes, the screen made up of what seemed to be three-dimensional shapes and colours that were in constant movement.

'We are transferring a great many passengers off Cloud Nine and onto Cloud Ten,' he explained. 'Where you walked through before you had your meal, where you met the captain, that was the main waiting lobby, which is why so many people were in there. Once the pressures equalise, the sidewall of that lobby retracts and we can start transfer. So that means that there are a few thousand people on that side of the cloud. Without monitoring that weight shift we could be in serious trouble.'

'So there are thousands of people on this cloud?' I asked.

The captain brushed his hand over the nub and a number appeared. It was constantly going down but when I first registered the figure it was roughly 85,000. Suddenly there was a bit of twenty-third-century data I could immediately understand. Numbers written as I understood them.

'You'll have to forgive me, but a lighter-than-air structure that can carry 85,000 people is difficult to comprehend.'

'We can carry 100,000 at maximum capacity,' explained the captain. 'In fact, wasn't it last month we had over that number when we evacuated the Tbilisi Culvert?' he asked Kirubel who nodded in agreement. 'But that was unusual and it was only for a short hop.'

Same old same old. One tiny question opened a huge hangar door that revealed a massive storehouse of further questions. The Tbilisi Culvert, what the hell could that be? I didn't even want to ask.

As I was thinking this, I had the realisation that while I was in London no one would have needed to explain to me what the Tbilisi Culvert was, I would just have known anyway. Here on the cloud, in contrast to any kind of experience I'd had to this point, I felt utterly lost and alone.

Once again I was faced with a stark choice I'd occasionally considered on my adventures. Give up and succumb to all-engulfing screaming madness and soil myself in a padded inflatable cell or just go with the flow. The second option was slightly more appealing although the first felt like it was constantly pulling at my sleeve.

6

NCE AGAIN, JUST AS HAD HAPPENED WHEN I arrived in Gardenia and the Squares of London, I was obliged to change my clothes. By this time in my journey I had almost forgotten about my chinos and polo shirt, my North Face lace up walking boots, iPhone and iPad, my wallet, money, credit cards, in fact my entire 2011 identity. It had just gone, it was no more.

I felt like I had been lost in the chaos and confusion of my journey for so long, and yet I still seemed to be alive. I was still Gavin Meckler, I was still from 2011, I should not have been on a man-made cloud 10,000 metres into the sky changing my clothes. But I was.

Kirubel, whose name I'd actually managed to learn and more importantly remember, had guided me into the room I had to change clothes in, although calling it a room was a bit pointless. A better description would be a smaller bubble off the main bubble I'd been sitting in which was mounted on top of a series of massive larger white bubbles below me.

But even calling it a bubble might be misleading, as before we entered it was nothing more than a kind of flattened bulge sticking out of the side of the main structure.

Kirubel had pointed to it from one of the windows of the control bubble. 'You see the small bulge on the side of the cloud,' he explained, 'that's a crew kit store.'

Try and imagine how little sense that made. I assumed I was looking at what he was referring to but it didn't really compute. Although by this time it was getting dark, or maybe it was just the shadow of Cloud Ten, I could just make out a vague bulge on the massive flank of the structure I could see stretching away from me, but I couldn't sense its size. It could have been the size of a sandwich or a double-decker bus; I had lost all sense of scale.

'Jane, can you inflate the starboard crew kit store,' said Kirubel over his shoulder. I think he was talking to the woman who'd been standing next to the captain. I glanced over and she held a hand up as if to say she was on it. I turned back to see the small bulge I'd been looking at kind of pop out like a balloon.

'There we go,' said Kirubel, 'I thought you'd like that, let's get you kitted out.'

He guided me along the corridor I had originally bounced down with the captain and there in the sidewall was a large circular hole. I felt certain it hadn't been there when I had passed by, but in my advanced state of confusion there could have been three naked and oiled female warriors standing and threatening me with spears and I probably wouldn't have noticed.

We entered this newly inflated bubble and it smelled so much like a tent pitched on grass on a sunny day I couldn't help reacting.

'Wow, what's that smell?' I asked.

'Yes, I know, it's a bit stale, the air comes from a central pressure bag. It probably hasn't been changed for a bit, I think we recharged over the Oxford Culvert before we picked you up,' said Kirubel.

'Is there any grass in the Oxford Culvert?' I asked.

Kirubel looked at me with a surprised smile. 'Yes, how did you know? The docking point is over a big lawn, it's a very pretty place,' he said. I nodded, I was feeling a little bit Sherlock at that point.

On the far side of the white spherical room I was faced with a pile of sealed clear bags attached to the outer wall. They were all about the size of the kind of padded envelope you'd get a DVD in, but when Kirubel sorted through them and opened one what came out was much bigger.

It was a dark cream kind of onesie with the strange blue pad on the back, the same outfit everyone I'd seen on the cloud was wearing. I assumed this was what allowed someone to slide up and down the fearsome elevators. How all this material could be crushed into such a small space was just another observation I had to log away. Even if Kirubel could give me an adequate explanation of how something like this was achieved I didn't want to know. I'd already experienced so many things like this I just shrugged and started to pull the one-piece suit over my clothes.

'You'll need to take off the suit you're wearing,' said Kirubel, 'the back pad needs moisture from your body to function.'

I smiled. Suddenly the repetition of experiences amused me. Once again I was standing in a small room with a tall African man and I had to strip naked in front of him. It almost made me believe in a supernatural, all-knowing God, and that he or she was having a bit of a giggle at my expense.

Anyway, I stripped off, pulled the new suit on and was intrigued to note that Kirubel turned away while I did so. He was giving me a bit of dignity, not staring at me and laughing, as had been my experience with Ralph and Akiki over in London.

The suit was a little bit baggy and droopy. I wriggled about in it to try and get comfortable. It really was an all-in-one job: the shoes were built in, slippers really, but even they were a little large for me.

Kirubel turned back to face me. 'Just press the blue patch,' he said, pointing to what looked like a small blue stain on the left forearm of the suit. I put my finger on it and felt the suit reduce and tighten, though not alarmingly as had been the case with the body suit I bought from Akiki, it was slow and gentle and it even made a vague hissing sound as it did so.

'That is quite cool,' I said.

'Are you cold?' asked Kirubel.

'No, sorry, I mean it is quite impressive, it's good, I like it.'

Kirubel nodded. 'I'm pleased.' He picked up the suit and shoes

I'd been wearing and put them in the empty bag my new suit had been stored in. He ran his fingers along the top of the bag and it reduced in size far more than the basic laws of physics would suggest. The Akiki suit was incredibly fine, so I would have expected that to fit, but the shoes here were solid and bulky. It was like watching magic to see how small the package became.

'We'll keep those here so you don't lose them,' said Kirubel. 'Now, the captain has asked me if I will escort you down to the transfer bay. There are people on Cloud Ten who want to meet you.'

'Ahh, okay,' I said. I felt slightly uplifted on hearing this; there were some people somewhere in this bonkers floating city who were interested in the fact that I'd just emerged into their world from somewhere they didn't seem to know about.

I found walking in my new suit a great deal easier than I had in my Squares of London get-up. Although Kirubel still held my arm I felt a lot more stable. We retraced the steps I'd taken with the captain and were suddenly faced with the strange lift arrangement.

'We will take the elevator back down to the lobby,' said Kirubel. 'Don't worry, you won't miss the get-off, it's the last stop, keep your feet tucked back as you go down but as soon as your feet touch the floor lean forward a little. I'll be waiting for you.'

As soon as he said this, Kirubel turned, laid back against the light blue material and just slid downward. He'd gone before I could say anything. I peered down the small opening in the floor and could see his head disappearing at what seemed a fairly alarming rate. I sensed a little vertigo as I could see down a long, long way. There was nothing else to do, I just had to copy him. I turned so that my back was facing the blue sheet, leant back and hoped for the best.

As soon as the pad on my back made contact with the material on the slide-cum-elevator I started to descend, slowly at first, but very soon it all felt a bit like falling. The inflatable floors passed me more rapidly. I could see people waiting to get on as I passed one or two of the floors but the sight was so fleeting I barely had time to register them.

I started to panic. What if I was meant to do something to slow this increasingly speedy descent? Had Kirubel told me something I'd forgotten? I felt my hands start to try and grab onto something in a pointless manner as the panic took over, but it was at that point I felt myself slow down.

'Lean forward a little.' I heard Kirubel's voice coming from below me. By this point my descent had slowed to a more manageable speed and as he appeared before me, smiling and holding out his long arms, I leant forward and felt a bizarre, almost organic uncoupling as my suit released contact with the light blue material behind me.

'That is bloody bonkers,' I said as I half stumbled into Kirubel's arms. He pushed me upright and smiled at me.

'I hope that means you like it,' he replied as he started walking me into the huge elongated balloon that I then knew to be the transfer lobby.

This time there was complete pandemonium in the space. The noise was overwhelming: thousands of people, literally thousands of them, all dressed in the same kind of weak custard-coloured clothing and many carrying large bundles strapped together. They were tangled together in what seemed complete chaos. I would hazard a guess that some were getting on-board Cloud Nine from Cloud Ten and an equal number were going the other way, but it all seemed a bit haphazard.

Through the melee I started to hear something which didn't quite register at first. It was a sound I knew but it sounded so incongruous in this helter-skelter of human concern.

It was the sound of a children's choir.

Staying close to Kirubel I slowly made my way through the packed crowds. There was no 'last train from Berlin' panic going on, there were no dumped babies crying or women weeping, everyone seemed fairly happy. Eager to move, but happy.

We got closer to the choir, who were standing on some kind of raised area at the far end of the massive tube, very near what looked like some kind of exit or connection to Cloud Ten.

'Can we stop and listen for a moment?' I asked.

Kirubel didn't say anything, but he stood motionless beside me making it clear we could.

I would guess I was looking at about 70 children dressed in dark cream one-piece suits similar to the one I was wearing. They were stood in orderly rows, small ones at the front, taller ones at the rear. In the centre of the maelstrom of chaos was a children's choir and their singing was enchanting.

I knew the tune, I'd sung it at primary school, it was John Bunyan's 'He Who Would Valiant Be' but the words were different:

Old man wind blows grit in our eyes,
Let him come hither.
See the cloud safe in the skies,
Come wind come weather.
When there's nowhere to hide,
There is no smoother ride.
We're safely tucked inside,
Our lovely Cloud home.

I was mesmerised by the sound and sincerity of these children. There didn't appear to be any teachers guiding them, they just stood and sang at the top of their lungs.

'That's so lovely,' I said as we moved away. 'Who are they?'

Kirubel turned back to look at the young choir, 'I'm not sure. I think they are children from the Manchester Culvert, from your country.'

I would never have guessed their country of origin, they

seemed to represent every race I'd ever seen and yet they were singing in English.

'The Manchester Culvert?'

Kirubel smiled at me. 'Of course, you have not yet seen a culvert, they are amazing constructions, very impressive even if you've seen them many times.'

Kirubel stood on what I took to be the intersection between the two clouds. There was an obvious material seam beneath my feet and the floor on the far side looked smoother, less billowy and a bit more solid. I stepped across and was relieved to find the floor far more as I would expect a floor to be. It was still spongy but not in the same bouncy way as the ones I'd been stumbling on up until then.

'Of course your old country doesn't have the really big culverts,' said Kirubel. 'Maybe we will see one of the really big ones. The Chicago Culvert is very big. Lalibela Culvert, that is where I'm from, that is very, very old. Was it not there in your time?'

'The Lalibela Culvert? No, I don't think I've heard of that. But then I haven't seen anything but these incredible cloud things.'

It had mystified me as to how I could be accepted so casually into this whole new world; no one seemed to be in the least surprised by my arrival.

'I understand,' said Kirubel, 'You have just come through the cloud portal.'

'The cloud portal?'

'Yes, we made a detour three days ago, we made sure we were nearby when we expected you and sent out spotter drones to escort you to safety. There are people on Cloud Ten who can explain. I only know what the captain told me.'

'But no one seems surprised to see me,' I said. 'In the other places I've been, I don't even know how to explain, but where I just left, London, a massive city called London, it was October in

2211. Anyway, they were all very surprised to see me. Many of them didn't believe where I'd come from.'

'You are not the first,' said Kirubel. 'You will soon understand. Come, I must deliver you to the committee and get back to Cloud Nine before the weather forces us to undock.'

I followed Kirubel through the huge crowds of people, barely able to take in what I was walking through. It was almost too big to take in. Unlike the vaguely tubular or balloon-like structures I'd been in on Cloud Nine, this was a vast white cavern. I could see many layers above me, kinds of smooth shaped balconies rising above me, possibly hundreds of metres high. Whatever I was now in was beyond vast. It soon became impossible to register that this machine, this structure, was floating thousands of metres in the air. I must have walked along with several thousand people and literally tons of packages being carried by them. As a pilot I knew one thing from experience: people are heavy when you lift them into thin air.

After many minutes of slow progress through the crowds we reached a large circular doorway in which stood three figures. A very short African man with a white beard, a tall blonde woman who looked worryingly thin and stared at me in a rather startled way and finally a rather suave-looking middle-aged white man with grey hair.

'Welcome aboard, Mister Meckler,' said the African man.

We shook hands and then Kirubel said, 'Gavin Meckler, this is Wekesa, he will look after you now.'

Kirubel pulled something from inside his suit and spoke to the old African man. 'We have his craft safely stowed and he's been through a full medi.' He handed over a small transparent thing about the size of a key fob. 'All the portal data is here, estimates suggest we have a three-month window until we can rendezvous with the portal again.'

'Thank you, Kirubel,' said the old African man. 'Give my regards to Captain Hector and we'll see you again soon I hope.'

'In calmer times,' said Kirubel.

'In calmer times,' said the old African.

At that, Kirubel gave me a friendly pat on the back and walked back into the crowd.

'Well, well, this must all be very strange for you, Mister Meckler, but we're very happy to welcome you onto Cloud Ten. We will soon be undocking from the other clouds, we need to get back upstairs fairly quickly,' said the old man, pointing upwards.

I was relieved to find out they had stairs on Cloud Ten, I didn't fancy trusting myself on the pale blue elevator sheets again.

'Wekesa means we have to get Cloud Ten to a higher elevation, there is a very powerful storm approaching and we need to get above it,' said the blonde woman. She had a fairly strong German accent but it wasn't this fact that made me momentarily pause my thoughts.

This was suddenly familiar. I had a fleeting thought and immediately a tall and rather intimidating woman knew what I was thinking. She smiled at me again and I found this slightly frightening.

'You have a kidonge, Mister Meckler. So do I.' she said.

7

'HIS IS ESSENTIALLY A SURVIVAL MACHINE,' said Wekesa. 'It can support a little over three million people for periods of up to two months without docking, ground charging or restocking.'

I said nothing. I didn't need to. I had met people like Wekesa back in 2011. They adopt a communication protocol that is described by the military as being in 'constant send' mode.

They never shut up, which in this particular instance was fine by me. Wekesa was giving me some serious data about the survival machine I was walking through.

'The outer skin, if laid flat on the ground, would cover an area of 82 square kilometres. The outer skin is a nano-porous, photovoltaic microfibre. Each square metre of the material produces 18 kilowatts when in sunlight and weighs 13 grams. If a one metre square section was to be tightly rolled, the material would be capable of supporting a little under 7,000 kilograms, which I'm sure you understand indicates it is very strong.'

Wekesa pulled a small sheet of cream material out of his trouser pocket and handed it to me. 'You can keep that,' he said.

By this stage I was used to the feeling of ridiculously light and thin materials. This was like having a sheet of semi-translucent gas land on your hand. Although my eyes could see it, the nerve endings in my fingers were far too crude and insensitive so I couldn't feel it.

I screwed it into a ball and it more or less disappeared. I let it unfurl on the palm of my hand and pinched part of it with my thumb and forefinger. This stuff was so light that even with the air movement produced by our very slow walk, it would have blown away.

'The structure is filled with slightly pressurised air which is warmed by a mixture of direct solar infusion during daylight hours and the compressed heat system during darkness,' said Wekesa. I made a mental note of that, I wanted to learn how you compress heat.

'The temperature of the air within the non-porous structure of Cloud Ten is 15 to 18 degrees Celsius warmer than the air outside, which gives the structure lift. The areas used by inhabitants of the cloud are kept at a constant 23 degrees Celsius regardless of exterior temperature. The entire habitable area within Cloud Ten is pressurised to maintain comfort, the system is capable of functioning at altitudes between 50 metres and 12,000 metres. We are currently rising at one metre every two seconds and will reach our necessary operating height of 10,000 metres in a little under three hours.'

During this fascinating monologue we had moved further inside the massive floating city. I was treated to the vision of vast interior halls without a straight line in sight, other than the floors we walked upon. Comparisons to a giant land-based shopping mall or impressive university building don't do justice to what I saw, this was larger and far more spectacular.

It did occur to me that whatever the reason the people of this 2211 had gone to so much effort to build a vast floating city, they could surely have created a simpler, more utilitarian design and it would have done the same job. This was a dizzying spectacle of immense depth, height and width. All around me were twisting forms of what I took to be inflated supporting struts but which were all made of the same basic texture and colour.

Everything I saw was the same vaguely cream colour, except of course the hundreds of thousands of people moving about.

Here was colour in abundance. Their clothes, while all being of the same cream functional base design, were adorned with an incredible collection of intense colours, some of the strapping and refinement seemed to be luminescent, glowing almost.

I stared around during our slow journey. The entire structure seemed to be glowing softly and although I could barely make out where I was, I could tell from the last glimpses of the outside world I'd seen from Cloud Nine that night had fallen on whatever part of the planet we were floating over.

'We are now heading to one of 20 residential sections,' said Wekesa. 'In this area we have requisitioned a sleeping pod for you. Each residential area consists of a little over one million cubic metres of habitable space split into sleeping pods, cleansing areas and medical and support services. Each section can sleep up to a quarter of a million people at one time.'

At this point Wekesa glanced at me as if checking for a reaction. All the way through his monologue my reaction had been pretty much constant. It could loosely be described as slack-jawed amazement, as if a Stone Age hunter was watching an A380 take off.

Wekesa almost smiled and then carried on. 'Sleeping is generally done in shifts. The occupants are informed of their sleeping period by their wrist strips.'

Wekesa handed me a small circle of cream material. 'You can keep this,' he said. 'It's your designated wrist strip. It will guide you during your trip on-board Cloud Ten.'

I inspected the band briefly, a thin, slightly glowing circle of almost non-existent material. I slipped it over my left hand.

'It operates a little like a kidonge,' said the tall blonde woman. 'Although it is a lot less powerful, it should help you understand what is happening.'

Her name was Theda, she was 49 years old and was born in Wolfratshausen just south of Munich and had a daughter called Ilka who was 22. If I'd never experienced the power of the kidonge this sudden influx of knowledge would have done my head in, but I just smiled.

'Thank you, Theda,' I said and patted my new wristband. 'This will be very useful.'

'The residential areas are situated in the upper sections of the cloud. In order to gain access we need to use the elevator, the elevator you need to use is number 20. It is this way,' said Wekesa.

He nodded down at my wrist. I glanced at the wristband, it had a number 20 showing in white numerics and a green arrow pointing slightly to my left.

Whatever concern I'd had about the elevator in Cloud Nine evaporated when I saw elevator number 20. As we rounded a corner of the baffling interior I was greeted with a sight that made my lungs stop working.

I saw another large hall, a gently curved atrium which appeared to slope up slightly. There were loads of people on the floor around me but up the far wall, a blue wall, thousands of people were going up and down as if it were the most normal thing in the world.

It was like the view from a traffic helicopter looking down on a busy five-lane freeway in Central Los Angeles. It looked chaotic and incredibly dangerous but not only was this a vertical freeway which disappeared beyond the ceiling of the space I was in, there were no cars.

Just people flying up and down in their hundreds.

We made slow progress through the milling crowds, which became more dense around the foot of the elevator. It took me a while to comprehend we were in a sort of slightly chaotic queue waiting to get on.

By this point I was feeling very hot and uncomfortable. I didn't want to go up this thing, the nearer we got to it, the more I tried not to look up.

Of course you can't help it, you just have to look, and I did.

I wish I hadn't, I could see so far up it was ridiculous, the figures sliding up just disappeared into tiny specks and the gap between the blue elevator wall and the floors above looked impossibly wide. How on earth would you ever get off!

'I will ride next to you to give you support and comfort,' said Wekesa. 'The first ride on a Cloud Ten elevator is sometimes a little disconcerting, even for people born in this era.'

Wekesa held my hand, turned me around as we neared the silent blue wall and leant back. Without much say in the matter I leant, back, too and instantly we started to climb. Being pulled aloft by your clothes should be a very uncomfortable experience, however, I was only barely aware that my body weight was being supported by the intricate design of webbing and supporting pads built into my flight suit, and anyway, I was far too terrified to be concerned by such trifles.

Foolishly I looked down as we slid upward. I saw Theda and the grey-haired man get on below us. I was too terrified to wonder who this man was, he still hadn't said a word.

I think Wekesa was still talking to me as we continued to shoot up the blue wall, but I didn't hear a word of it, I was breathing too fast. Just when I thought I was beginning to cope, a group of small children whooshed past me on the way down, they were singing as they travelled. They seemed tiny and not in the least perturbed by the fact that they were hundreds of metres up, sliding down a wall that was part of a giant balloon that was thousands of metres above the sea.

We passed what I took to be kinds of balconies as we continued our dizzying journey. The system was clearly not designed for people to get off at this point, as there was a very obvious safety wall running along the edge of these balconies, with behind them what I took to be offices or kitchens or schools. It was very hard to tell, we must have been travelling at urban car speeds; everything became a blur.

After a few more seconds the floors became more regular and closely spaced. We must have gone past dozens of floors, each one crowded with people waiting to go up or down, I had no idea which.

I felt Wekesa's hand pull me and I leant forward. We started to slow down and we stepped from the blue wall of terror onto a cream and slightly bouncy floor.

'We are now 2.3 kilometres higher than the main lobby,' said Wekesa, still on constant send. 'You will find the walking surfaces on the upper levels are more flexible.'

We waited for the others, they appeared moments after we got off and walked toward us.

'Did you enjoy that?' asked Theda.

'Um, I don't know how anyone could actually enjoy that. It was bloody terrifying, but I'll admit it is utterly amazing,' I said.

'I was also very impressed the first time I rode it,' said Theda.

'Come, I will show you your sleeping pod,' said Wekesa, who seemed to ignore everything except his explanatory monologue. 'All you need to remember is that you need to go to level 2011, we thought that would be easy for you to remember, and pod number 32, your age.'

I laughed a little, this was all so much more bonkers, brain-melting and utterly baffling than anything I'd encountered in Gardenia or London.

'Great,' I said finally, not wishing to offend my guides.

We approached another circular entrance and beyond, as far as I could see, on either side of a brightly lit and seemingly endless corridor were row after row of small circular units.

'Number 32 is here,' said Wekesa, patting what looked to me to be an inflated door in an inflated frame. It had a recognisable number 32 stenciled on the door, but the opening was at shoulder height and I couldn't see how I'd get up into it without some kind of handle or step, neither of which was immediately apparent.

Beneath it was another similar door, number 31. I didn't want to kick their fairly frail-looking door in as I clambered inside.

'How do you get in it?' I asked. Wekesa firmly grabbed my

 right wrist and put my hand on the door, It opened by flopping down, it inflated a little more and the inside of the door contained some sturdy steps.

'Like so,' said Wekesa, again with something that resembled a smile.

'Okay,' I said. 'Thanks.'

So, I was on a cloud as big as a city with possibly three million other floating souls. I had a sleep pod and a flight suit. I had met a woman who knew about a technology that only existed in another place which clearly most people I'd met on the clouds had no idea about.

To say the mystery was all-engulfing is to underestimate how baffling, terrifying and confusing this all was. I knew I'd survive the ordeal by simply not thinking about it. I knew if I thought about it for more than a second, I would go properly insane.

8

‘AVE YOU EVER HEARD THE PHRASE, “ANY sufficiently advanced technology is indistinguishable from divinity”?’ asked Theda when we arrived in a dimly lit corner of a busy and rather shabby canteen-type space on the same level as my sleeping pod.

‘No,’ I said, as I sat down at a wall-mounted table and chair arrangement that stuck out of the inflated wall. ‘It’s good though, I like it. I’ve seen more than my fair share of almost divine technology recently.’

‘I assumed you might be familiar with it because it was coined by a man from your era, a writer called Sir Arthur C. Clarke,’ said Theda, as she put three squashy liquid pillow things on the flimsy lightweight table. I was very relieved to see these containers had straws coming out of them. I didn’t want to embarrass myself trying to open the damn things like I had done in London.

‘Oh, right, yeah, I’ve heard of him,’ I said. ‘*2001: A Space Odyssey* and all that.’

‘That is correct. Well, Sir Arthur’s quotation came to me when I arrived here. That is how I initially responded to witnessing the technology we are surrounded by now, particularly the elevator. It was hard for me not to wonder if this was the work of gods.’

‘Wow,’ I said. ‘I have to say that hadn’t occurred to me.’

‘Oh, I apologise, I had assumed you would be open to the notion of gods having a concrete influence on the activities of humans.’

‘Um, no, sorry, I don’t.’

‘There is no need to be sorry,’ she said. ‘I am intrigued and clearly my grasp of your particular period of history is mistaken.

 I thought you would suffer from detrimental religious belief symptoms.'

'My wife does,' I said. 'Well, she did, 200 years ago.'

I was about to ask Theda exactly when she had arrived and where she had arrived from, but at this point we were joined by the silent grey-haired man. He had been with us the entire time but had been behind us in the queue for the plastic food pillows.

I had said farewell to the highly informative Wekesa by the blue wall elevator of terror; he had just leaned back and disappeared downwards, leaving me with Theda and the man with grey hair.

Up to this point the man had just stared at me and said nothing.

'Gavin, I'm sorry I haven't introduced myself, my name is Brad Dorschel,' he said, his American accent strong, his voice surprisingly deep for a man of such diminutive stature. 'I decided to remain in the background just observing for a while. I hope you didn't take offence.'

I smiled at him. 'Not at all, Brad. To be honest, someone staring at me and not saying anything is nothing new. I've been the object of rather a lot of interest lately.'

'I understand,' said Brad, 'I just needed to validate your existence.'

He held out his hand and I shook it.

I will admit now that I half expected to try and shake it and it would just disappear. I would discover that this perfectly normal-looking man was in fact made of some kind of gas or dark matter.

His hand was warm and solid.

'I'm the Chief Science Officer from the Chicago Culvert,' he said as he sat down opposite me. 'I'm a physicist, although I guess the best way to describe my specialty is if I use the term "theoretical physicist". That's the nearest discipline that would have existed 200 years back. Does any of that make sense?'

'To be perfectly honest with you, Brad, nothing makes much sense,' I said, feeling rather pleased with myself that I had used his name in my reply and forced myself to remember it. 'None of this makes any sense to me at all but I'm no longer surprised. I've been through so much weirdness that nothing has made sense to me for many months.'

'So you've done one hop from 2011 to 2211? Is that right?'

'No, three hops, Brad.'

'Three hops!' Brad seemed genuinely concerned.

'Yes, one to Gardenia in 2211, then another to London in 2211, and now here, wherever here is.'

'Well, this is the planet Earth, it's October 2211,' said Brad. 'And we're just off the coast of northern Siberia.'

'Are we?'

'Maybe I can explain this part,' said Theda. She smiled at Brad but it looked a bit forced. 'The technology we are experiencing here is extraordinary, we are presently travelling with the jet stream, our ground speed is about 300 kilometres an hour. In order to achieve this movement the clouds rise up, catch the jet stream and travel great distances at high speed. When they are approaching the desired destination, they reduce altitude and find winds that will hopefully guide them to the docking point. Their understanding and predictive technologies regarding the weather, storms, winds or stable conditions are very advanced. Often they have to wait for very strong winds to die away because the turbulence is dangerous at low levels. The surface winds can be very strong, much stronger than anything you or I have experienced.'

'We have occasional storm winds on the surface that can exceed 500 kilometres an hour,' said Brad. 'As you may be able to imagine, all pre-existing structures have either been destroyed or are very badly damaged. Here on the clouds we can live with the wind as opposed to struggling to survive it. You will learn much more about life on the surface soon enough.'

'Five hundred kilometre-an-hour winds! That's bonkers,' I said. 'Are you sure?'

'Gavin, we are very sure. Once you've had first-hand experience of wind speeds like that you tend not to exaggerate,' said Brad. He wasn't smiling as he spoke. He remained very serious.

'So, if we are on a cloud over Siberia, where was I when I came out of the real cloud, when I was escorted to Cloud Nine by the white doughnuts?'

'You were over central-southern England.'

'Would that be near Didcot?' I asked.

Brad stared at me for a moment. 'I'd have to verify that. I don't know the place Didcot. Does it have a resonance for you?'

'Didcot, well, it's just a town, well, it was back in 2011. It's the area where I originally entered the cloud.'

'I understand,' said Brad. 'Was there an existing power source there?'

'A power source? Yes, I suppose so, there was a massive coal-burning power station at Didcot if that's what you mean. It's enormous, you can see it for miles. Well, it was enormous for our period – back in 2011 it was enormous. Some of the things I've seen since I left have made it look a bit puny.'

'So you flew over the power source and entered an unusual cloud.'

'Yes.'

'And there was another power source on the other side.'

'Yes, a giant solar kite on a tether.'

Brad nodded slowly as if making a mental note.

'And then you went through the cloud again?'

'Yes, a few months later it reappeared and I tried going through it in the forlorn hope it would take me back to my era, back home. I now know that was stupid but that's what I thought it would do.'

'Did you fly into the cloud at the same angle?'

'I suppose so, yes. I didn't really think about it,' I replied. 'As I said, it was a bit stupid.'

'It's not stupid,' said Brad. 'It is, however, incorrect.'

I sat in silence for a while trying to take this in. You didn't need to be Inspector Morse to work out this Brad bloke seemed to know rather a lot about the cloud anomalies I'd been encountering, but he was better at asking questions than I was.

'So you understand how this happens?' I asked eventually.

Brad nodded.

'Wow,' I said. Again there was a silence.

Brad took a deep breath and held it. 'It's not an easy thing to explain and our understanding is still, as I have learned from Theda, rudimentary, but since the human race has started to be capable of generating ever-increasing levels of electrical power, we have observed that occasionally some inconsistencies are likely to occur, one of them being a momentary wormhole which has the side effect of ionic diffusion – massive electrical charges splitting water vapour, forming the clouds you have witnessed. Effectively, we have started to create accidental wormholes.'

As Brad stared at me with a serious face, there was something in his manner that made me want to giggle. I tried to suppress my amusement, but that just made it come out louder. Basically I laughed.

'Why is that amusing?' asked Brad with not a hint of a smile.

I know my eyebrows were nearly reaching my hairline but I was staggered. There was something about hearing the term 'accidental wormholes' being used by an American, not in a jokey, science fiction fashion but in all seriousness, it just tickled me.

'Sorry, I'm being a bit immature,' I said. 'It's the term "accidental wormhole"; for some reason I find it amusing.'

'Okay,' said Brad. He didn't seem offended. 'I don't want to burden you with too much information too quickly, Gavin, but if I suggest that our understanding of physics, of the mathematical laws that govern time and space have increased very dramatically in the last 200 years then you might be able to accept that the concept of the wormhole is no longer speculative or indeed amusing.'

This statement rendered me silent again. I didn't know how much they really knew about daft concepts like wormholes but Brad didn't strike me as someone whose job it was to confuse and befuddle some poor bloke who'd fallen through time.

'So did I fall through a wormhole?' I asked eventually.

'You didn't fall through one, you appear to have flown through one,' said Brad. He glanced at Theda. 'However, Theda did effectively fall through, using a paraglider.'

'You dropped through the cloud on a paraglider!' I said, looking at this stern-faced woman. She looked about as likely to strap on an unpowered flying machine as my gran.

'Correct,' she said. 'From the top of the Lichtturm in Munich.'

I stared at her nonplussed.

'The Lichtturm is a power tower in Nusslein-Vohard Square in Munich, just over 800 metres high, it's a reflected solar collector, 2,000 gigawatt capacity.'

'And you jumped off it?'

'*Ja*,' she said with a smile. 'We had noticed predictable cloud formations that contained numerous anomalies in their particle signals, it was decided that someone should attempt to enter the cloud to take some more detailed measurements. I volunteered to go.'

'Using a paraglider?'

'*Ja*, as you might recall drones have been outlawed for hundreds of years, but we had seen moving images of such devices, some of them from your period of history. We recreated one, it was very successful and although the experience can best be described as disturbing, when I came out of the cloud I realised very soon I was in a different place. I was no longer surrounded by the verdant squares of Munich, rather by a cold desert of wind-blown rock. I wondered for a moment if I had been transported to an alien planet but thankfully some human people rescued me.'

'Theda has failed to mention that she broke both legs on landing,' said Brad. 'If she hadn't been lucky enough to be spotted by some observant folks from the Munich Culvert she would have died.'

I sat in silence for a while trying, yet again, to take all this information in. Clearly the authorities in London knew a lot more about the cloud than they had let on to me. If they were trying to get through it in Munich, I felt sure there would have been people in London who knew about it. Everyone knew about everything in London 2211.

'So that means,' I said after a while, 'when I put this wristband thing on, I immediately knew all about Theda, but I knew nothing about you or Wekesa.'

'That's a very simple thing to explain,' said Theda. 'You have a kidonge, as do I. Through a quirk of electronics and communication protocols that are similar simply because they are created by humans, the kidonge can receive certain data from the band.'

'The kidonge can only receive certain data from the band,' I repeated. I felt the need to say this just to maintain my sanity.

'Correct. Here the band is used as a low-level information, identification and guidance system on-board the cloud, it allows the crew to monitor the whereabouts of passengers. However, as you can imagine, scientists such as Mister Dorschel and his associates are very interested in the kidonge technology.'

'So okay, you come from Munich. But forgive my crude twenty-first-century brain, would that Munich have been in the same time zone, world, reality, dimension, I don't even know how to ask it, but was that in the same world as the London I was in?'

'Correct. The same city but not the same historical period.'

Again I repeated what she had just said.

'I was born in 2355,' said Theda.

'You were born in 2355,' I said. 'That is quite hard to understand.'

'It is just a date, but, to help you understand a little more, I was born in the same dimension as you visited in London in 2211. If you had visited Munich that would be the same city I come from. It is the biggest city in Europe, including London. We have a very advanced research division connected to the power system. We managed to create what you call an anomaly by capturing the maximum amount of power and not releasing it into the grid, just for a few seconds. We had done it many times and each time the cloud formed, so the next obvious step was to explore the core of the cloud.'

'Okay,' I said, scratching my head furiously. 'So if I'd travelled to Munich a few days ago I could have met you?'

'No, I was already here, I've been here for two months.'

'Two months?'

'Yes,' said Theda with a smile. 'I rather like it.'

She rather liked it. She fell out of a cloud, broke both legs, left everyone she had ever known behind and ended up on a cloud with me, and the inscrutable Brad, and she liked it.

Brad spoke next.

'It is now accepted that there are many todays happening. You might like to think of it as a ring around the sun. There are many 2211s happening at the same time.'

'Brain's melting,' I said, rubbing my face. As usual Brad took little notice of my interruption.

'We don't know how many, most estimates seem to indicate 11. Before you came, we only knew of one for certain, the one Theda came from, but you have already confirmed there are two. Grenada and the cities of squares.'

'Gardenia,' I corrected. I felt slightly annoyed that he'd got it wrong.

'I apologise, Gardenia,' said Brad. 'We know they exist and I would suggest that in a few hundred years' time we will be able to travel between these worlds with ease. However, at present it is very precarious as you have experienced.'

'So you understand how I travelled here.'

'Not quite correct. We understand how you travelled from Gardenia to London, and from London to here, but we don't fully understand how you travelled from 200 years ago into now, the future. That is something we are learning fast, particularly since Theda has come here from the future. All this will greatly interest my research colleagues in the Chicago Culvert.'

'Oh Lord,' I said. 'Do I have to go to Chicago and be measured and prodded and scanned and dissected?' I said with a weary tone. 'I just want to go back home.'

Brad smiled at me and put a gentle hand on my left forearm. 'No one is going to do anything to you. We may want to talk to you, we may wish to inspect the drone you arrived in but no one is going to do anything to you. Your arrival here is fascinating, not entirely unexpected, but fascinating nonetheless.' He seemed genuinely enthusiastic about this. 'You're familiar with string theory, Gavin,' said Brad. I couldn't tell if it was a statement or a question. I'd heard of the term 'string theory' but it wasn't something I would claim to understand.

Brad took my silence as an admission of ignorance.

'String theory – I know for certain people were discussing it back in your times. That's how you're here, we use it all the time.'

'You use string theory?' I said. I knew enough about string theory to know it was a quirky notion discussed by particle physicists and involved inexplicable phenomena to do with space, time and dimensions and what happened before the Big Bang, but that didn't really help me.

'Sure,' said Brad. 'How else would you shift?'

'Shift? I don't know, I've flown through a bizarre cloud three times and my life has gone insane as a result.'

Brad patted me on the shoulder. 'Hey now, you're doing very well. You've been through three shifts, that's enough to burn anyone's synapses a little. But you've been shifting sideways and that's not good. I don't mean it's dangerous, I mean side shifting is fine if you were born in like, 2179, but for you this is not good. You need to go back, right?'

'Yes, I need to go back. I don't belong here.'

'You want to go back to where you left, to when you left That's what's going on here, that's why we were waiting for you. We're kind of confident that you will, that's what we're working on.'

I know I didn't respond. I know I was frozen mute as Brad was talking.

I was hearing someone speak who seemed to understand how I had jumped forward 200 years from way back in the twenty-first century. No one else I'd met on my ridiculous travels had much clue as to how this happened. An anomaly was all I heard in Gardenia, some mention of flocks of birds in London. But here on the cloud it seemed there was a complete acceptance and understanding of the process. I slowly took comfort in the realisation that no one here was particularly surprised or interested in seeing someone arrive from 200 years earlier because they knew how someone could. At least I assumed they all knew.

'We have one problem,' said Brad. 'And this one requires your complete co-operation.'

'What is it?' I asked. Somehow this didn't sound good.

'Although myself, Theda and some of the crew on-board Cloud Nine are aware of your origins, there are people around who, um, how should I put this …?'

'Are you talking about the Original Five?' I asked, feeling rather smug that I had remembered.

'Oh, Captain Hector has already informed you.'

'Well, kind of, the fact that there are five rubbish clouds around the equator, inhabited by weirdo's who blame me for everything that's ever happened in human history.'

'Something like that,' said Brad, with just the merest hint of a smile playing on his lips. 'So, the general populace knows nothing about your dimension of origin.'

'My what?'

'The fact that you were born back in 1979.'

'Oh, when do people think I was born?'

'2179.'

'Do they?'

'Well, the ones that have met you, yes. Any crew who have access to your tracking data will know this. The few dozen people who witnessed your arrival on-board Cloud Nine believe you to have come from another dimension but in the same time-line as the one we're in now. They do not know you come from the past.'

'And that's a problem?'

'General opinion on the actions of our forebears is negative,' said Brad flatly.

I nodded. 'Okay, so it's not just the Original Five clouds?'

'They have certainly taken the belief system to an extreme which is not helpful or constructive, but they have many sympathisers.'

'Oh, okay,' I said. 'You mean there are people on this cloud who might hate my guts, too.'

'There is a strong cultural thread that lays the blame for our current woes on the actions of your era and the ones preceding it. The actions of the people of the twentieth and twenty-first centuries have made our lives very complicated. Although there is very little logic to this way of thinking, it is the predominant meme. So the few scientists who know the facts are keen to keep them discreetly obscured for the time being.'

'Discreetly obscured,' I repeated, for no reason other than it struck me as odd. I had already been seen by thousands of people, I'd talked to a few of them.

'So, if I understand,' I said after some silent thought on my part, 'it's okay for me to say I came here from the Squares of London or Gardenia, but not that I came from Kingham in 2011?'

'Better not to mention Gardenia either.'

'Okay, so I'm from London in 2211. Is that what I should say?'

'If anyone asks, it's preferable that you try and avoid the topic altogether. As I'm sure you are aware, news travels fast, people are interested that Theda has come back from the future, they are interested that you have come sideways from another present. That much we think we can contain, but if people knew you came from the fossil age, there may be considerable disquiet. We don't want that.'

'No, we don't want that,' I agreed.

9

'HIS IS THE SUN LOUNGE,' SAID BRAD. 'YOU may wish to top up your vitamin D.'

For the first time in my guided tour of Cloud Ten, I saw something that could be described as anywhere near luxurious. Above me a deep blue sky and the strong warmth of the sun hitting my skin, all around me large cushions along with more structured day beds and large chairs. Many people seemed to be lying around and after a few moments I registered that they were completely naked. Old men, young women, children, teenagers, doddery old ladies all dotted about without a stitch on.

'I'd take advantage while you can,' said Theda, who was already halfway through removing her flight suit. She was German, so obviously being naked in public was second nature to her. I'd worked in Germany enough to know that they weren't ashamed of their bodies in the way British people were. This whole cloud had to be full of Germans – that was my explanation.

I didn't quite know what to do. I glanced at Brad who just nodded and said nothing.

'I will rejoin you later,' he said, and walked back the way we came.

I felt distinctly uncomfortable at the prospect of nudity even though my distant ancestors were supposedly from Germany, on my father's side anyway, the clue being in the name Meckler.

I shrugged and stripped off and surprised myself by feeling quite happy about it. I didn't stand out; I blended in.

'This is bloody weird,' I said to Theda, who by this point was stretched out on a day bed with a cloth over her eyes. Yes, that was the sum total of cloth-type products anywhere near her. Awkward.

'It is very important to the people here,' she said without moving. 'In the culverts there is very little direct sunlight and even less chance of taking time to lie in it. Every spare moment is devoted to maintenance and growing food so when they get a chance to spend time on a cloud, this is one of their most important activities, apart from dreaming.'

I lay back on a big cushion and realised that I wasn't actually exposed to direct sunlight or the elements; there was a barrier between me and the outside world. I couldn't see it but I understood it had to be there. We were many thousands of metres above the planet's surface, so if this area was open to the elements I'd freeze solid just after I'd suffocated.

It was warm and quiet, but not silent, I could hear murmured conversations going on around us. I saw in the distance what I took to be a family getting dressed, a man and a woman with two small children. They looked very happy as they joshed around with each other, the dad playing some tickling games with the youngest child as they struggled to get their suits on.

I lay back and allowed the sun's rays to warm me. In fact very rapidly it felt like they were roasting me.

'Intense,' I said as I rolled over. I felt quite proud of myself not ogling the various naked bodies around me. Being a product of the twentieth century, nudity had a sexual element to it no matter how above it all I tried to be. There was something about universal nudity that put the kibosh on such erotic notions. If you see a naked 22-year-old woman standing next to a naked 93-year-old bloke, something happens that isn't particularly erotic. Well, it wasn't for me.

'I feel like I'm cooking,' I said eventually.

'Don't worry, the canopy is a very effective UV filter,' said Theda. I glanced at her as she, too, turned over. I was at once appalled and fascinated and I wish I hadn't looked. I'm not saying this because she was repulsive or deformed, far from it; her body was lean and muscular and clearly in very good shape, but it just felt strange and a bit too intimate. I did flash on a couple of things as I looked away. One, what it would have been like to be next to Nkoyo, from the Squares of London, in the same circumstances, and then what it would have been like to be next to Grace from Gardenia.

I stopped myself thinking about that and sighed in relief because I was lying face down as the sun's rays scorched my backside. I felt bad because I hadn't even considered what it would be like to lie in the sun lounge next to Beth.

I tried to imagine Beth being naked on top of a cloud. It was impossible to imagine, she'd hate it, she'd think it was mad and would find the vision of hundreds of naked people who don't believe in God lying around in a plastic UV-shielded bubble perverse in the extreme.

'We are in a pressurised bubble on the top level of the cloud,' Theda said quietly. 'There are dozens of them dotted around the upper levels. Most of the passengers on-board will spend an hour a day in one of them, when they get back to their culverts their friends will often comment on the splendour of their cloud tan.'

'Okay,' I said, not really understanding anything she was saying. 'So people live in culverts all over the place because the winds are so strong, and they grow food and hunker down and try to survive and then every now and then a cloud passes and they get on-board and have a holiday. Is that an adequate description of life here?'

'I don't think it's a holiday, certainly not for children. They do most of their schooling while on-board a cloud. You may have noticed some large classrooms as we came up Elevator 20.'

'Classrooms?'

'Yes. As we went up there were some areas where we could not have alighted from the elevator, you may have seen them if you didn't have your eyes closed. There would have been a kind of balcony area and large rooms behind full of children.'

'I think I saw some balconies,' I said.

'Well some of those were schools, some are parts of the University of the Sky which is an international educational institute. Most of the research into technology and climate control is done while people are on here, so many of the people you will have seen on Cloud Ten are students, academics, engineers and scientists.'

'Wow, climate control, that sounds a bit ominous.'

'I would suggest it is essential work,' said Theda flatly.

'So from what you've seen, the climate is very different from your, um, your world.'

'Oh yes,' said Theda as she turned on her side, now facing me. I did glance but then I looked away and wished I'd chosen a cushion to lie on that was a bit further away. She didn't seem the least bit fazed to be lying next to a naked man she hardly knew.

'It is very harsh and the population is much lower. As far as I can tell from conversations I've had, it's not much above one billion.'

'Wow,' I said. That really did shock me. Everything back in 2011 predicted a massive increase in population, it seemed there were still plenty of people around in Gardenia and there were simply gazillions in the Cities of the Squares. 'One billion is nothing.'

'There simply aren't the resources to support more. Viable agricultural land has diminished to a few per cent of what it would have been in your era 200 years back. All coastal areas are either uninhabitable or flooded beyond use, sea levels have risen dramatically so you would possibly not recognise a map of the globe any more. It was hard enough for me and I know our sea levels are much higher than they would have been back in 2011.'

'And do they know what caused this weather?'

'Of course,' said Theda flatly. 'As Brad indicated to you earlier, they know precisely and they're not very happy about it. They dream about it, Gavin.'

'Dream about what?'

'About what it was like in your time, indeed in historical periods even before your era. I haven't told you this before, I feel I can predict your reaction so I have hesitated.'

'My reaction to what?'

'Here on the clouds they have the technology to record and create dreams.'

Theda looked at me. I was trying hard not to react. I wanted her to think I was not quite as backward and ignorant as I might initially appear. I failed.

'Quite so,' she said with a smile. 'You find that distressing.'

'No. Well, no, incomprehensible maybe.'

'They have dream recordings from before the winds. They really understand what it was like back in your day. When you sleep in the pods you will be able to dream about your time. I know what it was like. I have been there; I have experienced the past in a most convincing way. I think you will be surprised.'

10

ADMIT IT, I HAD A LITTLE PANIC ATTACK when I woke up in my sleeping pod. It happened before I was properly awake, I felt I couldn't breathe and my arms and legs started lashing about. I thought I was having a nightmare that I'd been buried alive; I was trapped in a small box and I couldn't get out. It all got rapidly worse when I realised I actually was in a small box and couldn't quite recall how I got into it.

I had claustrophobia I suppose. I don't know for sure because I'd never had it before, but there was something about the low levels of light, the closeness of the walls and ceiling that just got to me.

I was also very aware of movement. I think that may have been what woke me with such alarm. I became panicked and very confused, I was trying to work out why I was trapped underground but falling. I went through all sorts of mental contortions trying to work it out; maybe I was in a self-flying machine as there were no controls. I needed something to grab and steer with. There was nothing.

I eventually managed to control my fears and climb out of the box and my mental state went from screaming panic to deep embarrassment in an adrenaline-fuelled heartbeat.

I was getting out of sleeping pod number 32 on floor 2011.

As usual I had no idea what the time was, where I was or if I would be able to ask anyone to help me. The long corridor outside my sleeping pod seemed deserted. Everywhere I'd been on Cloud Ten had always been busy, always full of people and yet suddenly I was alone.

I stretched and yawned, scratched my head and tried to work

out how to respond to this utterly bizarre moment. I could just get back in my cosy pod and wait for someone to come and find me.

That's when the memory of my dream hit me and it was like being hit by a bus. That's the thing; I'd just been on a bus going down Oxford Street in London. I think it was a hybrid bus, certainly not something I'd ever been on in real life, but the dream was so vivid I wasn't sure what was real and what wasn't.

I was on a bus in London and outside the wind was howling along the street, the rain was horizontal and I could see people walking along struggling with their umbrellas.

I could feel the fabric of the seat I was on. It was incredibly detailed and real, all sorts of images from my dream came back to me and this wasn't an experience I was used to.

I don't deny that I have dreams, I'm sure I do, however, I very rarely remember them when I wake up. I hadn't remembered this one when I woke up, I just felt trapped and enclosed in a box. It was only after getting out of the pod that the vivid memory started to return. It was frightening because it wasn't a hazy memory of a dream, a sequence of events that made no sense. It was more like being in a movie, created by someone else but featuring me. I was actually experiencing the events. Everything around me, the fabric of the city, the bus, the people on the street, the taxis, the cyclists, the shops and buildings were all very familiar. It was Oxford Street. I distinctly remember looking in the window of Boots and seeing a very fat girl looking at make-up. It was London back in my era, no doubt about it. Other than the hybrid bus, everything was as it should be.

I felt a bit sick and wanted to be anywhere but on a damned cloud floating above Siberia. I started to shuffle down the corridor of sleeping pods as the previous day's experiences started to come back to me: the explanation of the cloud, northern Siberia, Theda and spooky American Brad and the sun lounge, Theda naked and hearing cryptic information about the weather and dreams that had been recorded and could be played back. It didn't really help.

Then a figure suddenly appeared at the far end of the rows of pod doors. It was a young woman dressed in the regulation flight suit but with a kind of orange shawl around her shoulders. She walked past me giving me a cursory nod. I turned and watched her continue on her way. She stopped, put her hand on a pod door and it immediately opened. It was only then I realised it was number 32. She was getting into my pod, well, the pod I'd just half fallen out of.

I stood motionless as she very expertly clambered inside and the door closed behind her. Had she been coming to see me? Was she some kind of sexual companion that the spooky Brad had arranged? Was I meant to go back and join her?

It may seem ridiculous now, but this place was so weird anything seemed possible. Nothing I'd previously experienced in any of the time zones, realities or bizarre cities I'd been in could have prepared me for waking up on a massive man-made cloud and having a young woman climb into what had effectively been my bedroom.

Then I remembered Wekesa had explained to me that people sleep in shifts. Somehow the woman must have known I'd vacated the pod and she could get inside and sleep there.

My nose wrinkled involuntarily. I hadn't exactly tidied up when I'd got out. I was in such a panicked state I had literally just clambered out. I stared at the long rows of doors trying to remember if I'd left anything in there. I patted myself up and down, I didn't have anything except for the suit I was wearing and the band around my wrist, but I hadn't exactly left it fresh and tidy.

'Don't worry, Gavin, the pods are self-cleaning,' said Theda. She was suddenly standing beside me. I looked up.

'How do you do that?' I said.

'Do what?'

‘Creep up on people like that. Where have you come from?’

Theda gestured over her shoulder. A pod door was just closing behind her and I assumed that was where she was sleeping.

‘I don’t think I was creeping,’ she said. ‘I was sitting at the back of the bus and so when you got off I knew you had woken and I decided to join you.’

‘What bus? You mean the dream! Were you having the same dream?’

‘Yes.’

‘How? That is sick, you were on the bus with me?’

‘Yes, I kept my distance because I thought you might find it too disturbing, if I had sat next to you and told you we were both dreaming in the same place you might . . . ’

‘Might what? Go mad?’

‘Yes, something like that. It is very confusing and I don’t wish to add to your stress. I am finding the experience of being here and the power of the dream machine just as stressful as you.’

‘I think I might have gone mad. I feel burnt out, I don’t know what to do.’

‘Try to relax, you are not in any way damaged, just follow me.’

I followed Theda as she walked back along the corridor. I was very grateful for her company as I wasn’t sure which way to go, far less what to do with myself.

Once we’d reached the kind of vestibule area near the dimly lit canteen I started to remember some of my travels the day before. The shape and structure of the cloud was so confusing I could not seem to get my bearings.

I normally had a good grasp of buildings I was in, I understood how they fitted together and I could generally find my way around them. The cloud threw that skill out of the window. Nothing looked that familiar as we walked through the now busy vestibule. Even calling it a vestibule is pointless; it was more a kind of big balloon with a lot of smaller long, thin balloons going off it in various directions. One thing I did notice was that the lighting seemed more intense than it had the night before.

'I have no idea what time it is,' I said.

'Time is flexible,' said Theda flatly. She carried on walking almost as if my asking about the time was annoying and childish.

'That really doesn't help,' I said, bouncing along the unstable floor. 'I can't deal with theoretical physics right now.'

'I am not trying to confuse you. It was decided to schedule your sleep periods to avoid exhaustion so you went to sleep when it was appropriate for you to sleep. If you want to know what time you went to sleep it was about 11 o'clock in the morning, but that was morning above the Krasnoyarsk Culvert, in what you would know as Russia. It is now three o'clock in the afternoon in the Calgary Culvert, that is, in what you would have known as Canada.'

'Yes, I know where Calgary is,' I said. 'So we've moved from eastern Russia to Canada while I've been sleeping and dreaming about a bus on Oxford Street 200 years ago.'

'Yes, correct. We are now descending to try and make a docking at the Chicago Culvert. No doubt it was the movement that woke you.'

I obediently followed Theda into the canteen and joined a long queue heading toward what I took to be a kind of server area. Even here, somewhere I'd been before I'd slept, seemed bizarre and almost dreamlike in its complexity and confusion. There was a queue but it was almost as deep as it was long. It was basically a crowd of people all facing the same way, a bit like an audience at an open-air rock concert, however, it was quiet and very orderly.

'All the food on-board is paste- or liquid-based,' said Theda as we waited. 'It is not very nice but is perfectly nutritious.'

'I'm not sure I'm hungry,' I said.

'You need to eat. There is no knowing if we can dock at

Chicago, that is why all these people are here, they will all be getting off if we can make a docking.'

'You seem to know a lot about how things work around here,' I said as we shuffled forward a little.

'I learn fast,' said Theda. 'I have been here two months, one month in the Munich Culvert, the rest on the clouds. This will be my first time in the Chicago Culvert.'

'I know you've been here two months,' I said, 'I can just about understand that.'

'I fell through the cloud nearly 200 years after you left London,' said Theda, as if this information was just that, information, not a mind-shattering revelation.

'Okay,' I said, really wishing I could sit down. I felt a little dizzy.

Theda turned and looked at me. She almost smiled. 'I can understand how you would find such information difficult to digest, I will try to explain in simple terms,' she said as we slowly shuffled forwards.

'I studied your case along with a great many other people. It was very interesting and garnered a great deal of attention. As you may know the first manifestation of shifts also happened in London, the sighting of swallows long thought to be extinct.'

I remembered being made aware of this when I was at my first press conference, the one I cried at.

'Your arrival was obviously much more interesting, as was your departure. After you had left there was intense interest both on a personal level from all the people you interacted with directly, and from the global scientific community. So from the moment you were witnessed disappearing into the cloud until the time I left, vast resources and intellectual capital have been expended on discovering how this phenomenon could take place. How a human being and a machine could fall through time and how we could utilise this system to benefit the species.'

'Blimey,' I said eventually, and that was it. I certainly couldn't speak and by this point we had shuffled to the front of the enormous queue. I was handed three soft sachets of liquid stuff by someone so young I assumed school-age children did all the cooking.

That said, there wasn't anything to actually cook, they were just handing out identical pillows with different black labels on one side.

'Breakfast for time shifters,' said Theda with a big grin. 'We need to descend to the loading bays fairly soon. Do you wish to have breakfast here before we go down?'

'Oh, right, we have to use the elevator again.'

'I'm afraid so, in fact more than one.'

'Maybe I'll wait until we go down then,' I said, not fancying the prospect of losing my breakfast all over the people below me on the terrifying blue wall of doom.

I followed Theda through the crowd until we were in another similar wide queue that was heading toward the distant blue wall. Again I could see people sliding up and down and I tried to convince myself that this was all normal and there was nothing to be concerned about.

'So, you didn't know any of the people I met in London?' I asked as we slowly moved forward.

'No, if you think about it that would be doubtful, they would all have to be over 200 years old, but I read a great deal about them. Clearly you made a very big impression on Doctor Nkoyo Oshineye, she spoke about you with great affection and emotion.'

'Did she?' I said, I couldn't help feeling a little buoyed by this news. 'I always had the impression she found me a little bit annoying.'

Theda smiled at me. 'Ready?' she asked, as she turned around and stepped back toward the blue wall behind her. 'Just keep your eyes shut, that's what I do.'

We had made it to the front of the queue and all around us people had turned their back on the blue wall and were dropping like a torrent over a waterfall.

I turned my back on the wall, clutched the three plastic breakfast pouches to my chest and felt my clothing engage with the wall.

The descent on Cloud Nine was bad enough, but that was gentle and slow in comparison with this vertical human highway. I felt the wind rushing past me as we slid down, initially following Theda's advice and keeping my eyes tightly shut. Curiosity got the better of me however, and I couldn't help having a peek. I soon discovered that as long as I didn't look down it was okay, I was just looking out at floors rushing past, the balconies and wide walkways. Just as Theda had described I caught glimpses of brightly lit school rooms full of kids, people running about playing sports, large lecture theatres and everywhere crowds of people.

I imagine the descent took all of two minutes but it felt like an hour and as we emerged into the main lobby where I'd first seen the elevator I nearly screamed. I must have been more than a hundred metres up as the vast arena of the crowded space was revealed to me; to call it a dizzying spectacle is a pathetic attempt at describing the experience. Nauseating horror at the prospect of instant and painful death would be slightly better. However, almost as soon as this terrifying scene took the breath out of my lungs, I felt a slow but powerful deceleration as we neared the floor.

'Lean forward a little,' said Theda. I glanced at her. Her eyes were still tightly closed and I copied her as she moved her head and shoulders away from the shimmering blue wall.

We slowed more violently until my feet made contact with the floor of the vast atrium with barely a jolt. I walked forward as best I could, knowing there were bound to be others right behind me.

'Okay, come with me and we'll have a look at the scene below us,' said Theda. 'This is my favourite part of the cloud.'

Again we made slow progress through the seemingly endless crowds of people that were slowly milling in one direction. It was very difficult; they were all heading out of the atrium area while we seemed to be crossing the flow.

I think I must have said 'sorry' and 'excuse me' many hundreds of times as we slowly made our way toward a small opening in the side of the space. As soon as we'd cleared the crowds we moved faster.

'Can you sense that we are still descending?' asked Theda as she walked briskly along a slight downward slope in the long white balloon corridor.

'I think my senses are fried,' I said. 'Where are we going?'

'The lower observation deck, hopefully we will have time to have a look before we disembark. I am taking a risk, this is not something I normally like to do, but since my initial journey through the anomaly cloud I have been less risk-averse. Have you found this to be the case?'

I was almost running now to keep up with the tall figure striding slightly ahead of me. 'I don't know,' I said. 'Maybe you're right, I certainly don't feel the need for the kind of planning and control over my life I used to worry about. I just do things and then weird stuff happens. Maybe I'm getting used to it.'

'Exhilarating isn't it?' said Theda with a big toothy smile, 'Down here.'

I was faced with another blue wall, this one only wide enough for maybe four people side by side, a kind of B road of vertical human highways.

Theda almost threw herself against the blue surface and immediately disappeared down the chute. I hesitated for a moment, said 'Oh fuck it,' and followed her.

Thankfully the descent was over in a few seconds and I found myself in the centre of a circular room with a handful of people all looking out of large windows around one half of the space. The windows were clearly designed for looking down as they were sloped outward. A reassuringly stout support rail you could lean on ran horizontally at waist height above the floor. I stumbled about looking for Theda, but when everyone wears much the same outfit it's hard to pick an individual out from a crowd.

'Gavin, over here!' I heard, and turned to see Theda by one of the windows. 'Look down there,' she said, pointing down. '*Mein Gott*, that is impressive!'

As soon as I joined her I saw what she meant. A giant curved wall, no, more like a small mountain range stretching away into the mist. It was smooth, curved, shining, man-made and vast beyond comprehension. To one side a plain of light brown dirt, rocks and what could have been broken pieces of concrete. To the other side, beneath odd-looking transparent dome structures was lush vegetation, the domes surrounded by low protuberances of baffling design and even more baffling purpose.

'The Chicago Culvert,' said Theda. 'The largest culvert on the planet.'

11

I DON'T WANT TO GO ON ABOUT THE CLOUD Ten elevators too much, but they are very difficult things to forget once you've been on them. The internal ones are challenging enough; I think for me it was the total lack of any mechanical support, no handrails, footrests or padded hydraulic safety enclosures. You literally slid up and down a blue sheet and relied entirely on a bizarre system of electro-magnetic materials that you just had to believe wouldn't fling you to your doom.

I had understood that Cloud Ten was so ridiculously vast that it could not 'land' in any conventional way. It could only come within about 50 metres of the Earth's surface if the winds were low enough, which I had to assume they were because we were clearly approaching the surface.

While I was looking down on the eye-popping spectacle of the Chicago Culvert I felt a tingle on my left wrist. It was the band I was wearing – it had gone a bright red colour.

'We have to go,' said Theda. 'Brad is waiting for us.'

Once again we shot up the short blue elevator and made our way back along the tubular corridor to the huge atrium at the foot of Elevator 20. By this time I could sense that one side of the wristband was tingling. Although at that moment I didn't know why, after a little thought as we made our way through the still slow-moving crowds I realised it was tingling in the direction we were headed.

The tingling faded when I made out the diminutive figure of Brad standing by one of the bizarre candy-twist inflated supports that dotted the structure we were in.

'We have a limited window for descent. Currently the weather is calm and we need to get off here,' he said, grabbing my arm and pulling me into the slow-moving crowd. 'Did you get a chance to see the abutments?' he said, as we slowly shuffled forward.

'I think so,' I said. 'I couldn't understand what I was looking at but it was very big.'

'It's an engineering miracle,' said Brad proudly, 'the biggest abutments on the planet, 90 kilometres long and just over one kilometre high.'

'Yep, that sounds big,' I said.

'It's covered in over 40 million carbon ceramic tiles.'

'That's a lot of tiles,' I said.

'It's a work of beauty as well as life-saving protection for the culvert,' said Brad. 'But first, I urgently need to explain about the exit elevator. You need to listen carefully.'

'Exit elevator?'

'Yes, it's just the same as the elevators you've used on-board, the only difference being that the logistics needed to get this many people on and off the cloud requires discipline. As soon as we make contact with ground you must stick with me, we will be turning to our left and we must make our way very rapidly into the clearing area. Don't hang around looking up and around. For a first-timer it is a spectacular sight but I really need an assurance from you that you will resist the temptation. Move fast, stick with me, Theda will be right behind you. Okay, Theda?'

'Good for me,' she said, and gave me a reassuring pat on the back. 'You will be fine, Gavin.'

By this time we had neared yet another blue wall. This one clearly only went down, as there was a large inflated kind of cushion just above head height running along the top. The cushions glowed a dull green colour and made a noticeable humming noise, the sort of noise made by very powerful electrical equipment; it was a low and dangerous hum and it didn't make me relax.

All the time I was trying to take this in, we were nearing the blue wall; however, at that moment I noticed there was another identical wall on the other side of the tubular corridor we were in. There were hundreds of people appearing up that one and rapidly moving off into the central area of Cloud Ten. They didn't look happy or terrified, just determined. Although the people popping up the inbound elevator were as diverse as everyone I'd seen on the cloud, the white members of this group looked paler, if anything a little pallid and ill.

The crowd I was shuffling along with all looked a bit healthier and happier. Maybe the cloud was like a holiday camp, the sort of place I remember my parents describing: bizarre ex-military camps that were converted into makeshift holiday resorts after World War II. I wondered for a moment whether if you stood by the gates of a holiday gulag back in the 1950s and watched the people leaving passing the people arriving, that a similar contrast would be visible. I decided this floating holiday camp was probably a little more extreme.

The people in front us were turning and descending in their hundreds on either side but due to the sheer numbers it still took a while for us to get up close.

Before long we neared the opening and I could feel warm air rising out of the opening that people in front of me were disappearing down.

Brad grabbed my arm and pulled me forward as we moved along the row rapidly until there was just one row of people with their backs to the wall. They all leant back in unison and immediately slid out of sight.

'Turn,' said Brad. By now at least I was used to the sensation and fell back against the wall.

'Stick with me,' Brad shouted as we descended. I gave him the thumbs-up sign as I knew there was no way I could talk. I was right.

This descent was even more terrifying than the last. For a start the blue wall was not static. In all my previous experience with this ridiculous transportation system the wall had been still and I just had to accept that whatever was holding me wasn't going to fail. The big difference to the internal elevators was that this blue wall billowed and twisted quite violently – I now assume it was from the winds but at the time I just felt just sheer terror, I didn't think anything. Sometimes it felt like going down a kids' slide, as there was something beneath me that I was sliding down, but the next moment I was literally hanging maybe 80 metres in the air with seemingly nothing holding me there.

Below me I could see crowds of people moving in one direction and next to them another long line moving in another. For some bizarre reason it reminded me of films I'd seen of vast parades in Communist countries like China and Soviet Russia; no individuals, just huge masses of people creating patterns with their precise, regimented movements.

As the blue sheet billowed again I felt a strong movement of warm air blasting me in the face. Warm and very dry air thundered in my ears and everything suddenly seemed violent and dangerous.

At one point the giant blue wall more resembled a thin bed sheet blowing in the wind on laundry day. My eyes were dazzled by what I saw. On another elevator I spotted thousands of people going up into the cloud. I heard screams of terror from children, I heard shouts from men, everything chaotic and panicked.

'Ready?' shouted Brad. I glanced down, beneath me I could see long lines of people moving off to my left but we seemed to be coming down right on top of them. A bald man's head looked as if it was directly beneath my feet.

At this point I realised many things in a split second. The blue elevator sheet I was attached to was part of Cloud Ten, it was joined on and Cloud Ten was moving. This meant the bottom of the blue elevators were also not static, they were moving across what looked like a large paved area sunken into the top of the Chicago Culvert.

They were moving across this paved area at speed.

'Lean forward!' shouted Brad. I did so, and my feet made contact with hard ground. It felt like someone had just hammered the soles of my feet. I felt heavy and had the wind knocked out of me.

'Go, move! Fast!' Brad shouted and I followed him. We moved at a slow jog, there were hundreds of people in front of him all moving in the same direction. We were jogging in a line alongside the blue sheet, in fact we were running at an angle to the sheet because it was moving towards my left shoulder all the time.

'Don't look up!' shouted Brad.

'This is fucking crazy,' said Theda, who I sensed at once was right behind me. 'Keep going!'

I heard a noise to one side of me; a small Chinese woman landed right next to me and started moving at the same pace as everyone else. She barely batted an eyelash. She had just slid down a hundred metres of flapping blue electro-magnetic sheet and started walking briskly with the crowd.

Moments later an African man who was taller than me appeared to my left. It was literally raining every ethnicity of humanity around me and still we kept moving.

Everyone was moving as fast as they could, young and old, some people carrying small children, everyone's face set in grim determination.

At the same speed that the whole chaos and terror of the descent had started, it stopped. We ran under a substantial concrete lintel and entered an enormous hall where the massed ranks of people descending from the cloud spread out like a bucket of water spilled on a kitchen floor.

'That was immense,' said Theda. She was still half pushing me forward, but the pushing turned into a series of slaps on the back. 'I cannot believe we survived that, was that not seriously immense, Gavin?'

'It was, it was very immense,' I said, now almost running to keep up with the briskly walking Brad.

'But this should be very interesting,' said Theda as we approached a group of people standing to one side of a vast space we had entered. They looked eager and a little solemn but not particularly threatening, all of them wearing similar floor-length brown robes.

'Our greeting party I believe,' said Theda discreetly.

I stared in bemusement as we approached; they looked a fairly raggle-taggle bunch, some tall and thin, some short and stout, men and women, old and young. Most of them were smiling, but as we got closer I noticed a few of them looked a little frightened.

Brad joined them and turned toward us with one arm outstretched.

'Commissioners!' he bellowed. 'May I introduce you to the two most remarkable people on the planet right now. Theda Meckler and Gavin Meckler.'

There was a small smattering of slightly embarrassed applause. I almost took a bow, but glanced at Theda who had her hands together in front of her like someone at prayer. I copied her as inconspicuously as I could, which I admit would not have been very inconspicuous but I didn't want to stand out. It was only after I stood up straight that the introduction I'd just heard registered. Theda Meckler. She had the same name as me.

Why hadn't I noticed that when I got all the information about her through the kidonge?

I somehow knew immediately that this wasn't my error; I would just have known her name was Theda Meckler. I wouldn't have to wonder. She had somehow blocked that piece of information from me. I didn't know why but I really wanted to find out.

12

'ELCOME TO CHICAGO!' SHOUTED A VERY SHORT Japanese woman. 'I hope your journey was uneventful.'

'It was very relaxing,' said Theda, adding in a much louder voice, 'thank you, Commissioner.'

'And how about you, Gavin, did you have a relaxing time on Cloud Ten?'

I smiled; this little woman was so unthreatening and charming I couldn't help it. 'Uh, yeah, it was okay.' Her face looked perturbed, so I shouted, 'Yeah, it was fine. Thanks.'

'So, let us retire from the noise and bustle. We have some solid food waiting, you may wish to chew something again.'

'Chewing would be good,' I shouted.

The commissioners, whoever they were, made a gangway for us, staring at us all the while as we passed between them. At this point we were in an enormous low-ceilinged building, well, maybe the ceiling wasn't that low but it looked low because the room was so vast. It had to be many thousands of square metres in size but it was hard to tell, it was very dimly lit. There were what looked like natural daylight openings in the ceiling and some artificial lighting around the wall we were near, but the thing that jangled my nerves was the noise. It was very noisy; the small Japanese woman had been shouting at us, she was standing right in front of us and I could still only just hear her. So many people in a big room with low ceilings meant the acoustics were pretty terrible. It was the first time I'd been able to articulate a criticism of any technology or structure I'd seen since leaving 2011.

Where some of the hallways and atriums on Cloud Ten had been breathtaking in their elaborate and enormous vision, this building was ultra-utilitarian, almost like a military facility. No decorative embellishments anywhere.

We passed through a very wide, low opening and into another low-ceilinged room. This one had a large circular table in the centre beneath what I took to be a natural light opening above. Along one side of the room was a kind of buffet, but again it was all displayed in regimented rows of black containers. There was nothing gentle or pretty to look at.

The crowd of commissioners followed us but stood around the walls looking at us as we wandered about. I tried to stay next to Theda, who seemed to absolutely tower above everyone else in the room.

The Japanese woman emerged out of the brown-clad throng. I noticed the cloth she was wearing was very fine. It wasn't as if all these brown-clad people were a bunch of monks in crudely woven tunics, the material was very fine and light.

'Now we can hear ourselves think,' she said. 'Allow me to introduce myself: I am Michiyo Nishimura, I sit on the Council of Commissioners here in Chicago. We are a community of just over four million people and, as I believe Doctor Dorschel has explained, not everyone in the culvert knows the full details of your arrival. However, in this room we all know and there is great excitement among our small scientific community. I want you to feel assured that you are both very welcome here and I want to underline the fact for you, Gavin, you are safe here.'

'Gavin is fully aware of the threat posed by the Original Five,' said Brad. I nodded to confirm this, which was of course ridiculous as I had no real idea of who the hell the Original Five where, how many sympathisers they had, if they had secret agents
hidden in small terror cells on Cloud Ten or even in the Chicago Culvert. I was dimly aware of some clouds called the Original Five, that was all.

Michiyo made a small, almost imperceptible bow to which I

 responded with a low bow. I'd worked in Japan and knew all about bowing; however, my movement caused a small ripple of mirth among the other brown-clad commissioners. I grimaced.

'Do not worry, Gavin,' said Michiyo. 'There will be many things we don't understand about each other but we will both learn fast enough I'm sure.'

She turned toward the long table with the black food containers and gestured gracefully. 'Please help yourself to food, we have been awaiting your arrival and will join you if that is acceptable.'

'Thank you,' said Theda.

'Yes, thank you very much,' I said. A short African man handed me a large black plate. It was incredibly lightweight and my forearm jerked up a little when I took possession. My muscle memory must have assumed it was going to be heavy because it was so large, so I did that arm jerk thing. Again this caused amusement to the crowd of people staring at me.

'Forgive us, please,' said Michiyo kindly. 'We are all so fascinated to meet you, we are fairly isolated here and have never previously had visitors from the other dimensions, let alone other historic periods.'

Over the next few minutes I slowly put things on my plate, all the time watching how other members of the small gathering did theirs. I didn't want to pile up a great mound and then notice that everyone else was eating a mere morsel, but the plate was so big. The reason for this became apparent when I saw that everyone arranged small piles of the different ingredients in a neat pattern around the plate.

I say different ingredients – it was all vegetables and fermented curds, beans and salads, not exactly the burger and chips that I had visualised when told there would be something to chew on.

'Your journeys here must have been spectacular and full of anxiety,' said Michiyo, when we had sat down on small stools around the circular table. 'It is very hard for us to imagine what you have been through.'

I just nodded, it was such a relief to not be the sole centre of attention. Theda held forth in her slightly clipped German accent while I stuffed my mouth with perfectly adequate vegetarian food. I'm not saying it was rubbish – it didn't have quite the complexity of flavours and freshness of Gardenian cuisine or the reassuring familiarity of the printed food I'd had in London – but it was better than the creamy grey paste I'd been sucking on in Cloud Ten.

'And, Gavin, for you this must have been even more terrifying. Had you never seen clouds before in your world?'

I glanced around the large circular table. Everyone was suddenly looking at me and of course I had my mouth full of salad.

I wasn't sure what I could say. I didn't know for sure if some of the Original Five people were in the room. I had no idea who all the people were; they could have been mad axe murderers for all I knew, just waiting for their chance to express their anger at the destruction wrought by my generation.

'It's okay, Gavin, you can speak safely here,' said Brad calmly.

I chewed faster, swallowed and hoped I wouldn't spit bits of salad onto the table as I spoke.

'I'd seen clouds, yes, well, obviously, you know, we had clouds. We had everything, you know, clouds, sea, mountains, rivers and stuff. But it wasn't like this. We could be outside any day of the year, you know. I mean we had weather, it rained a lot in England, where I'm from, that was normal, but there were sunny days that weren't too hot, and cold days that weren't too cold. I suppose you could call our weather benign, it was calm most of the time. There was the hurricane in 1987, when I was a kid. A tree came down in our garden and crushed my dad's shed, my brother and I thought it was great but my dad's lawnmower was mashed up so he wasn't too happy.'

It was too late, I was rambling. I wanted to stop but everyone was listening. All I really wanted to find out was why Theda hadn't let me know she had the same name as me. I wanted to know if there was a connection but I couldn't bring myself to ask her in front of all these people. While I was thinking this, my mouth was still going, blabbering out nonsense.

'I mean, it wasn't that different, you know, back in 2011, well, I don't really know what it's like here, I've only seen the clouds so far. They are incredible, I mean we only had clouds made of water vapour, not ones people live on. It's very difficult to understand, I mean, it wasn't as if people weren't talking about things like global warming and stuff back then, they were, loads of people talked about it, they had big conferences in places like Copenhagen saying they were going to do something about it, they had worldwide agreements on things like carbon emissions but it didn't seem like people were actually doing anything about it other than talking. Some people were saying that the weather would change due to what we were all doing back then, but it was normal, what we were doing seemed normal to us. I'd never seen a world where there wasn't, I don't know, like cheap, abundant energy. I want to say to you that not everything we did was wrong; we were making amazing jumps in technology and our understanding of the world. I know it will seem crude and ridiculous to you now, I mean, I can look back at the people who made early steam trains and water pumps and be amazed at how crude and imperfect those things were, but I admire them, too. They didn't set out to destroy the world by burning coal; they set out to make the world better. They didn't know what the long-term consequences would be and neither did we. That's all I want to say really. Oh yes, and I'm really sorry for the mess we seem to have made for you,' I said.

'Thank you, Gavin, that is very interesting,' said Michiyo. 'This information is very useful to us. If it is acceptable to you, I would like you to tell us a great deal more. Not now, you need to rest and acclimatise to life in the culvert, but over the next few days my team would very much appreciate all the information you can give us about the past. We live in very different times. The only thing I can say now is welcome to the Anthropocene.'

13

HAVE A POWERFUL MEMORY OF WATCHING *The Empire Strikes Back* when I was about 12. My dad had a VHS copy of the film and it was a big treat one winter Sunday afternoon to sit in front of the telly and watch a proper film with no advertising breaks.

For some reason the early scene where the rebels close the outer doors on the ice planet Hoth had a lasting emotional impact on me.

'Close the outer doors!' shouted someone dressed in an orange jumpsuit. People ran about getting ready for the outer doors to close because night-time temperatures on Hoth were not to be messed with.

Luke was still out in the icy wastes. He was going to die! Thankfully Han Solo found him before it was too late. He used Luke's lightsaber to cut open the belly of the dead Tauntaun and then stuffed Luke's half-frozen body into its stinking stomach cavity to keep him warm. That was also a moment burned into my memory.

However, I never wanted to be Luke or Han. I wanted to be one of the rebel technicians behind the closed outer doors. They knew you had to close those outer doors before the freezing storm killed everyone; they understood things and knew what to do.

During the afternoon of my first day in the Chicago Culvert, a very similar scene was played out in a very frightening and real way. It was nothing short of spooky, almost as if there had been some kind of subconscious meta-memory leaking back into the mind of George Lucas in the 1980s.

Michiyo and a few of the other commissioners took Theda

 and me through a maze of dark corridors, down a couple of flights of steps that I would guess, from the sound our feet made on them, were made of some kind of carbon composite, and into a large hangar area.

As we stood looking around this vast hall, Michiyo explained that we were actually under what they called the Outer Abutment: the giant tiled mountain range I'd seen from Cloud Ten.

On one side of this enormous space was an opening to the outside world and what I saw through that opening was distressing.

A sun-bleached blasted rock desert for as far as I could see, which due to the deep blue sky and clear air was quite a long way. Not a trace of vegetation, no hint of a man-made structure, just a great open expanse of rubble going on forever. The sky above seemed clear and blue. It wasn't cold like the ice planet Hoth, in fact the wind blowing in through the wide doorway was hot, dry and unpleasant.

There was so much going on it was impossible for me to take it all in. Although very few people were in the space it was still incredibly busy. Machines, walking machines, were going in and out of the doorway non-stop. These multi-legged robots, most about the size of small cars, didn't have some bloke dressed in orange overalls driving them; they were sleek, efficient and clearly fully autonomous machines. The ones passing me by as I stood in the wide entrance were carrying enormous piles of some very smooth black sheet material on their flat backs.

'Do not fear them,' said Michiyo. 'They are aware of your presence, they will not harm you but it's best we leave them to get on with their vital tasks. They have to work very fast.'

We stood at one side of the entrance as I stared slack-jawed at the mechanical mayhem going on around me. The bots kept their distance, skirting around us as we stepped onto the broken ground just outside the culvert. Here the wind was hot, dry and very strong.

'It is best we go no further than this,' said Michiyo. 'We may need to return at any moment, the weather patterns are highly unstable.'

I nodded my understanding. The noise around us was intense, but even from this sheltered vantage point I could assess the true scale of the structure I had been in.

As far as I could see in either direction was a massive man-made mountain of black plates or tiles disappearing into the distance. In the far haze I could see machines working but other than us I did not spot any signs of human life.

All along the culvert protection abutment, multi-legged robots too numerous to count were busy clearing rubble from the lower areas by picking it up piece by piece with their numerous arm-type appendages and flinging it many tens of metres away. The piles they were creating were then being crushed flat by large autonomous caterpillar tracked machines fitted with enormous backhoe digging arms. They also had some kind of spray attachment fitted to the rear, which dispensed a thick grey goo over the rubble. It was guesswork on my part but I assumed this was to secure loose particles that would otherwise be picked up by the wind, causing damage to the outer walls.

These activities were noisy and to my human eye utterly chaotic, they made no sense to me. It seemed like a pointless activity; the bots weren't making anything or if they were, it just looked like a mess, like an endless quarry that produced nothing. These weren't mining machines, that much was obvious. They weren't extracting ore, they just seemed to be expending huge amounts of energy pointlessly moving stuff about.

Michiyo pointed to an area above us and to our right. I spotted a cluster of multi-legged machines busy replacing a large area of black tiles. I say tiles, they were each the size of a double bed but because the wall before me was so vast, when in place they looked like tiny mosaic tiles.

'We had a severe impact up there during the last storm so we have to repair it before the next,' she shouted. 'The bots work whenever the wind is low enough for them to carry out the task.'

'It seems fairly windy at the moment,' I shouted as the air thundered around us.

Michiyo smiled. 'Gavin, believe me, this is a calm day.'

Theda was busy talking to one of the other commissioners in German so I couldn't follow what they were talking about, but I could tell it was an explanation of some sort – they did a lot of pointing and nodding.

I turned back to Michiyo. Something she had said when we were eating our rather plain vegetarian lunch had concerned me.

'Michiyo, what was that term you used when we were eating? You welcomed me to something, you used a word I don't know.'

'The Anthropocene.'

'The Anthropocene?'

'You've never heard that term?'

'No, what does it mean?'

'This,' said Michiyo, spreading her small arms wide, 'is the Anthropocene.'

She held the pose for a while, I suppose for dramatic impact, although that kind of thing is usually lost on me. I was looking at a diminutive Japanese woman standing on a dusty rock-strewn vista with a hot wind blowing around her.

'Okay,' I said. I was none the wiser. 'So, um, are you telling me this Anthropocene is a bad thing?'

Michiyo smiled at me. 'You don't know, do you?'

'No, I don't know what you are talking about,' I replied as calmly as I could. I was beginning to feel irked, she was using a word I'd never come across before and expected me to understand it. In my experience that is not how you learn.

'The Anthropocene is an epoch, part of the geological timescale. I believe it was coined in your era by a man called Eugene Stoermer.'

'I've never heard of him,' I said dismissively. I wanted to imply that whoever he was, he wasn't big news in my day.

'As is often the case,' replied Michiyo, 'there are people in every era who realise something profound but who are ignored by their peers.'

I nodded my understanding. She had a point.

'For the last 66 million years our planet has been going through the Cenozoic era, the era of mammals. The most recent epoch within that era has been the Holocene.'

'I've heard of the Holocene,' I said. Michiyo nodded and smiled sweetly.

'The Holocene is the epoch which ended around the time period you come from. It was the epoch when human beings became the dominant species on earth. We now know the epoch ended about 250 years ago as human activities started to make measurable changes to the lithosphere. From that point on we entered the Anthropocene. The word's roots are Greek, *Anthropo* meaning human and *cene* meaning new.'

'So what are you telling me, is this—' I waved my arms around, '—this mess was caused by human activities?'

'Sadly that is correct. We have had to adapt to it. It has not been easy but we are getting better at it.'

I stared out at the bleak landscape before me trying to understand. It was hopeless.

'Every time I have to think about this my brain goes mushy,' I said eventually. 'In the world Theda comes from, I don't know what it's called but in that world, the weather had changed from my time, I mean it was a lot hotter in London than it had been back in 2011 but it wasn't like this. And in Gardenia it was hotter but again, it was green, with trees and farms and clean rivers. If this is the same world I come from, what the hell happened here?'

'It's very complicated,' said Michiyo with a kind smile. 'The temperature here is about 12 degrees Centigrade hotter than 200 years ago, and about six degrees hotter than in the cities of the Squares or Gardenia. Here there are no polar ice caps, there is no longer a temperate region. What you would have known as the tropics is now either a swathe of uninhabitable desert or very warm and highly acidic oceans. In the deserts even culvert communities cannot survive because of the intense heat. Our weather has become very extreme and very violent. We are making progress to control the global climate but it is going to take many generations before we start to see a change. We are surviving, that is the important thing. We are surviving.'

Suddenly above the din of the machines and the roaring wind in my ears I heard a siren sound, a series of high-pitched bleeps.

'We must retire immediately,' said Michiyo, grabbing my sleeve and pulling me back into the entrance. 'The outer doors will soon be closing.'

I flashed again on the scene from *The Empire Strikes Back*. The outer doors would be closing, the night was coming, or in this case I guessed a storm was coming.

We stumbled across the broken ground as machines ran past us in serried ranks. The noise was overwhelming, the high-pitched beeps were a constant and painful reminder that something bad was happening. All around me dozens of low, fast-moving walking machines were funneling into the dark interior of the culvert. I looked around and saw on the distant horizon what looked like a huge brown wall; it was fairly obvious this was a sandstorm, or maybe a rock storm of fairly gargantuan proportions. It filled the horizon and the horizon was very big, I must have been able to see for hundreds of miles as there was nothing on the ground above ankle height.

Just before I entered the structure I glanced up and caught a glimpse of what must have been Cloud Ten. It was already thousands of metres in the air but it still looked huge; a vast white ball of cloud. It really did look like a thunder cloud from this point, if I hadn't known what it was I don't think it would have immediately registered as a man-made object.

'Come, we have no time,' said Michiyo, with some alarm in her voice. 'We are in danger.'

As we passed the threshold Michiyo pulled me to one side. I noticed a bright pink line painted on the smooth graphite floor which ran around one side of the space.

'You are safe here,' she said. 'I think you will enjoy seeing the bots pack away.'

Although at that moment I didn't know what she meant, when I understood I did indeed enjoy it.

Many hundreds of these bizarrely animal-like multi-legged walking machines entered the space and formed neat rows on one side of the hall. They rapidly folded their legs away and closed themselves down. They could store themselves so closely that once they had settled they just formed a solid block of seamless machinery.

As soon as one layer was complete, the next row of machines climbed on top and did likewise until, after a few moments there was just a large, dark complex wall that fitted together beautifully.

Once this wall reached the height of the stone ceiling, another one started. Within about four minutes the entire space, empty when I'd first seen it, was packed solid with now silent machines.

Then the noise really started, as a truly gargantuan door started to slide down from above. It had to be ten metres thick and the mechanics controlling this leviathan of closure devices rumbled and squeaked. With a nerve-jangling thump it finally stopped and my ears were ringing with the sudden silence. The siren beep stopped and everything was still.

'Well, you had a little of everything there,' said Michiyo. 'You got to see the repair bots at work and you got to witness a storm closedown. The perfect end to the perfect tour, is it not?'

'I guess so,' I offered. 'But I saw some kind of storm front that looked like it was miles away. Surely we had a bit more time? I'd like to have seen it.'

Another discreet smile from Michiyo confirmed that my grasp of the elements of this world was slight. 'The storms approach very fast, it will still be over a hundred kilometres away but it'll hit the abutments in the next few minutes.'

I think my silence at this appalling piece of information signified that I was awestruck.

'But now,' said Michiyo. 'We have to vacate the machine hall as it will be pressurised to help support the door, we would not survive if we stayed in here.'

I followed Theda and the other commissioners as they made their way around the now solid wall of repair bots and back into the long corridor. As we moved along I became aware of a low thundering noise.

'I take it we are hearing the storm,' said Theda. Michiyo merely nodded and we walked in silence as the distant rumble intensified.

After a considerable walk along endless low-lit passages, Michiyo showed us into a small, dimly lit and rather spartan space.

'This is our last available guest apartment,' she said. 'We are very full at the moment, I'm afraid it is fairly basic but has all the essential amenities.'

She walked across the space and lights came on all around her. It wasn't that bad, but again it had a very bare and slightly military bunker feel about it.

'Washroom in there,' she said, pointing to a narrow doorway in the far wall. 'And sleeping pods on either side. You may wish to freshen up before we convene later today, we have much to ask and much to explain.'

'Thank you,' said Theda.

'Oh, yeah, thanks,' I said, not entirely sure what I was thanking her for.

Michiyo made an almost imperceptible bow and left the room.

'Wow,' said Theda.

'Yeah,' I agreed. We stood in silence for a moment. Well, we didn't talk but things were not silent.

'Just listen to that wind,' she said, after we had stood motionless listening to the rumble. I couldn't be sure but it did feel like the whole structure was vibrating a bit.

'Are you sure that's wind? It could be machinery. You know, air conditioning or something,' I said.

Theda shook her head. 'No, Gavin, that is a wind the like of which we cannot imagine.'

'I'd really like to see it.'

'That is not possible, if you were exposed to the exterior even for a second you would be blown away and torn to shreds by flying debris. You saw those carbon ceramic plates the machines were fixing. They are ten centimetres thick, they are made of the strongest material available and they still shatter. The impact from airborne debris is awesome.'

'But aren't there any windows we can look out from?'

'Gavin, there is no transparent material strong enough to withstand the constant bombardment,' said Theda, as if explaining to a child why you can't stand in the middle of a busy motorway. 'The only safe place during a storm is either in a culvert or on a cloud. The climate here is nothing short of lethal.'

I sat down on a hard chair that was built into one wall of the room. There was nothing soft or comfortable-looking around.

'I'm not going to pretend I understand what's happened here, are we on Earth? I mean, the same planet I was born on. It feels like we're in some other universe.'

'Well, we are in another dimension, but this is the same Earth, the same planet at the same position in the galaxy and at the same time as the Squares of London you have just come from; however, it is very different in many other respects. Maybe if we both just sit calmly for a while you can absorb some of what I have learned since I've been here.'

'You mean through the kidonge?' I asked.

Theda nodded and sat on the opposite side of the room, her head upright but her eyes closed. She took a deep breath.

'Just try to relax,' she said.

'But what about your name?'

'Just relax, you will understand.'

'Why didn't you tell me your name was Meckler?'

Theda didn't answer. She sat motionless. After an agonising and frankly annoying silence she said very quietly, 'Relax.'

Her suggestion was about as much use as asking a five-year-old to relax after he's eaten a tube of brightly coloured sweets and drunk a couple of cans of fizzy pop.

No chance.

14

THE THING IS, I DID RELAX.

I relaxed too much; I fell asleep. I once again want to point out that this sudden daytime sleeping habit was very unusual for me. Before I went through the first wretched cloud over Didcot Power Station I cannot remember having a nap during the day, ever.

It's just not something I do.

I can only put it down to nervous exhaustion or to the terror of sliding down the blue sheet, or the mind-buggering experience of living on a bloody cloud.

Or it could have been the horrendous reality of the storm that was still raging outside the colossal structure I was in and of course the fact that, by this time, I was alone in a very hostile world when all I had been trying to do was get back home.

But far more mystifying than any of that was that when I woke up yet again I knew a whole load of new stuff, something I never discovered during my stay in the Squares of London.

The kidonge works when you are asleep.

When I awoke I was alone in the small room. Theda's sleeping compartment was empty, she must have slipped out while I dozed and I had no idea where she'd gone. She could have left a note, not that I'd seen any paper or pens in this bizarre storm ditch.

As I woke, I knew much more about the world of culverts and clouds. I didn't have to think about it or try and understand a new deluge of information, I just knew it like I'd known it for years.

I knew why Theda's family name was Meckler. That bit made

my head spin. I knew it as if I'd known it all my life and yet I also knew I hadn't known it before I fell asleep.

She was called Meckler because when I'd been scanned in Rio de Janeiro they had used my data to print sperm. Yes, they printed a whole bucketful of Meckler sperm.

Excuse my French, but how fucked up is that?

I knew there were loads of Mecklers knocking around a hundred years after I left London, mostly male children, but Theda was one of the few female German Mecklers.

Apparently my sperm was really popular in Munich. I knew this like it was just something I'd always known. I knew it like it was something amusing I could say at parties: 'Yeah, my sperm is really popular in Munich.' Not that I would ever say that but I don't know how else to explain it.

This knowledge was preposterous and it made me want to go back to Rio again and inform them that I thought it was a diabolical liberty.

It was distressing enough having this sudden influx of personal knowledge but that wasn't the half of it. I also knew, although saying 'knew' doesn't really describe the sensation you have, but I just understood what had happened in the world I woke up in and it wasn't a very pretty story.

The previous 200 years of this world were profoundly different to the histories I'd learned in Gardenia or the Squares of London; profoundly different and not in a good way.

Essentially, from around 2015 onwards, the global climate changed far faster than even the most pessimistic projections made by climate scientists in my era suggested.

I'm not going to lie to you, I was a climate sceptic back in 2011. Not a denier, a sceptic, there's a really important difference.

It wasn't like I was some God-bothering nutter from the American Midwest who believed President Obama was a Muslim Communist who wanted to force people into poverty to placate his green fascism, or some other swivel-eyed-loon theory, but a lot of the science I'd been aware of at the time seemed very easily refutable.

When temperatures rise, so does CO_2; it had happened before in pre-human history, there was ample evidence to back that up from ice cores drilled out of the Arctic and Antarctic shelves.

There seemed to me to be no reason why it couldn't happen again. That was the bottom line: which came first, temperature or CO_2? Could it be the sun? A natural cycle? It wasn't clear to me.

The annoying CO_2 argument seemed a bit flakey and flimsy, but maybe it was the company I kept. A lot of engineers working in the mining industry and particularly in coal extraction do not make a likely group of CO_2-obsessed eco-warriors. Personally I was always open to debate on the matter whereas a lot of my work colleagues were fervent and often angry climate change deniers. They kind of had to be, their jobs were dependent on those industries continuing their work.

However, in this timeline at least, I was badly mistaken and all those scientists with their computer projections, weather satellites and global temperature monitors were proven very right. In fact they were proven to have been far too optimistic.

Colder winters, stronger storms and hotter, drier summers affected large swathes of the Northern Hemisphere. They also had to deal with heavier rain, larger tidal surges, terrible floods, typhoons of greater strength, and hurricanes of greater size than had ever previously been recorded.

In North America, the central belt came under increasing attack from mind-numbingly huge tornadoes and crop-destroying drought but still no one did anything to change the way they extracted and produced their energy. They continued to dig and drill and burn for years.

In the Southern Hemisphere, the winds became hugely destructive, temperature records in places like Brazil, Africa,

 India and Australia went off the scale. Droughts meant crop failures, crop failures led to hunger, hunger led to lower birth rates.

It was just disaster after disaster.

Somehow, through the first 30 years or so of this horrific turn of events, my generation continued as if nothing was happening. That was until things started to really go wrong. The costs of maintaining the old political and economic order just became unsustainable and things went from bad to worse. The cost of maintaining the oil and gas extraction equipment when massive storms ripped the structures to bits clearly put a bit of a crimp on their enthusiasm to continue.

In the history of the world in Gardenia, the collapse of the old order, while I'm sure disturbing for the people who lived through it, seemed essentially non-violent and gentle. It took a long time and the human race slowly adapted to their new environment.

The history I'd gleaned while in London 2211 appeared to be a continuous period of economic and political stability as women slowly took over the management of the planet.

In this world – for a start there was no name for it, it was just the world – the previous 200 years had simply been a battle for survival.

There were no big wars, merely countless little ones, but even the wars stopped because it rained too much or it was too hot, too cold or too windy to do any proper fighting. You wouldn't covet your neighbour's house because it had either been blown down or flooded, you wouldn't covet their fields because they'd been turned into a rock-strewn scorching desert or saltwater wasteland. There was nothing to fight for, the only worthy opponent was the weather, in particular the wind, and that needed fighting around the clock.

A hundred years before I arrived, most of the structures built by the human race in the previous thousand years had either been destroyed or damaged beyond repair by the ferocious winds; it was during this period that the culverts started to be constructed. People dug in, literally digging themselves into enormous ditches to get out of the wind.

I think of wind as being quite benign. I can recall standing on mountain tops in Wales and Scotland when I was on family holidays as a kid and laughing at the force of the wind. My brother and I would try and lean into it as it flapped the sleeves of our windcheater jackets. Those winds were probably 60 or 70 kilometres an hour. That's strong if you're a scrawny 12-year-old kid, a sudden gust can blow you off your feet.

A 500 kilometre per hour wind is something else. That kind of force can pick up rocks and carry them hundreds of metres until they smash into things. It can tear down buildings and scatter the rubble for hundreds of miles. I don't even want to think about what it could do to human bodies, to animals, to forests and prairies.

There are only two ways to survive a wind like that: get out of it or float along with it.

I was staggered that anyone had survived, even if the information I suddenly knew was only half accurate. The tragic truth of course is that far fewer survived than you might wish for, but it wasn't just the wind and weather that decimated the population.

One of the things I didn't know when I left Kingham in 2011, but which was very clear from this history, was that the population drop in certain key countries was enormous and catastrophic and it had already started back then.

I had grown up in a world where the 'population explosion' was a constant topic. There were always reports about how the population, particularly in the developing world, was exploding. The global population had doubled in my lifetime from three billion to six billion. What I didn't know was that in Europe the population was dropping, even back in 2011. Also in Japan and Russia in particular, people had just stopped having enough babies. In every country that allowed women to be educated even to a rudimentary level, and in every country where basic health services were available, the birth rate dropped rapidly and the seemingly inexorable increase started to level off.

By 2093 an actual drop in population was finally accepted as being a problem. The global population peaked at around eight billion in 2056 and then started to reduce.

One hundred years later in 2156, global population was back down to three billion, and by the time I arrived on this ravaged world it was down to a paltry one billion.

There were multitudinous reasons for this decline, the main one being the weather. It just got worse.

By 2110 most coastal cities had been abandoned and although I'd never really thought about it, I suddenly knew that the vast majority of the world's biggest cities were on the coast. The sea level had risen enormously. I had woken up that morning knowing many different sea rise estimates from different organisations but they were all over ten metres, some as much as 15. I knew that to have been the case in both Gardenia and the Squares of London, but if you combine sea rise with catastrophic storms you can get serious problems in your seaside villa.

I knew that coastal areas were uninhabitable because of the tidal surges and the saltwater invasion. With winds as strong as were commonplace on this earth, during bad storms seawater could be blown inland many tens of kilometres, meaning that any coastal agricultural land was decimated.

What was also clear was that even in these extremely adverse conditions something in the human spirit persevered. The culverts were small oases in this sea of chaos, and there were thousands of them all over the place. Some were built into mountain ranges, some almost buried in deserts. The technology employed to save water, reduce temperatures and protect against the wind were, as I saw on the Chicago Culvert's outer abutments, incredible, ingenious and effective.

As I sat ruminating on all this stuff I could still hear the distant rumble of a storm outside. I was desperate to experience what such a wind was like, I wanted to find some place in the culvert where I could safely go outside and see it.

I stood up, stretched, took a couple of big breaths and headed for the door.

15

I WALKED FROM THE ROOM AND BACK ALONG the corridor we came down when I arrived. I remembered some parts of the journey clearly, although all the corridors looked much the same. They were wide with dull grey walls, low ceilings and very soft lighting.

After a long quiet walk along empty corridors I got to a T-junction and I couldn't decide what to do. For a start, the far bigger corridor I'd just arrived at was very busy, like a tunnel at a London Tube station during rush hour. Hundreds of people were walking past and no one took a blind bit of notice of me, which was fine.

My problem was that I had no idea where to go and, more importantly, what to do. There was nothing for me to do other than be examined and tested by a short Japanese woman and strange commissioners who wore brown floor-length tunics.

I remembered how frustrating that feeling was when I got to the Squares of London and figured out there was nothing for me to do, to contribute there. The more I saw of this place, Chicago, if indeed that was really where I was, the more Gardenia stood out for me as being a place I wanted to be.

I leant against the wall for a while just idly watching all these short, slightly anxious and thin people walk past me in droves.

As I stood there I realised something that surprised me. I wanted to go back to Gardenia more than I wanted to go back home.

All I'd ever said to people was that I wanted to go back to 2011, to Kingham, to Beth, but allowing myself to actually consider what I really wanted made me suddenly want to go back to Gardenia. To Grace.

I wanted to see Grace and live in that peaceful world where I could actually do stuff that helped. I could fix things, maybe even build things and I could see Grace and my child.

I don't know why this feeling emerged, I don't remember contemplating it before, I had just had a kind of official line that I always used if the subject arose. 'I want to go back home,' which I did.

I had wanted to go back because I knew what I was doing back in 2011, I knew who I was and where I fitted in. I felt so tired of being the freak, the weird person who fell through the clouds.

I buried my face in my hands because these thoughts gave me very strong feelings and that was still something I wasn't used to dealing with. My heart rate had increased even though I was motionless, I felt slightly dizzy and all I was doing was thinking.

Somehow, for 32 years before I went through the clouds, I had never been able to do this. Of course if something external happened, if my mum told me off or another boy at school hit me, then I would react to that moment. If Beth shouted at me for being uncommunicative I sensed a kind of low-grade physical reaction to that, but I could never stand on my own and just think about something and get upset.

I had a strong sense that if I just let these thoughts, desires and emotional feelings run away with themselves I would start going insane and that was a genuinely frightening prospect.

I somehow knew that if I went mad, it wasn't like dying or sleeping, it wasn't as if the 'me' that I was aware of would just stop being and I would turn into a deranged person. I could sense that the pain I was feeling now, the longing to escape from this distressing place, would overwhelm me and I'd be drowning in pain. Not drowning to death, just lost in a swirl of emotion and feeling stuff, but still be me. A me with no escape.

I rubbed my eyes with the heels of my hand and coughed, took a big gulp of air and stood up.

I would deal with the world around me. I would try to take it in and deal with it, I would try to find out how to get back somewhere; home, Gardenia, I didn't care, anywhere but this blighted ditch on this even more blighted barren world.

I noticed that a lot of the people passing by along the corridor were carrying bundles of vegetables, some had large sacks slung over their shoulders and a few were carrying what appeared to be boxes of fruit. I decided that while I was stuck in the Chicago Culvert I might as well try to discover how they fed themselves, so I walked in the opposite direction to the flow to see where the shops where, if indeed they had shops in Chicago.

As I made my way through crowds of people, I remembered the old Chicago, the twenty-first-century Chicago, the Windy City. The irony of that twentieth-century nickname made me smile. However windy it had been when they built those huge towers, it was a lot more bloody windy now.

I'd visited Chicago for an engineering consultancy job back in 2008. The memory was still fresh for me, even though the actual trip had taken place over 200 years ago.

On my first morning in the old Chicago I sat in a huge office on something like the 23rd floor of a glass tower near the State Street shopping centre. It was glorious: the morning sun was glinting off Lake Michigan as I drank American coffee and discussed a huge mining project due to start in Brazil with a couple of very funny old engineers.

It was a happy memory: I was young, full of energy and excitement at the scale of the project. The memory of this visit made me feel something. Although the memory was a happy one, the feeling I was sensing was sadness. I smiled as I walked along; having a little bit of time to myself had allowed me to reflect on these insights. Once again I could sense a feeling fairly quickly after I had it, a skill I'd clearly learned when I was in the Institute in London.

Those two old engineers back in 2008 weren't evil, they didn't want to destroy the world. They were just digging for manganese ore in Brazil. They weren't even drilling for oil or mining coal, they were just extracting raw materials from an area that was fairly desolate before the digging started.

Actually, now that I remember, it had been an area of rainforest, but by the time we planned this mine the trees had long been felled and burned. Remembering that didn't make me feel much better. The important thing was, none of the people I worked with then wanted to destroy the world, they wanted to make it better. Okay, so it could be argued that the companies they worked for had one intention and that was to make as much money as possible in the least amount of time and with the least regard for the long-term impacts of their activities.

I couldn't argue with that, especially not after seeing the state of the planet outside the carbon ceramic bastions of the Chicago Culvert.

More than anything else I'd witnessed in any of the dimensions I'd visited, the sight of a wind-blasted debris desert had hammered home to me the importance of long-term planning. The process of assessing the full impact of any particular activity and weighing those things very carefully was certainly not something I'd ever considered or been encouraged to consider during my training or subsequent career in engineering.

I made my way slowly along the corridor trying my best not to get in the way. The vast majority of people were walking in the opposite direction so it wasn't easy.

Eventually I discovered where they were all coming from.

Something you don't often expect to walk into after you've had a bit of a think about the state of your soul is a giant greenhouse full of trees. But that's what I was confronted with when I emerged from the end of the corridor.

I managed to find a corner of the balcony I'd walked onto so I could get a good look at this place without being in anyone's way. A flight of wide steps led up to this balcony and that's where the crowds were coming from, a seeming endless stream of people slowly making their way up the steps and off down the corridor. On the opposite side of the enormous space I could see the same slow journey being made on a similar structure of steps and balconies by even more people.

Below me, and stretching off into the distance, were multiple layers of verdant gardens, intensive vegetable cultivation on stepped beds that looked like they could be moved and stacked. Directly beneath me were rows of carefully manicured fruit trees and everywhere, hundreds of people working.

A greenhouse, that's not a very good description, try a massive glass structure covering an area the size of a small town. This place was on a par with the London Museum of History where I'd seen my Yuneec hanging as an exhibit, so it was big.

I glanced up and knew at once I was looking at something I'd never seen before. The sky was brown, not blue or grey, not white clouds or low grey rain clouds. It was a dirty brown whirlwind going overhead at such speed I had the sensation that the structure I was standing in was moving fast, like when you're on a stationary train and another train moves but you think it's you. It was a dizzying sight.

Through this swirly dirt haze I could see the bright sphere of the sun. It was very high in the sky, which gave me some indication of the time, either late morning or early afternoon. Whatever time it was, I shouldn't have been sleeping.

I then became aware of a background noise that had increased in intensity as I emerged into this vast and busy space. I stood still trying to work out where it was coming from. It sounded a bit like rain on a metal roof, the sort of noise you get when you sit in a motionless car during a storm. It didn't take me long to work out this was grit landing on the substantial transparent panels high above me. It was loud and it was terrifying.

I looked back down at the people working in the giant greenhouse; they were paying no attention to the maelstrom going on above them.

So I was seeing the storm raging outside and it was utterly horrific, it didn't look real, nothing I had ever previously witnessed on planet Earth was anything like this. It was instantly obvious that anything standing in the way of this onslaught would be immediately destroyed if it wasn't protected by huge constructions covered in the hardest and most resilient materials.

I assumed the roof I was looking up at was well below the tops of the ramparts outside. This really was a window looking up from the bottom of a ditch.

'There's your storm,' said Theda's voice right behind me. As always it took me by surprise. Maybe it's just me, I don't know why but people have always been able to creep up on me and say something clever and make me jump. I was certainly fully immersed in staring through a transparent roof structure 50 metres above my head at a swirling dirt storm of doom. I mean, it's not something you see every day.

'Well, I find it encouraging that you don't know everything, Theda,' I said, trying not to acknowledge the shock she'd just given me. 'You told me there was no transparent material that could withstand the onslaught of the storm.'

'We are at the bottom of a very deep hole,' said Brad. This time I really did get a shock, I suppose because Theda was so tall and Brad so short I genuinely hadn't seen him. I jumped when he spoke but he didn't seem to take offence.

'Oh, right, yeah, of course,' I said trying to disguise my alarm.

'The debris you see flying across the sky is mostly the lighter particles, dust and small pieces of grit picked up by the wind. The larger pieces are currently smashing into the abutments you saw earlier.'

I nodded. I didn't really need this explanation, it was pretty obvious what was happening.

'Thankfully the days of the truly destructive storms seem to be behind us. Thirty or 40 years ago you would have seen very large objects flying through the air. This structure does have a protective canopy that can be closed but apparently it hasn't been used in years.'

I nodded again. The two people, a very tall woman and a very short man, just stood looking at me.

'How did you know I was here?' I asked, when the realisation struck me. I hadn't spoken to anyone, seen anyone I recognised or told anyone or any system where I was going. More to the point, I didn't know where I was going. I was just stumbling along.

'You have a kidonge and thankfully you are still wearing your flightband,' said Theda. 'It wasn't hard to find you. If you want to be alone, just take off your band and leave it in our room.'

'Oh, right,' I said glancing at the thin band that was still wrapped around my left wrist. 'Of course.'

Brad was just staring at me, he didn't say a word. It was awkward, his look didn't transmit hostility or even annoyance, I don't know what he was thinking, but I didn't get the impression he was totally thrilled to be in my company.

'So,' I said eventually, 'what's occurring?'

As I was soon to find out, something rather important was occurring.

16

T WAS A PROPER BIG SCREEN IN A LARGE dark room. Okay, well that sounds like a cinema, but the large room I entered with Theda and Brad wasn't a cinema, it was a meeting room of some kind and it contained a great many people.

They were sitting on simple benches that circled a small area that was slightly brighter. That said, the whole room was fairly dark, like pretty much every room I'd seen in the Chicago Culvert.

I was shown to the slightly brighter raised area near the centre of the room, but unlike my experiences in the Squares of London I wasn't the sole focus of attention. I was with Theda and I was very relieved for her to take the lead.

There was a semicircular bench on a raised plinth and Theda sat down on it as if she knew what to do. I sat beside her and stared around the room.

The crowd were all busy chatting to each other, some of them looking at Theda and me as if they were viewing monsters or ghosts, a look I had grown used to receiving.

'Good afternoon, everybody,' said Michiyo Nishimura, who was also standing on the raised plinth thing. The room fell silent as soon as she spoke. This time Michiyo was wearing a kind of golden cloak over her brown floor-length tunic and she looked quite regal.

'Thank you for attending, and thank you in advance for your contributions. As we all know we are graced with the presence of two extraordinary people, Theda and Gavin Meckler, and as you also know they are related, although not in any conventional way.'

Michiyo smiled at me and put her hand on my shoulder as if to reassure me. I was grateful that I knew about the situation regarding Theda's heritage before she spoke. If I'd found out I was effectively Theda's dad while exposed in front of so many people it would have been awkward to say the least.

'In traditional biology Gavin would be Theda's great-grandfather, although indirectly he is her father. This is obviously confusing for us as, I'm sure Theda won't take offence in me pointing out, she is Gavin's senior by 17 years. Such is the paradox of time and multiverse shifting without control.'

By this stage in proceedings I was an old hand at hearing bizarre and baffling explanations of concepts and technologies utterly beyond my comprehension. I sat beside Theda with a set expression on my face. I was trying to convey the impression that I knew all about this multiverse stuff: I'd been there, I'd done the shifting thing, I was a space and time veteran, baby.

That didn't last long.

'It is clear from our initial discussions with Gavin Meckler that he has no understanding of his role in these historic events. He is the perfect example of the accidental tourist, the lost soul in a complex and challenging multiverse. Theda Meckler, on the other hand, has a very good grasp of what is at stake and we are very grateful that she took the risk to come back to visit us.'

That put me in my place. Being the numpty in the room didn't sit well with me, I was more used to being the one who had to explain complicated things to numpties.

'However, as he may be starting to understand,' she turned and smiled at me kindly, 'Gavin is of vital importance to our research. Over the last few days we have been recording his dreams both here and on Cloud Ten. We will feed them into Calmer Times so everyone can benefit from the information.'

A pause there, while you imagine my reaction to this news.

'We have managed to extract some wonderful data about his era and in particular the energy systems at use. Obviously we have some historical records of this, but the actual human experience of what it was like to live when surrounded by such dangerous and crude technology is hard to manifest. Now we have the ability to dream in a verified and exact copy of 2011.'

The gathered audience seemed happy with this revelation; I was feeling increasingly baffled and not a little annoyed.

'You've recorded my dreams?' I said.

Michiyo turned to look at me. 'Yes, Gavin, they are wonderful and we are very grateful. We are going to play one now.'

The light in the room shifted slightly and suddenly I was in a bus, except it wasn't a bus, I was still in the room with all the people. The image was sort of 3D but it was all-engulfing, if I glanced to my left and right I was totally in the bus but it was semi-transparent. More chilling was the fact that it was exactly like the bus on Oxford Street dream I'd had in the sleeping pod on Cloud Ten. No, far more than that, it actually *was* my bus dream.

I screamed.

The bus image around me froze for a moment and I felt Theda's hand on mine, gentle and reassuring.

'It's okay, it's just a recording, look behind you.'

I turned and saw a frozen image of Theda sitting at the back of the bus, smiling at me. She was also sitting next to me on the low seat in the middle of the room.

'Don't be frightened,' she said. 'Think of it like a television.'

'Television didn't look like this,' I said under my breath.

'May we continue?' asked Michiyo. I saw Theda nod, she continued to hold my hand.

The bus all around me started to move again. I could see the street outside, the horizontal rain, the people with their umbrellas fighting against the wind.

It was only then that I realised there was no sound to accompany this image, I was still hearing the ambient sound in the room, of which there was very little until Michiyo spoke.

'All the dreams we have recorded will be available for study and they are fascinating. We can learn a great deal about our past from this resource and I think we should all thank Gavin for his generosity.'

There was a polite round of applause from the gathering as the image of the bus faded away.

I glanced at Theda who was looking at me kindly.

'That was intense,' I said.

I felt her gently take hold of my hands, and I discovered they were shaking uncontrollably. I find it hard to convey the experience of seeing a dream I could barely remember rendered in such sharp focus. It bore down into the very core of my being. I felt nauseous and I know I was sweating.

The lights in the room changed.

Michiyo stood up and started speaking again.

'I would also like to thank Theda Meckler for her insights into a problem we are facing. As some of you will already know, Theda has numerous neural enhancements, which we have studied closely. Theda, would you like to explain?'

Theda stood up and turned around the room, smiling.

'To start with, I would like to try and put to rest some of your completely understandable fears of this type of technology. I know you have had some bad experiences with enhancement technology and I think you are wise in your decision to restrict its introduction. However, as with all technologies, there are benefits and costs and if those are measured and controlled in accordance with pre-existing guidelines then these developments need not be negative.'

Theda glanced at me and smiled.

'Gavin is a very good example of how neural enhancement technology can be beneficial. When in the Squares of London he was issued with what was known, sorry, *is* known, as a kidonge. This is effectively a micro data transmitter and receiver that rests somewhere in the human body and is completely benign. What it enabled Gavin to do, even with his understandable limitations, was engage in the world around him in a far more immersive way. His knowledge of other people was instant and encyclopedic, his ability to understand social, political and technical advances from his own era was hugely improved and, most importantly of all, he suffered no negative side effects. Is that a fair description, Gavin?'

I wasn't expecting a question. I was worrying that my understanding of the social, political and technical advances I had experienced wasn't quite as encyclopedic as Theda had suggested.

'Yes, that's fair,' I said. I didn't want to say anything but felt obliged to reply.

'Obviously,' Theda continued, 'my enhancements are more advanced, the kidonge was the first universally accepted enhancement system and this was swiftly followed by more directly engaging neural systems, brain enhancements if you like. These mostly focused on memory and sensory inputs. I am, for example, able to sense very subtle changes in electrical activity and brain chemistry in individuals in my immediate vicinity. For example, I know there is one person in this room who, strictly speaking, you would probably prefer to be elsewhere.'

There was a short pause as Theda's statement rippled through the room. 'Noshi, I'm referring to you.'

People started looking either side of them, craning around and eventually finding the culprit.

I followed their gaze and my eyes fell on a very diminutive figure sitting at the back of the circular auditorium. I couldn't make out if this was a man or a woman.

'I mean no harm,' said this person. I decided on hearing the voice that he was a man.

'Noshi, I have to ask you to leave, I think you know why,' said Michiyo.

The person called Noshi stood up and left the room without further comment. There was a great deal of discussion among the audience from that moment. I watched Michiyo stand in the centre of the space in silence, she seemed to be waiting for the hubbub to die down, which it eventually did. What made me worry was that I didn't know if the hubbub died down due to millennia-old human group behavioural norms or because of some freakish brain control weirdness from Theda.

'Please continue, Theda,' said Michiyo once the silence had descended.

'Thank you,' said Theda. 'I think that was a good example of the benefits of enhanced systems. I want to explain one or two things though. Obviously this kind of enhancement gives someone in my position a lead in a world where enhancements are limited. It puts me in a position whereby, were I so inclined, I could use these extra abilities to cause harm or give me an unfair advantage over others less well endowed. However, in Munich this is not the case. From birth to death we all have such systems and so no one individual has an unfair advantage, we are all equal in ways that have never previously been experienced by the human race. There are no people in our city without great intelligence, knowledge and prodigious memory abilities. This allows us to live together in a very peaceful and creative way.'

Theda paused there. No one clapped or did anything. She slowly turned so she could take in the whole room, she certainly had the audience's attention, the silence was all-engulfing.

'So the question is, how do we explore the possibilities of me helping you utilise these technologies in order to better counter the problems you are facing? That is part of the reason for my journey here. Thank you.'

Theda sat next to me as the gathering clapped wildly and whooped and yelled. She was a bit of a star.

Michiyo took the floor again, this time gesturing for people to calm down.

'Thank you so much,' she shouted above the din, 'I am so

happy to hear that response. We will now have a look at the latest findings from the dimension teams.'

I leant closer to Theda and said, 'That was pretty cool.'

Theda looked down at me with a big grin.

'Why, thank you, great-grandfather,' she said, 'but now, Gavin, just look at the image system, this may really help you understand what's happened to you.'

I know Michiyo was speaking at this time but I couldn't understand anything, it was garbled nonsense to my ears, a muffled sound coming down a long tube.

'The image system,' I said.

Theda lifted one of my hands and gestured toward the dull brown patterns that were on display behind Michiyo.

Something clicked as I looked at it, but it was almost a subconscious click. It was as if I had knowledge of something without understanding it. I don't want to claim that I was instantly aware of the basics of shifting between one universe and another, although there was a visual representation of multiple overlapping circles which I supposed in my ignorance could be something to do with it.

The huge screen covered one side of the room. I had to move my head to scan the whole thing as it was so full of information. Thousands of text boxes far too small for me to read appeared and disappeared beside various circles, the whole screen was a bedazzling waterfall of information, the background was brown and the lettering was in a kind of dull ochre so it was all rather soothing.

Concentrating on this gush of data seemed to help me recover from the distress of reliving my dream with a room full of people. All I wanted to do was forget the experience as soon as possible.

I doubled my efforts to understand what I was looking at. Occasional words or phrases Michiyo was saying started to emerge from the confusion.

I eventually realised that the large circles were moving slowly. I was seeing a continuously moving ring of overlapping circles that spun gently across the screen. I then started to see further rings linked to this central group, these were in a lower ambience and not initially visible to me.

As I stared at this screen I slowly became aware that I wasn't staring at a screen. It was an image, certainly, but it wasn't coming from a light source projected against a flat surface. It changed its shape and form as I studied it, the rings I had first noticed became smaller and more closely packed, and the connected rings or circles below and above became easier to see.

What then lifted my slow brain was how this bizarre pattern grew before my eyes. It seemed as if the image changed as my understanding of it increased. I want to describe the experience as spooky, which it was, but it was also fascinating and highly immersive. New rings appeared, floating in space before me, either running up above the original ring of circles, or down below them.

With more careful observation I could sense that these smaller and harder-to-see circles were moving at slightly different speeds to the central ones, so a large bright circle that was overlapping a smaller dull one beneath it would, after a few minutes, have moved on and be intersecting with another dull circle.

Then I noticed something in a text box that caught my attention. The word 'Gardenia' was linked to one of the central circles. I suddenly felt dizzy again. Gardenia did exist! That's what this information was telling me, literally telling me, no one else, just me. Somewhere, somehow, Gardenia existed.

'Mister Meckler,' said a voice, immediately snapping me out of my reverie.

'Yes, sorry, yes?' I said without thinking. I was looking around like a stunned mullet, it seemed everyone in the room was looking at me.

'We wondered how you felt about the proposal?'

There was a deathly silence in the room, my brain went blank, there was nothing, I hadn't heard anyone say anything.

'He wasn't listening,' said Theda flatly. There was a reaction from the room. I think it's fair to say it was a negative reaction.

Theda stood up and bowed a little to the large crowd of brown-clad people around us. 'I think I can explain, and I hope Gavin won't take offence.' She raised one long slender arm towards the images I'd been looking at. 'He was so intrigued by the theory presentation he didn't hear a single word that has been spoken. I think it would be unfair to judge Gavin on this failing, you have to understand that the concepts you are familiar with considering had been mere theory discussed by a very small handful of scientists at the time he left his home.'

'Indeed,' said Michiyo. I smiled weakly at her and for the first time in my life I think I got a look from an Asian woman that was openly disdainful.

'What we wanted to know, Gavin,' she said, after taking a deep breath, 'is simple. Are you are prepared to return to 2011?'

Again I was unable to answer. I think I may have wanted to shout 'Yes!' or even the more snide 'What d'you reckon? Fuck yeah!' but nothing came out.

'What we also need you to consider is the danger. There are unknowns involved and, as you might be able to understand, we are scientists – we don't like unknowns. One thing we are certain of, is that it is too dangerous to go back from here.'

'From here?' I managed to finally ask.

'When you were not able to listen to me, I was explaining what happens to the central nervous system during reverse time-hops. There is a lot of electrical activity which will affect everything that passes through. Your brain will be affected, Gavin, possibly fatally. You may not go back to a dimension you recognise and you would have no memory of anything you've experienced here. In fact, you may have no memory at all, you may emerge completely blank, effectively a newborn.'

'That doesn't sound good,' I said, trying to make light of it. Michiyo's expression informed me there was no making light of anything.

'You would be brain-dead,' she said flatly, 'so you cannot go back from here.'

Guess if I suddenly found the ability to respond to the utter nonsense I was hearing? You guessed right, not a word passed my wide-open lips.

'You will have to side shift before you drop shift,' said Michiyo, making less and less sense with each utterance. 'We can explain the details later, but we have discussed the proposition at length and have come to a unanimous agreement. We cannot allow you to go directly back from here.'

17

‘KAY,’ I SAID AS I SAT DOWN IN OUR APARTMENT with Theda and Brad. ‘I’m focused, I’m concentrating, I’m not distracted and I’m not dreaming. Can you please explain to me who those dimension people were and what they were talking about? Because I’ll tell you right now, I did not understand a word.’

I was a little agitated – no, that’s not complex enough. I was experiencing an unusual concoction of emotions and I was aware of them as I was experiencing them. I was angry, yes, I mean, they had recorded my dreams, they had invaded what can only be described as the last sanctuary of human dignity. The dreaming mind, for goodness’ sake, even the Nazis didn’t do that, even Stalin couldn’t record your dreams.

However, mixed in with this righteous anger was a swirl of other emotions. It’s exhausting being in touch with your feelings, I still wasn’t used to it. I was also excited, elated, terrified and of course utterly confused.

Brad sat on the low bench on the opposite side of the small room and smiled at me.

‘I will try and explain,’ he said. ‘I hope my explanation won’t make things more confusing for you. I’ll use the simplest language I can to illustrate what we understand.’

‘That would be good,’ I said. I did feel very alive, very focused and I felt no embarrassment staring at Brad. At that point in my journey I was newly famished for knowledge. Even in my confused state I could sense something fairly momentous going on.

‘I am going to assume you know where the traditional three dimensions are?’

'What, wait, *where* they are?' Already I didn't understand. 'How do you mean *where* they are?'

'The three dimensions we are all aware of as human beings: left, right; forward, backward; up, down. The three dimensions of space,' said Brad, gesticulating each direction with small arm movements.

'Oh, yes, okay, yes, with you,' I said. It was the language, not the concept that confused me.

'You will, I'm sure, understand that we need three coordinates to locate an object in space.'

'Yes, longitude, latitude and altitude,' I said, wishing to convey that I wasn't a Stone Age moron.

'Correct. So if there were more dimensions, you would need more coordinates.'

I nodded, less certain about what he was implying.

'As I'm sure you are also aware, the human race is not physiologically equipped to observe those dimensions, but that does not mean they don't exist.'

'Doesn't it?' I asked.

'No,' said Brad. 'The idea of multiple dimensions has been around for many hundreds of years in terms of mathematical concepts. After Albert Einstein developed his theory of general relativity – you've heard of Albert Einstein?'

'Yes,' I squealed, trying not to sound annoyed and failing.

'Of course you have. Forgive me. So it has been observed that his theory works for any number of dimensions. It doesn't have to be just three. Many years ago scientists started to understand the existence of extra dimensions because of string theory. String theory was for many years what we called a "candidate theory" for unifying quantum mechanics and gravity. This is quite simply because these two things seem to require extra dimensions of space in order to make sense mathematically.'

There was a silence. I glanced at Theda who was standing by the doorway looking at me. She didn't respond. She was waiting for this colossal block of information to make an impression on my reptilian brain.

'I don't know anything about quantum mechanics,' I said eventually. I wanted them to know I wasn't stupid. I felt stupid and out of my depth but my pride was hurt. They had such a huge advantage over me, 200 years of scientific research and development in Brad's case, and something like 400 in Theda's, plus she had a computer brain with terabytes of power and zettabytes of memory. To paraphrase the thick kid at the back of a primary school class, 'It's not fair, Miss!'

It really wasn't fair. I couldn't help myself, I blurted, 'I know a great deal about mechanics, hydraulics, electronics, leverage, power-to-weight ratios, traction, newton metres of torque, even good old horsepower.'

'That is wonderful knowledge and it should help you at least start to comprehend what I am explaining,' said Brad kindly.

'Okay, but I never studied quantum mechanics, I don't even know what it means.'

Again Brad actually smiled at me, then he said very slowly, 'The reason we have developed an understanding of extra dimensions is because they might actually have implications for our world. They help to explain properties of matter that we've observed; they may even help us to repair our damaged home. So allow me to explain.'

Brad extracted a piece of white material from his pocket and got down on all fours. He then drew a simple stickman figure on the smooth black surface of the floor. I watched in fascination at this world of advanced materials and mind-boggling graphic representations Brad was drawing on the floor with a piece of chalk.

'I'd like you to try and imagine creatures that live in a two-dimensional universe. That is all they know, two dimensions, up and down, left and right. In their universe there is no forward or backward.'

'Okay,' I said, impressed that he'd drawn a fairly well-proportioned stickman upside down for him but the right way up for me.

'These creatures would have the same trouble conceptualising three dimensions that we once had when we tried to understand more than three. So what would these creatures see if a three-dimensional object passed through their universe? If a ball, a sphere, passed through this flat universe they would only see a series of disks that grew in size and then decreased in size.'

Brad drew a circle next to the figure. 'They would still not be able to comprehend three dimensions.'

I smiled at this point. 'I totally get that,' I said. I looked up at Theda with a big grin on my face. 'Really, I can actually understand that.'

'Clever Gavin,' she said in what could have been a patronising manner, but it was somehow reassuring and kind.

'So we are capable of understanding a two-dimensional world inside a three-dimensional world, but it is very hard for us to conceptualise more than three dimensions.' Brad stood up and spread his arms wide. 'So, for example, if a hyper sphere, a four-dimensional sphere, passed through our universe —' he waggled his arms around a bit; I wondered if he was simulating what a hyper sphere would look like, if he was it wasn't working for me, '— all we would see was a series of spheres that grew in size and then decreased in size. The fact that we don't observe those extra dimensions doesn't mean they don't exist. They are hard to conceptualise but we can calculate them mathematically.'

'Can you?'

'Yes we can, we do, we have been doing so for a long time,' said Brad. 'That is why we understand how you came here, that is why we understand how Theda came here. Much of the basic research was done in your era. Particle physics gave us the key to understanding and that was well developed even back in 2011.'

'CERN,' I said, 'I knew a few of the engineers who helped build it.'

'Did you?' said Theda. 'That is incredible.' She was smiling and shaking her head. 'Did you ever meet Brian Cox?'

'Um, no, who's he?' I asked. 'You mean the actor? The bloke in the Bourne Trilogy?'

'No, I mean Professor Brian Cox. You will find out who he is when you go back,' said Theda, still smiling.

'Well, I met some people who'd worked at CERN, but they weren't the scientists who worked there, more the engineers who helped construct the tunnels and the infrastructure of the project. I never went there myself.'

'It is good you know of the work at CERN,' said Brad, 'because that's where they first discovered Kaluza-Klein particles.'

'Oh blimey, I don't know what they are, I don't understand again,' I said in despair.

Brad sat down on the bench again. 'Please don't worry about that, Gavin. You have no need to understand Kaluza-Klein particles in any detail, all you need to know is that these particles have mass and their mass reflects extra dimensions.'

'That doesn't help.'

'These particles were the initial key,' said Theda. 'Proof if you like that other dimensions exist and that there are methods of communicating between them.'

Brad nodded and said, 'Once we had proof of extra dimensions, all we needed to do was find out how to explore them, either mathematically or through direct, physical interaction.'

He pointed at me as he said that. So I was proof of direct physical interaction. Fair enough.

'One of the reasons we believe our research into this area is in advance of other dimensions,' said Brad, 'by that I mean places you've been, Gardenia and London, places on the same horizontal timeline, you understand?'

'Yes, I understand.'

'Well, once we were able to survive the storms, we had a lot of time on our hands. We've been able to spend large amounts of time thinking. As long as we have enough to eat and are safe from the storms, our minds have focused on this issue with an end goal of understanding what went so catastrophically wrong in this dimension and hopefully discovering ways of rectifying that.'

'Okay,' I said after a short pause, 'so you want me to go back to 2011 and do something about it all, change history so you don't get the storms?'

This time both Brad and Theda smiled at me and there's no point trying to gloss over it. The smile was one that an adult gives to a baby when the kid rubs chocolate biscuit all over its cherubic face and gurgles in delight. It's not a horrible moment, in fact it's quite charming, but you've just asked the baby to explain how to understand long division and all you get back is a chocolate-covered mush.

'No, we don't want you to do that and more importantly, even if you could steer events of such gargantuan scale, the results could be far worse. Any tiny change in the timeline will, as I'm sure you can understand, have utterly unpredictable consequences. We have to deal with enough of those already.'

'Okay, so, I go back to 2011, to my home, to my era, and then what?'

'Then nothing. You live your life, you maybe procreate, you die,' said Theda as if she was giving me a list of basic tasks.

'But what about everything I've seen? Everything I've learned since I came through the first cloud?'

'You cannot take that knowledge back with you,' said Brad.

'Why not?' I asked. I was outraged, what were they going to do, give me electric-convulsive therapy and fry my simple mind?

'I'm not saying we won't allow you, I'm saying it is not possible. Your mind cannot contain all the information you have been exposed to. It would kill you. It's not to do with psychology or sanity, it's to do with electronics. The synapses in your brain cannot deal with the flow of electrons it will encounter as you down-jump. What you have done so far is jump forwards and then sideways. Both of these activities result in the electrical activity in your brain being considerably reduced during the transition but that only results in temporary tiredness. Travelling back to 2011 from here would create a fatal increase in synaptic connections, the actual tissue in your brain would fry and you will be brain-dead, as Michiyo explained. That is why you cannot go back to 2011 from here.'

I burst out laughing. I'd felt the laugh building all the time Brad was talking. What he was saying was so preposterous that I imagine a few of my synapses had fried anyway and the fact that I could maybe go back home 'but not from here' was utterly baffling.

'There was a joke I heard years ago,' I said when I managed to regain my composure. 'A young couple on holiday in the countryside – I know you don't have countryside anymore but I mean an open area outside a city – anyway, they are travelling around in a car, a mechanical, wheeled, ground-based transportation unit, and they are lost. So they stop and speak to an old man who is leaning on a gate. They ask him directions to a certain village. The old man says he knows the village, but he says – and then of course I've got to explain to you the social and class system for any of this to work – but the old man has an old accent, a way of speaking which defines him as being local, of not having travelled far from his home, so with his strong rural accent he says, "Oh, sorry m'dears, you can't start from here."'

I'd adopted my best West Country drawl to deliver the punchline. The response was total silence from my audience of two.

'You can't start from here,' I repeated.

'I don't understand,' said Brad.

'Neither do I,' said Theda.

I buried my face in my hands for a moment, then slowly looked up.

'You are saying I can go back to 2011, but I can't start from here.'

Brad nodded. 'I see your confusion here, Gavin,' he said calmly. 'Indeed, you can start your journey from here, you can transverse dimensions from here and go back from your original dimension.'

'Wait. What?'

'The dimension you originally jumped to. The one that was connected to your timeline at the moment you passed through the original cloud. You have to go back to Gardenia.'

18

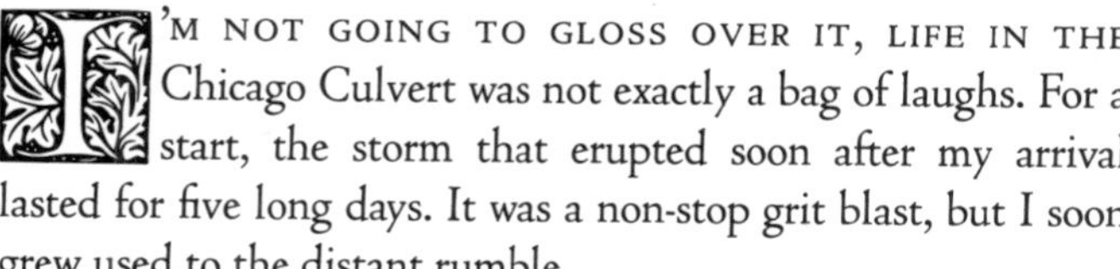

I'M NOT GOING TO GLOSS OVER IT, LIFE IN THE Chicago Culvert was not exactly a bag of laughs. For a start, the storm that erupted soon after my arrival lasted for five long days. It was a non-stop grit blast, but I soon grew used to the distant rumble.

There was one moment when I heard something a bit more ominous, a massive thump, which seemed to shake the foundations of the whole structure. I discovered later that it was caused by a very large lump of concrete from some devastated bridge that had been half buried a few hundred metres from the outer culvert walls. The vicious wind had finally lifted this multi-ton missile out of the surrounding dirt and hurled it at the walls.

'A big repair job on that one,' was all Brad told me.

However, during these five days I learned a great deal about the lives of the people of the culverts. The occupants were from all over the world; they all seemed to be in transit from somewhere and on their way somewhere else.

The ones in transit had travel plans that were simply that: travel plans. Eventually they hoped to get to the Beijing Culvert or the Moscow Culvert or somewhere I'd never heard of. They simply had to wait for the weather, not only the immediate local storm we were trapped by, but suitable conditions to allow the arrival of one of the clouds, one that was hopefully going the right way.

However, there was a fair-sized community of people who, to my ear at least, were American, possibly natives of Chicago, born and bred in what had once been the USA.

One of them I had seen before and I was initially very wary of him or her. This was Noshi and he or she told me more about life in the culvert than anyone else.

When I say he or she, that's only because I'm still not sure which one Noshi was. It clearly wasn't a problem for him or her. I think I'm going to refer to Noshi as him but I want to underline the fact that it really wasn't clear to me.

He was very beautiful, at a guess a mix of African and Asian, quite tall, slender with a dark honey skin tone. He had wide shoulders, long limbs and a very feminine narrow waist.

Noshi was either a very masculine and attractive woman, or a very feminine and attractive man. That might make me sound like I'm a bit of a Betty Bothways, which I don't think I am. Well, I didn't until I met Noshi.

I would challenge the most confidently heterosexual man not to find something faintly alluring about him.

I met Noshi again on my first day working in the garden. I didn't apply for a job or add my name to a waiting list to work in the garden. I didn't get paid to work there but I had very little else to do.

Noshi was the first person I spoke to when I arrived on the work floor and I recognised him immediately. It was hard not to.

'Hello, Gavin,' he said, 'I'm very pleased you are going to help us in the garden.'

So he already knew I was going to be working there. I only knew that morning when Theda introduced me to a very old woman who, I assumed, organised the work shifts in the garden dome.

I felt a little guarded, saying anything to Noshi at first, mainly because of what had happened at the meeting in the circular room where they played back my dream.

When Theda pointed him out and he was asked to leave it gave me the clear impression that there was something seriously amiss. I suppose because I didn't have a clue what it was I found it easy to ask him why.

'I am still considered a renegade,' he answered.

'A renegade?'

'Yes. A person who doesn't agree with the majority decision. I have changed my mind but they are still upset with me.'

'Who is?'

'The Culvert authorities, the people in the room with you the other day.'

'Oh, right, and what didn't you agree with?' I asked.

'Many things, but certainly neural enhancements, holding back technology like that when we have to live like this. I used to think that it wasn't a very sensible idea.'

'I see,' I said carefully. Here I was trying to understand a disagreement way above my non-existent pay grade. 'Do you have any of these enhancements?' I asked.

Noshi looked a little shocked and then he laughed. 'Me? No, I don't have anything like that. D'you think I'd be weeding pulses if I had upgrades?' He laughed again.

'I think you already know enough about me to understand that most of what's going on is a mystery to me,' I said. I was feeling quite confident I could be honest with Noshi because he'd heard my story in the circular room. Not only that, he was probably the least threatening person I'd ever met.

'I used to live on Cloud Four,' he said as he weeded a long box of vegetable seedlings. 'I left many years ago but because of that, the authorities don't trust me.'

'Oh, right,' I said, 'so you are from one of the Original Five.'

'Not really. I lived on Cloud Four because they picked me up from the Da Lat Culvert when I was 12 years old.'

'Oh, right,' I said. 'So you don't think that everything that's gone wrong here is, well, my fault?'

Again Noshi laughed and reached out to touch my arm. 'No, Gavin, don't be silly.'

Noshi was very kind to me and only once did I sense any kind of sexual vibe coming from him. I couldn't tell if he was gay or straight, never mind which gender.

Noshi and many other local people seemed to be the main

 workforce in the massive protected garden that I ended up spending most of my waking hours working in.

It was a delightful environment. It smelt gorgeous, it was generally lighter than the rest of the culvert and it didn't feel so claustrophobic. I had taken a great dislike to the low stone ceilings in the living quarters, so being in a large airy space with a very high semi-transparent roof was a blessed relief.

Up until my entrance into the cloud over Didcot Power Station, I don't think I'd done any gardening other than planting some cress seeds on blotting paper when I was at primary school. It was never something that interested me and even though my mum grew flowers around the dull lawn of her back garden, it wasn't something I'd grown up being involved with.

Since working in the gardens at the Institute in London I'd started to develop a genuine interest in planting regimes, drip-feed irrigation, hydroponics and the many related skills required for producing gargantuan amounts of food in very small areas.

They had that down to a fine art in the Chicago Culvert, it was essentially industrial-scale gardening in many ways similar to the arrangements I'd seen in the Squares of London. However, this system was highly mechanised, each bulging bed of vegetable growth was on a slowly rotating mechanical rig that brought the soil surface to the right height for human crop management.

The towers containing these slowly rotating beds were tens of metres high and there were many levels of gantry where workers could give the plants attention and check growth.

Noshi initially showed me how to work on one of the long narrow beds of densely packed root vegetables. It was easy to reach the whole soil surface from a standing position, mainly thinning or weeding around the new shoots. It was fiddly manual work and by the time I'd finished one bed it would all be a bit uncomfortable. However, as soon as I was bending down to reach the last offending weed, another bed would come down the rack and I'd start working on that. Beans, peas, pulses of all sorts, some plants I'd never seen before. Some of them not in soil, just held in a mesh with their roots exposed but covered in a fine mist.

'What are these?' I asked Noshi, who was working on the next slowly rotating machine to mine. The plants that mystified me looked like miniature pea pods but longer and thinner, growing on a bit of a scrawny stalk.

'You don't know what those are? For real?' he exclaimed. Thinking about it, if Noshi was a woman she had quite a deep voice.

'Beans?' I suggested weakly.

Noshi laughed and embraced me, 'You are so funny.'

He reached up and plucked a little bean pod from the unfamiliar plant.

'Lentils,' he said. 'These are the Masoor variety. In the same bed we have green Puy lentils, yellow lentils, Richlea lentils and at the end over there, Macachiados.'

'Lentils,' I said, 'well I never. I've heard of them, I've eaten them but I've never seen them growing.'

Noshi ran his hand through the lentil plants as he walked back to his station. 'They are kind of important, very high levels of protein, we use them as a base stock for a lot of the food products. They grow fast and these varieties are very hardy. One day, maybe not in my lifetime, but one day, maybe they can grow outside again.'

That made me stop and think. I'd not really considered it but of course nothing could grow outside. It really hit me at that point. The human race in this world was literally hanging on by the skin of its teeth. Nothing was growing outside, it had all been levelled by the winds. The effect this must have had on the environment had to have further exacerbated the climate in ways impossible to imagine back in 2011.

'Have you ever lived outside?' I asked, as I got back to pulling little weeds out of the soil beneath the dense rows of lentil plants.

Noshi looked at me and smiled. He had such a beautiful and indeed peaceful, confident smile. 'No, never. My grandfather remembers living outside but he lost a lot of his family in the early storms. He's from Da Lat Culvert. Have you heard of Da Lat?'

'Yes, I think so, it's in Vietnam,' I said, 'Southeast Asia.'

'I guess so. Anyway, we've had to live in culverts for many years. When the weather is kind I like to run in the rubble, just to feel the sun. I like that very much.'

'Wow, so you only ever go out of the culvert when you know the weather is calm.'

'Of course,' said Noshi with that enigmatic smile again. 'Many of us go running or walking when the weather is calm. We find things in the dirt, things from the old world. People like to collect old things if they are not too broken. Look at this.'

Noshi reached into his pocket and pulled out a small item, which he leaned across and gave to me. I stared at it feeling slightly dumbstruck. It was a die-cast model of a Ford Anglia, a toy car. It didn't have any wheels and the paint was badly chipped. It had at one time been painted white and was clearly a couple of hundred years old.

The thing that made me start was the fact that it was a Ford Anglia, a British car from the 1960s. It was a model of the same car I'd seen in the Museum of History in London. I think I only ever saw one real, running Ford Anglia back in 2010, sometimes classic car clubs drove through Kingham village as they wound their way through the Cotswolds and I'm sure I remember seeing one drive slowly past, leaving a trail of white smoke in its wake.

'That is amazing,' I said.

'Do you know what it is?' asked Noshi, it sounded like he truly didn't know. I knew I had to be careful; for all I knew Noshi could be a sleeper for the Original Five. This could be a test, a trick to see if I blurted out my true origins.

'I think it's a child's toy. I've seen one in the Museum of

History in my home city. It is very, very old, like 250 years old.
I think it's a model of a thing called a car.' I said carefully. When confronted with something as bizarre and unexplained as a model Ford Anglia I felt compelled to explain.

'What does it do?' asked Noshi.

'Well, I don't think it actually does anything. It's a toy, a child's toy.'

It was fairly clear that Noshi didn't have a clue what I was talking about. 'A toy, you know, a thing for children to play with. Didn't you have toys when you were a child?'

'I had a lizard,' said Noshi, 'but it died.'

'Right, I see,' I said. 'Okay, well this is a model, a miniature model of a real car, d'you know what a car is?'

Noshi shook his head. 'Okay, well, way back in the past, hundreds of years ago, people travelled around in cars. It was a simple machine for moving around in. In the old days you could go outside, the winds were not strong, you could go outside at any time you wanted and if you wanted to travel a long way you got in one of these.'

Noshi made an odd face, which I took to mean he thought I had to be joking.

'No, I don't mean one of these actual things, this is just a small version of the real thing. The real thing was big enough to get in, it was a machine that could move along. You see these shapes here,' I said, pointing to the empty wheel arches where the wheels would once have been. Noshi nodded.

'That would have had wheels when it was new,' I explained. 'So that meant it could go along the ground.'

'What, over rubble without legs?'

'No, they didn't have rubble, they had roads, long smooth strips of road all over the world, everywhere, and thousands of these machines to move them.'

Noshi gestured to the next bed of lentil plants that had appeared in front of me. I handed the model back to him.

'A car,' he said.

'Yes, a toy car.'

'Thank you for explaining it to me. I have wondered what it was for years. I found it many miles from the culvert when I was running.'

I shook my head in bewilderment. Noshi struck me as an intelligent and aware person but he clearly knew nothing about the world that had been ravaged to rubble by hundreds of years of brutal hurricanes.

But it was spooky, a Ford Anglia. Why had I seen that car in two different time dimensions? It had to mean that wherever I was, whatever weird time warp connected reality, hyperspace alternative dimension world I was in had a very similar history to both the Squares of London and Gardenia.

Of course I wanted to ask Brad about this, but he was nowhere to be seen. Since I'd spent a few days working in the garden factory I hadn't seen him.

Later that day I moved to another area with Noshi, where we picked hydroponically grown lettuces, thousands of them. We stacked them into boxes and other people loaded them up into stacks and walked out of the garden factory with them balanced on their heads.

I never once saw a walking machine inside the culvert, they were clearly only used outside the walls of the facility, but it did strike me that this very labour-intensive aspect of life in the culvert could have been done by machine. They had plenty of sophisticated machines at their beck and call. I pondered this as I washed my hands and arms after a long day's gardening. Maybe they just chose to grow food like this because it was so beneficial to their mental health. I imagined it would be easy to go a bit stir-crazy, locked away in this cocoon of safety month after month while the elements went apeshit outside the walls.

'I'd like to go for a walk outside, when the weather is calm,' I said to Noshi as we climbed the metal stairs out of the garden factory. 'Not sure I could keep up with you if you were running, but the glimpse I got of the outside before this storm was amazing.'

'I will walk with you if you like,' said Noshi. 'The weather will be better in three days, we can go then. Many people will leave the culvert then, it will be nice to see the sun.'

'How do you know it will be sunny?' I asked. It was late October by this time and I'd assumed the winter would be setting in. I knew that Chicago had once been a very cold city in the winter.

'Oh, it will be a hot sunny day. We always know exactly what the weather will be like, that is something we learned to do many years ago. Sometimes it is too hot, sometimes it will be too cold to go out for long, but in three days' time it will be just fine.'

19

'I HEARD TODAY THAT THE STORM FINISHES AT 3:14 tomorrow,' I said to Theda a few days later. She had just washed her hair and was using a very bizarre little ball of material to dry it. I assumed she was drying it; she was rubbing the small ball over her head, which seemed to leave her short, mousey hair very dry.

I was sitting on my little chair cleaning under my fingernails with a bit of wood I'd found in some of the soil I'd been planting shallots in. Life in our little apartment had become reassuringly domestic.

'Yes, I heard the same information today,' she said without looking at me.

'So, does that mean a cloud could come and visit?'

'I imagine it's a possibility, although I have been working with the dimension committee so I have been a little preoccupied,' she said as she finally finished rubbing her fluffy hair and sat down opposite me. She smiled. 'I think we are in the same ship. We would both like to go home, is that not correct?'

'Yeah, although it's the same boat.'

'Sorry?'

'The old English phrase is, "we're in the same boat", not ship.'

'It means the same thing does it not?'

'Yes it does,' I said. I enjoyed this little moment simply because it was simple. It was the sort of conversation that could have happened in any century for the last thousand years, two people with different native tongues learning the intricacies of each other's language. Of course it would have been simpler if it had been two people from the same time period, the same dimension in space–time, the same bloody world. It would have been simpler if it didn't involve an utterly baffling relationship requiring me to think of this older woman as my great-granddaughter. I preferred to think of Theda at that moment as just a German woman with fluffy hair who claimed we were in the same ship.

'I'm going out for a walk tomorrow as soon as the winds drop,' I said. Theda looked up at me a little alarmed.

'You mean you are going outside the culvert?'

'Yes, not on my own or anything brave and foolhardy, I'm going with Noshi.'

'Noshi!'

'Yes, Noshi. He's fine, he's very charming and kind, I know he was once from one of the Original Five clouds but he's left them now and I can tell he's not one of them.'

Theda just looked at me without saying anything.

'I work with him when I'm gardening,' I added. 'By the way, you've got to try his apples, they're bloody amazing.'

I handed her an apple I'd carried back from the garden dome. 'Noshi told me it was okay to take a couple.'

'Thank you.' She took a bite and chewed for a while, nodded and said, 'Well, he can grow a good apple.'

'Hydroponic apple trees. The most bizarre things I've ever seen,' I said.

'You have to be careful, Gavin. You and I are strangers here, we don't know the intricacies of Noshi's history, who he is in contact with. We don't know where his true allegiances lie and why he asked you to go outside the culvert with him.'

'He didn't ask me, I asked him,' I replied. By this point I was getting a bit indignant; Theda wasn't my mother and I wasn't ten years old.

'I want to see what it's really like, I only got a glimpse when we all went out before the storm, I want to see what's happened to the world.'

'I don't think it's a good idea,' said Theda. 'If the weather is calm and a cloud is able to make contact, we need to be ready to go. Noshi could have befriended you in order to ... '

'To what?'

'I don't know, to maybe delay your departure so the Original Five can capture you?' Theda's confidence faded as she was saying this. It was as if as she spoke she understood how ridiculous the notion was.

'I don't know, Gavin!' she wailed. 'I am worried for your safety. Is that so bad?'

'No, it's very kind of you,' I replied.

'Out of all the millions of people in this culvert, you become friends with a member of a subversive group, does that not make you a little anxious?'

'Okay, fine, I'll be careful, okay? Noshi does not strike me as a heavily-armed member of a violent terrorist cell. He's a gardener. Anyway, this is all speculation, we need to know if a cloud is due to arrive, don't we?'

Theda smiled at me. 'You are correct, we need to know. Let us find out.'

So we left the small apartment and I followed Theda along the endless low-ceilinged corridors. I assumed she knew where we were going because I wasn't concentrating at all, I was just walking alongside her.

'So you want to get back to Munich in 2411?' I asked.

'Yes, of course.'

'Oh, right,' I said. 'I hadn't really thought about it, I assumed you'd just jumped through the cloud on a kind of one-way ticket.'

'It was a risk, we knew that, but from what I have gathered here, combining our understanding of the science involved and the very advanced knowledge the people here have developed, it should be possible for us both to get back home.'

'Can you go straight back to Munich from here?'

'At the correct time, yes I can.'

‘So why have I got to go back to Gardenia?’ I asked, feeling somehow cheated, that I had got the super economy ticket with more stopovers.

‘I jumped back in time. I cannot damage my brain returning from here, the damage has already been done.’

‘Oh, so you did suffer brain damage coming here?’ I asked. Theda had not struck me as someone who was anything other than super bright.

‘I was very confused when I first arrived, I did not know where I was or who I was. It is the memory stored in my hardened enhancements that allowed me to reconnect with myself. You do not have such enhancements.’

‘I’ve got a kidonge.’

‘That is not the same, that is not protected from current surges and will be disabled on your return journey. When I arrive back I will remember everything. You jumped forward, if you go back to 2011 any changes you have made to your brain could have very dire consequences for you.’ Theda stopped walking and looked at me. ‘Not only that, it’s a safety mechanism for everyone. This moment here, now, it is very delicately balanced, it is surely easy to understand how the actions of one person could spread and alter over many years.’

I think I grimaced because I didn’t really understand. Of course if I went back and started a nuclear war or introduced a lethal virus that wiped out the human race things could get sticky down the line, but I was hardly in a position to do either. Theda started walking again. ‘That is why you need to go back from the place you first landed in. From Gardenia.’

We walked in silence for a moment. My mind was blank and I felt quite calm. I was slightly surprised at this because in my previous experience when I didn’t understand something I would get very anxious. Now, because it seemed my very existence had been taken completely out of my control I felt very relaxed. Not only that, I *knew* I was feeling relaxed as the relaxed feeling swept through me. I did allow myself to ponder if this newly aware state of mind would also exist when I got back to 2011. If I got back.

We went through a low door and along another corridor. It took ages. We might have walked a couple of kilometres by the time we entered the final corridor. This one had glass panels down one side and inside the small rooms we were passing, groups of people seemed to be sitting around talking. It was almost like a university campus except the ages of the people were too varied. Some of them were kids, some were old women, ancient-looking blokes and a few teenagers here and there.

Theda stopped outside one of the glass-fronted rooms and waited. 'Brad should be finished soon, we will wait here.'

I looked into the room we were standing outside and there was Brad. It looked like he was in full flow and he was gesturing in the air. I noticed everyone in the room with him was looking at his gestures and studying what looked to me to be empty space.

'He's using the same graphics system we saw in the conference room a few days back, the time you did not listen to anything.'

I smiled at the memory. 'The thing with all the swirly circles?'

'Yes, exactly like that.'

'But I can't see anything from here.'

'No, you won't be able to, not unless you are in the room. It has a very limited range, specifically so when you are not intended to see anything.'

'That sounds a bit ominous.'

'No, it is not ominous, it is not being hidden from you, it is being kept from some of the people who live here in this time. Because life is rather hard here it is feared that many people would try to do as you and I have done, migrate to an easier, more amenable dimension.'

'So the people in there are learning how to jump from one dimension to another – is that what Brad does?'

'In a way, yes. That is a research group, all the people in there are very advanced scientists.'

‘Some of them look like kids,’ I said, looking at a girl who could not have been more than 12.

‘They are usually the most brilliant thinkers in this field. They have no fear of the technology or the theories, they are all involved in developing technologies which it is hoped will help us to understand the science and aid the communication between dimensions.’

‘Wow, so you mean it might be possible for people here to talk to people in say, Gardenia or the cities of the Squares?’

‘Yes, it is possible now, here. The only problem is that the technology in other dimensions does not always exist. The understanding of the vagaries of space–time and a multidimensional universe are not, well, they are not yet universal. If you think about it, in my dimension, the one you just came from, it took a further 200 years from your arrival for us to understand or even accept the possibility of other dimensions.’

‘Okay,’ I said, leaning against the wall opposite the conference room. ‘So even though they live in ditches and float about on clouds here, their science is more advanced.’

‘Correct.’

I sighed. I understood that I was at the same point in time, well, the same year at least as I had been in Gardenia and the Squares of London, but what I didn’t comprehend was how these people in the Chicago Culvert could possibly have developed such incredible scientific knowledge. I’d seen breathtaking technologies and scientific do-dads in the other dimensions I’d visited. The people of the clouds didn’t have tethered satellites, maglev transportation systems, massive self-powering mega cities or kidonges. But they understood particle physics and string theory like I understood hydraulics and pump actuators.

It had to be down to the environment they lived in. They were battling the elements to a degree the human race had never faced before, they were stuck underground for the vast majority of their lives. I suppose they could have got drunk, had parties, fornicated and debauched themselves as the storms raged outside. What it seems they had done instead was a lot of thinking.

The glass door hissed and Brad emerged as it slid away. The rest of the group stood behind him, some of them clearly whispering to each other as they realised who we were. Once again I was grateful for the presence of a very tall woman from the future – Theda definitely got most of the attention.

'May we talk briefly?' asked Theda.

'Of course,' said Brad. He turned to the small group behind him. 'Would you excuse us for a moment?'

The group wandered off, occasionally giving a glance back to us as they departed.

'Gavin and I were wishing to ask you if you have any data on the next cloud arrival.'

Brad nodded and started to walk in the opposite direction to his departing group. 'I have been very involved, as you know, Theda, very involved in the dimension sub-committee, however, let us have a quick look in MT1.' He turned to me and smiled, 'That's the culvert meteorology and transportation department. I think you'll like this, Gavin.'

We went through another doorway and down some steps into a long corridor with an even lower ceiling. At the end was a huge door that looked like it was made of stone. Brad stopped outside.

'I just have to inform you, Gavin, I am slightly worried. One of my students was asking a lot of questions about you today. Have you said anything to anyone in the culvert?'

'No,' I said, glancing nervously at Theda. 'I've been very careful.'

Brad rubbed his chin for a moment. 'Mmm, interesting. Clearly word is spreading. The student I'm referring to was actually born on Cloud Three, he's a fascinating young man who is clearly in conflict with his family, however, we cannot be too careful. His questions were very pointed, although I have the feeling he's not certain of the exact time period you came from. Some of his research notes were about a war between England and Germany in 1914. Does that mean anything to you?'

'Well, the first and second World Wars,' I said. 'They were a bit of a nightmare.'

'Mmm.' Again, Brad did the chin rubbing. 'He seems to think you come from that era, but that was a little before your time.'

'A lot before my time, my great-grandfather fought in World War I,' I said.

'Well, hopefully we can get you on a cloud and away before this becomes a problem. Let us proceed.'

The huge door that looked like stone slid open with ease as Brad approached.

Once past the door we were faced with another even longer flight of stairs, down into the proper bowels of the Earth. Once we got to the bottom we turned right, through another of the stone-like doors and into a room that, even at this stage of my travels, really took me by surprise.

I want to underline that my general emotional state during my stay in the culvert could adequately be described as stable, even flatlining. Nothing phased me, no new weird technology had any effect on me whatsoever: walking repair bots, floating clouds, massive culverts covered in carbon ceramic tiles, weird brown 3D projections of impossible-to-comprehend time and space-defying dimension concepts. It was all much of a muchness until I entered the Chicago Culvert's meteorology department.

There, in front of me, was the world. A ten-metre-high solid planet floating in the middle of a huge space. It was complete with visible atmosphere, ridiculous detail in the land masses, seas and cloud formations and to top it all off, it was rotating very slowly.

Standing and sitting around the room were a small number of people who seemed busy in conversation, but not with each other, however. They seemed to be talking to some distant party. They weren't using microphones or any visible equipment I could see, they were looking at the globe and talking, some of them in languages I wasn't familiar with.

'We need to stay back,' said Brad, 'they are in communication with the clouds and there is a bit of high drama at the moment because they are looking for an ambient window for the launch of Cloud Eleven.'

'From the Beijing Culvert?' asked Theda.

'Correct,' said Brad. 'Let's circumnavigate and have a look at the weather conditions.'

We walked around the side of the room along a slightly raised walkway. I could not take my eyes off the planet before me. I was trying to understand how it floated so serenely above the floor. It looked utterly solid, I felt certain it wasn't a projection, it was a solid object that must have weighed hundreds of tons.

'Just incredible,' I said as we walked around a dark, raised section of the circular room.

'We are very proud of it. This is the most secure part of the culvert.' Brad turned to me and whispered, 'I mean secure from the weather. We don't suffer from terrorist threats or possible war-like aggression from other people. I know this was often a problem back in your era.'

I nodded my understanding.

Brad then continued without whispering. 'This is the world's most advanced weather prediction system, we can predict weather up to six months in advance with 98 per cent accuracy down to the last kilometre. What we are seeing here is the weather pattern for next week.'

Brad pointed to the globe. I could easily identify the coast of China, although I did notice that all the landmasses were coloured brown, not green. The sky over where Beijing should have been looked clear to me but there was no sign of a city on the surface of the slowly spinning blue–brown planet.

Far away, south of Japan, there was a vortex of clouds over the Pacific, the sort of weather pattern I would have recognised as a hurricane. I then noticed these cloud patterns made up the majority of the cloud formations and some of them were continental in their scale.

‘So, it’s looking good. Cloud Eleven is three times the size of Cloud Ten, it’s going to take four days to inflate and during that time when it is still tethered to the ground it is in great danger from winds. The construction was completed a year ago and they have been waiting to launch all that time.’

‘Wait, three times bigger than Cloud Ten?’ I said, ‘But that’s inconceivable.’

‘Not really, the systems and structures have been designed to steadily get bigger. The residents of the Beijing Culvert are already constructing the chassis of Cloud Twelve, that will be over 200 kilometres across.’

I had to hold my head; it felt like it was going to melt. A man-made, lighter-than-air structure more than 200 kilometres across. I suddenly wanted to stay in this dimension just to see something like that; a floating mega city was something worth hanging around for.

‘One moment,’ said Brad. He leant forward and spoke briefly to a woman who was standing just below us. She glanced at him, smiled and glanced at me. Her smile was rather flirtatious. Well, I thought it was. She nodded and said something to Brad.

He stood up and turned to me. ‘Professor Glynne said that as it’s for you, Gavin, they will return the map to the present time so you can see current weather conditions here; let us circumnavigate again.’

‘You are very lucky,’ said Theda. ‘I have spoken with Professor Glynne before, I don’t think she would make such a concession for me.’

I smiled. I didn’t know what to say. It felt odd, the fact that although no one seemed to pay me any attention, they all seemed to know who I was. It was very unlike the experience in London, here it was all understated and quiet, as was the room and the giant spinning world within.

I followed Brad around the raised walkway until the North American continent came into view. It was hard to pick out at first as the western half was covered in one arm of a truly vast weather event. The centre or eye of the storm was between the Californian coast and Hawaii, but the cloud arms almost covered half the Pacific and half the American land mass. I had never seen any weather pattern like it.

'Three hundred and fifty kilometre per hour winds,' said Brad. 'A bird storm.'

As I heard Brad explain, a question started to develop in my mind, it was answered before I could say anything.

'A bird storm doesn't have birds in it,' said Theda. 'It's called that because of the shape of the two storm fronts that circulate around the ultra-low pressure area in the centre. The outer tips of those cloud-wings you can see? That's the danger zone. Winds at that point can reach 500 kilometres per hour.'

'See there?' said Brad, pointing to the sphere. 'Just above the mouth of the Mississippi, that's Cloud Nine.'

I stared at the giant globe and couldn't make anything out. That's when I got another shock. Suddenly the globe expanded beyond comprehension, virtually filling the space it was housed in. The surface was suddenly mere inches from my face and there, in perfect focus, as clear as day, was Cloud Nine.

'So it's not far and it is hoping to head this way,' said Brad.

At that point Professor Glynne walked up to us. Her head was actually inside the Earth, so it was a bit confusing until the giant solid-looking planet shrunk back to its original size.

'Just as well you are not a meteorologist, Doctor,' she said with a kind smile. 'Cloud Nine is travelling away from us at speed. It will not be able to make contact with Chicago at this time. We are hoping another cloud will be able to, if they come in from the north, but as yet we have no solid data on this.'

'So, I've got time to go for a walk?' I said, turning to Theda.

'Yes, Gavin, it looks like you have.'

20

UT OF ALL MY ADVENTURES IN THE FUTURE multiverse, I found walking with Noshi to be nearly the most embarrassing.

Not that he was unpleasant and, indeed, referring to Noshi as 'him' maybe doing her an injustice, I'll never know. However, as we left the culvert with a sizeable crowd of similarly adorned people through an enormous sunken doorway, Noshi held my hand.

It is probably not hard to imagine how awkward I found this. Not that I have anything against holding hands and I think I may have done so once or twice with Beth when we went on early dates, but it has never been something I make a habit of.

No doubt I held my mum and dad's hands when I was a toddler, I don't recall, but I have never walked along with another man and held hands.

Maybe that's a bit sad. I have seen Italian men and Arab men holding hands as they stroll along and it looks fine, I may have had a couple of 'blimey, they must be gay' thoughts, but I quickly got used to the sight. In fact on a purely intellectual level I think it's a good thing, much better than walking along punching someone, but I have to admit walking hand in hand with Noshi made me a little tense.

It also took my focus off the experience I was having walking away from the culvert and being engulfed in the stultifying heat.

After countless days of windstorms ravaging the planet, the air was suddenly very still, thick and hot.

There was not a trace of cloud in the sky and it was easy to get disoriented on the vast brown plain beneath my feet and the shocking blue dome above my head.

After about an hour of walking and holding hands, Noshi let go.

'I think you'll be okay now,' he said, and of course it was only at that moment I realised what he'd been doing.

He wasn't holding my hand in a gay way, or a patronising way or even in a 'culture I don't understand' way. He was holding my hand to ensure I didn't fall over.

The ground we were crossing was very uneven; we had been walking over piles of broken rubble for miles. This was not easy, there wasn't a smooth flat walking surface available, the whole place was riddled with potholes and trip hazards.

Every now and then as we trudged on I would spot a very unusual shape breaking the horizon. The endless flat nothingness that surrounded me meant my eye was naturally drawn to something out of the ordinary. As we got nearer to some of these peculiar landmarks, I understood them to be large pieces of concrete or the twisted remnants of a steel beam.

The concrete had been grit-blasted into smooth, almost sculptural shapes, the steel I-beams and reinforcement rods were polished smooth and shiny.

My fascination at these objects meant I slowly fell behind Noshi, who ploughed on as if he were walking through a picturesque park on a Sunday morning.

I glanced up at him every now and then just so I didn't lose sight of him. I had to concentrate on where I put my feet all the time as the landscape was so difficult to navigate.

I could see that Noshi had reached the summit of a low hill. I'd seen it looming in the distance for what seemed like hours – the generally flat brown landscape made judging distances very hard.

There were no trees or buildings to pass to give you a sign that you were actually making headway. Noshi had been ahead of me for much of the walk, he was very fit and clearly used to getting across the barren, broken terrain I'd been stumbling over.

I was wearing amazingly competent walking boots that Noshi had brought with him to my tiny apartment early that morning. These were the first boots I'd really liked since I left 2011 and without them I think my feet and ankles would have been cut to ribbons.

We had been walking across a broken wilderness of hundreds of years of industrial output, mashed, crushed, broken and flattened by forces beyond the control of mere mortals.

It was hard not to be depressed by what I saw. The waste was overwhelming, there had been such unfathomable destruction over such a long time it was impossible not to feel your humanity crushed by the horror.

Strangely though, and I suppose this was a perfect example of the indomitable nature of the human spirit, Noshi seemed to be thoroughly enjoying himself.

'You get a great view from up here,' he shouted down to me as he stood on a lump of what I imagined was once part of a building.

I eventually managed to clamber over the massive lumps of concrete, some of them having sand-blasted bare metal reinforcement bars jutting out from the broken surface.

I stood up next to Noshi once I'd made it to the rugged pinnacle. I was breathing hard and my vision was slightly impaired by the peculiar goggles I had been told I must wear. However, what greeted me was a sight I shall never forget.

A massive vista of barren, sandy brown destruction. Nowhere did anything break the skyline by more than a couple of metres, just proper, post-apocalyptic devastation as far as the human eye could see, which from where we were situated was many hundreds of kilometres.

The sky was crystal clear blue, blue beyond comprehension, such a deep blue colour it almost made me weep.

'Can I just remove the goggles for a moment?' I said. 'I want to see what it really looks like.'

Noshi looked down at his wrist, scanned the horizon and nodded.

'Just for a moment,' he said, 'but the light will hurt, it's very bright.'

He was right, as soon as I pulled the goggles up to my forehead I was dazzled by the brilliance. I managed to squint for a few seconds to get an unimpeded view. The sky was an even deeper blue than I'd seen through the goggles; it was such a clear sky, a prehistoric and untampered-with blue.

'It's sort of beautiful,' I said after a long silence.

'I think it is,' said Noshi. He handed me a white cushion of liquid, a newly inserted straw stuck into the top. I drank and of course, as is often the case with me, I only realised how thirsty I was once I started drinking. Rather like realising I'd had a feeling a couple of hours after I'd had it.

On my left forearm was a read-out built into the suit. Not some plastic add-on, it looked like a series of numbers printed on cloth in matt ink but it was constantly changing. The air temperature was 48 degrees Centigrade, my heart rate was at 138 beats per minute and that was all I needed to know. It was hot, the air was still and I was knackered.

'There's not really anywhere to sit in the shade is there?' I said with a half-hearted chuckle. Noshi didn't respond and I held the now empty liquid satchel down by my side because I felt a bit guilty. I had downed the lot without a second thought.

'Is there any area, like a valley or something, where there's still stuff around that's, well, recognisable from, well, from before?' I said.

Noshi shook his head. 'Not that I've ever seen. Not around here that's for sure. If you travel a long way east there are still some big hills and the eastern side of those still have some organic growth dug in between the rocks. Moss, lichen and the like, nothing big like a bush or tree but from a distance it can look a bit green.'

'But there are no buildings?'

'No buildings. Other than culverts, there's nothing.'

'It's terrible,' I said, 'it's so, utterly terrible.'

I pushed away grit and small bits of rubble with my boots and managed to clear enough smooth and relatively flat concrete to sit down on. I could feel the brutal heat of the sun on my back as I finally relaxed. Even though the suit was made of some highly reflective material, the heat still made its way through.

Shading my forehead with my hands, I stared at the ground between my legs and a tiny bit of movement caught my eye. It was an ant, a tiny little ant clambering over some bits of rock. Then I saw another and another.

'Wow,' I said, 'look at that, there's still things living out here.'

I glanced up at Noshi, who seemed to be very happy standing in the blazing sun just looking at the flat view before us.

'Sorry, did you say something?' he said eventually.

'I was just commenting that there is something living out here. Look. Ants.'

Noshi squatted down and stared at the ground. 'Oh, yes. Well, there are still insects. They live deep down. Cute little critters. I've seen cockroaches too, but nothing that flies.'

'What about birds?'

'You mean like birds that fly?'

'Yes.'

'No, not outside a culvert, we don't have any birds.'

'Wow. What about, like, rabbits and furry things that live underground?'

'No, nothing, there's nothing for them to eat,' said Noshi waving his arms around.

'So there are no animals or birds anywhere?'

'The Topeka Culvert has a big animal sanctuary. They've got a big laboratory and holding pens, they've got many animals there. I've never been but I'm sure you could go visit.'

There was another long silence. It was eerie being outside and hearing nothing. Not even a light breeze. The Earth was still and effectively dead.

'Everything I've learned since being here is really hard to deal with,' I said eventually, almost to myself. Noshi sat down beside me and I turned to face him. By this time I'd gotten used to the fact that 99 per cent of his body was covered with a silvery blue bodysuit and a pair of bug-eyed goggles. He pulled the suit down from his mouth and I could see he was smiling.

'I'm amazed that you seem so happy,' I said.

'I have a good life,' said Noshi. 'I don't know much about what it was like in history, I found history made me sad so I didn't learn much. Things are getting better, the really big storms don't come so much, we get more days like this when we can recharge and dry out, when we can mend things and build new things. It's not so bad.'

'So you don't know much about what happened in the past?' I suggested.

'We were taught it when I was young, about the smoke and the flames and the destruction, the wars and the cruelty and how stupid everyone was. I don't really understand why people were so stupid with each other. It seems crazy. It made me sad to think about it so I didn't pay much heed. Did you like history over in your world?'

'I think it's important to know about what people did in the past, you know, so we hopefully won't repeat the bad stuff but also so we can learn from the good stuff.'

'I think it may be a bit late for that now,' said Noshi. He looked at me and smiled, his face, what I could see of it, was so calm and peaceful. I was also wearing a one-piece suit although very different to the dull cream flight suit I'd been wearing. Mine was a kind of translucent blue colour, complete with built-in gloves and tight-fitting hood. There was a backpack which reminded me of some of the clothing tech I'd worn in the Squares of London, you just picked it up and it sort of wrapped itself around you.

We looked like two blue mime artists lost in the desert, but I was very grateful to wear it. Clearly to have been out there in shorts and a T-shirt would have resulted in serious heat stroke and sunburn.

'When you were on the cloud that picked you up from Vietnam, what was that like?' I asked. I wanted to find out more about that period of Noshi's life but had never had the chance to ask before.

'Cloud Four, it was frightening at first. That's where I learned a lot about history. No one had explained anything to me before that.'

'Why was it frightening?'

'Oh, the early clouds are very simple, you could fall off them if you weren't careful. Only a small central part is pressurised so they can't go very high. If they get caught in a storm it can be very bad.'

I nodded as he spoke, getting images of ancient sailing ships on the high seas.

'And did you meet Ebrikke?'

'Ahh, yes, Miss Karensdottir, I know her. She is an amazing woman,' said Noshi. 'She is also a very angry woman. You know, she is the one with the many enhancements?'

'Yes, I've been told about it. She's a bit frightening isn't she?'

'No, not frightening, she knows a lot about why we live like this, and she is very angry about it. She is right but I always said to her, being angry doesn't help.'

'That's very wise,' I said with a smile.

'She didn't listen. You see, many of the people on the Original Five think she's right, they agree with everything she says and because I didn't, they considered me a renegade and dropped me off here. And then when I came here everyone in Chicago

 Culvert thought I was a renegade, they decided I was one of the Original Five so they don't trust me. I am just the original Noshi.'

I laughed again. He was so sweet, how could anyone be scared of this person?

Suddenly my vision was lost, everything went a sort of sandy-brown colour as some kind of explosion happened somewhere near. I jumped in shock as I had no idea what it was. As the dust dropped away I saw Noshi once again. Both our suits were covered in brown grit, not sand, it was coarser than sand which meant it dropped off without difficulty. I sat low on the lump of concrete and stared about in terror.

'What the hell was that?' I whispered.

'A twirly tail. It's nothing to worry about, they happen all the time, I could see it coming.'

Noshi was pointing off into the distance and I couldn't quite believe what I was seeing. A sort of tall stick of brown dirt skittering across the plane like a mini whirlwind.

'That's a twirly tail?' I said, as it seemed to disperse and fade before my eyes.

'Yes. It's the heat, it creates a lot of strange effects like that.'

'But you saw it coming?'

'Yes, well, my sensors did, yours would have too, a little yellow mark at the top of your goggles, didn't you see it?'

'Um, no I didn't, I just got a face full of dirt,' I said. 'But thanks for telling me.'

I tried to see anything resembling a little yellow mark on my goggles, but I couldn't see anything.

'Where is the culvert from here?' I asked. I had no way of judging my bearings, no idea where I might be on an old map of the world.

Noshi pointed to my left. I turned and looked, right on the horizon was a vague shadow, a kind of smudge.

'Can you see it?' he asked.

I nodded. 'So we've come quite a way.'

Noshi glanced at his sleeve, 'Fourteen kilometres,' he said. 'But I'd like to press on, I want you to see the lake.'

'The lake?'

'Lake Michigan, there is still some of it left and walking on the lake bed is very easy.'

So we set off again, me always lagging behind as I carefully negotiated my way through the rubble.

After another hour of walking I could make something out on the flat horizon. A different colour, something in the distant haze that could have been water.

Soon the ground became oddly smooth and we moved much faster. It was such a relief after the rough ground we'd been walking on.

'This is the lake bed,' said Noshi. I could finally keep up with him and we walked on at a good pace.

'Where we stopped on the hill, that was once downtown Chicago. The culvert is in what would have been Arlington Heights. Have you heard of that?'

'Yes, I think so,' I said. 'It was a suburb of Chicago.'

'Correct, and this was once Lake Michigan, but the water level has dropped a great deal. Sometimes it comes back, sometimes it's very empty.'

'How can the level drop so much?'

Noshi pointed up. 'The sun dries it out. Sometimes when we get a heavy rainstorm it fills up, but if there's a strong wind the water is spread over a very wide area. We have sometimes had floods right up to the culvert abutments.'

After a few more minutes of walking we reached the edge of a large body of water. It was flat and smooth, dazzling to look at because of the brutal sun but nonetheless delightful.

'Wow, Lake Michigan,' I said. I squatted down at the water's edge and looked at the muddy liquid lying still and motionless at my feet. 'Amazing.'

21

T'S NOT AS IF I'D NEVER BEEN WALKING OUTSIDE on a summer's day and spotted a distant rain cloud before. It's a common sight and especially in the jolly old UK back in the day.

When Noshi pointed to a distant cloud on the horizon above the flat wasteland that had once been a vibrant city, it was a rather different experience.

We'd been walking back toward the Chicago Culvert for over two hours. The sun was beginning to cool a little as it approached the western horizon and a very slight breeze had built up, which was a blessed relief as by this time I was utterly exhausted.

'Is that dangerous?' I asked, feeling slightly exposed in the middle of the rubble field. Although we could see the ramparts of the Chicago Culvert I could sense there would still be a couple of hours of stumbling to get to safety.

'No, not dangerous, we don't want to miss it,' said Noshi. 'I had hoped we'd see it, it was one of the reasons I wanted to get you out here today.'

'Is that, wait, it's not a storm?' I stuttered. The cloud on the horizon was huge, a white fluffy upper area catching the light of the sun, the lower parts dark grey and slightly ominous.

'Cloud Eleven,' said Noshi, 'the biggest, ever.'

I tripped over at that point. My own fault – I was staring over at Cloud Eleven to my right and didn't see a massive lump of rock sticking up out of the ground.

Noshi helped me to my feet.

'You okay?' he asked kindly as he held my arms.

'Yeah, I'm fine.' I was fine, just feeling slightly awkward at the sudden intimacy.

Noshi glanced at his sleeve. 'We need to move fast, I'll steady you and don't worry about getting too hot, we'll soon cool down when the cloud is overhead.'

From that point on we almost ran over the endless rubble. Noshi held my left arm with a vice-like grip and pulled me along.

I kept looking around at the approaching storm cloud. It soon filled the northern horizon and for some reason I found it terrifying. Although I knew this was a man-made behemoth and wasn't designed to crush all that came before it, it was so huge and I felt so vulnerable it was hard not to slip into a bit of a panic.

I also had no idea how it was in the vicinity. I'd heard they were trying to launch it but was sure they had said it was built in China. How had it got to Chicago?

I wanted to ask so many questions but there was no chance, I was out of breath and concentrating hard on not falling over and breaking my leg. Grunting and panting were the only noises coming from my mouth.

As we finally got near the door in the culvert abutments, the cloud was directly overhead and it had become ominously dark. However, my terror started to dissipate as we joined a large crowd of people who had emerged from the culvert entrance and were standing around looking up at the slow-moving monster above us.

Then it started raining.

Not just a bit of drizzle, this was a full-on torrential tropical downpour and it started instantly.

'Just made it!' said Noshi. He pulled up his goggles and pulled back the hood of his suit. I did likewise as the cool water pummeling our heads was an incredible relief.

We mingled with the large crowd of people standing around the entrance, everyone staring up, their mouths open in what I took to be a moment of awe. I spotted a teenage girl holding a plant in a small pot. She was laughing as the rain drenched her and the plant.

The grey mass floating maybe 500 metres above our heads was dispensing millions of gallons of water; I saw torrents falling from outlets placed at regular intervals along the underside of the cloud.

'Don't worry, it's all been filtered,' said Noshi, who by this time was also standing with his mouth open and his tongue out.

'What?' I said. 'It's waste water?'

'Sure,' said Noshi, 'they rain onto the culvert to top up our tanks.'

I opened my mouth and stuck out my tongue like everyone else. If I was going to get typhoid, malaria, cholera or guinea worm disease I would not be alone and what's more, the cooling effect of the artificial rain was heaven-sent.

I had been sweltering all day under the brutal sun. I'm sure the body suit had protected me from harmful rays and it certainly kept me cooler than any twenty-first-century clothing I could have worn, but I'd walked for miles and had sweated like a spit roast pig all day.

Standing under a cool shower was a near-divine experience. Noshi leant toward me and touched my left sleeve. Suddenly the water penetrated the suit as if it wasn't there. I felt completely naked.

'Oh, wow!' I shouted, as the water started to cool my worryingly overheated body. 'This is amazing!'

Somehow the material had instantly transformed from a totally impermeable membrane into something that resembled fine linen. The relief was immense.

As I stood there soaking, I noticed that the cloud above me was now hardly moving, in fact it looked totally motionless. It also seemed to be lower than when I'd first seen the rain start to fall, it looked to be just above the ramparts we were standing beside.

I'd been in the Chicago Culvert for so long, hiding away from the brutal elements, working in the garden with Noshi, eating fairly unpleasant food and sleeping in my pod every night. Time had just slipped by, I was surviving but not really living, not until I escaped into the arid terrain with Noshi and saw the devastation.

It was as if I'd just woken up from a long sleep. I felt invigorated and inquisitive again, I wanted to do stuff, go places, see things and understand what the hell was going on and what was in store for me.

'Gavin!'

I turned and saw Theda standing just outside the doorway into the culvert. She was holding a kind of umbrella device above her head protecting her from the constant deluge.

'Come, we must prepare to leave!'

22

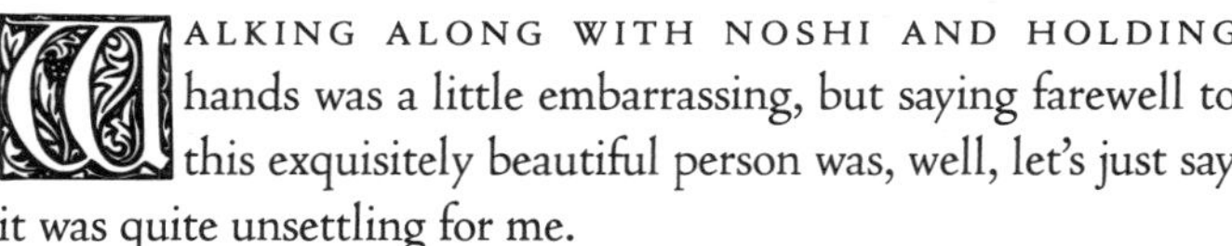

WALKING ALONG WITH NOSHI AND HOLDING hands was a little embarrassing, but saying farewell to this exquisitely beautiful person was, well, let's just say it was quite unsettling for me.

Not altogether in a bad way. I don't mean I freaked out or found the experience repugnant, it's just not something I'd ever done before.

'I am going to miss you, Gavin,' said Noshi as he embraced me. That was awkward enough, but when he released me he stared right into my eyes, moved forward and kissed me on the lips. I didn't resist even though I felt very awkward; I knew Theda was watching us.

To paraphrase Katy Perry's 2008 song: I kissed a man and I liked it. Well, I kissed someone I thought was a man, someone who could have been a man.

'That's so sweet,' said Theda when the kiss finally finished.

I feel uncomfortable just recalling this moment, but it happened and there we are. I may as well admit that I felt stirrings when he kissed me. Who knows what would have happened if Noshi and I had more time together.

'I want you to keep those boots,' said Noshi, as I started to take them off. 'You can't wear them on the cloud, but maybe afterwards, maybe when you get back to your home time.'

I held the boots up and admired them. They were amazing, very supportive and rugged and even after all the trudging and tripping I'd done in them they looked brand new, unscratched, perfect.

'Thank you, Noshi,' I said. I wanted to give him another kiss but I couldn't quite bring myself to do it.

In the meantime, Theda was rushing about collecting her few belongings. She was almost girlish in her excitement, jumping up and down on the spot screaming, 'Cloud Eleven, I cannot believe we are going to go to Cloud Eleven!'

Noshi was laughing with her, I was grinning but I didn't really know why.

I wasn't so convinced that going back onto a cloud was such a good idea even though I understood it was, theoretically at least, the start of my journey home. It was a difficult choice I'll grant you, but I had grown used to being safe in the Midwestern ditch that was the Chicago Culvert.

I'd also grown used to spending time with Noshi. We'd worked all over the garden together, he'd shown me the many layers of underground areas and intensive crops growing under incredible light panels powered by, according to Brad, a 50-gigawatt geothermal system which powered half the culvert – the other half coming from solar collectors that could be retracted to protect them from the storms.

Although my exploration of the culvert had been fairly limited, it was clearly an enormous place, which safely housed possibly millions of people. The technology in evidence was anything but crude, it was solid and reliable but not in the least attractive. Everything was highly functional and without embellishment, which made prolonged exposure to this environment rather dreary. There was very little natural light, very little music, there was nothing that resembled theatre, dance or entertainment, well, not that I experienced.

Generally the mood in the culvert seemed subdued, no one seemed to laugh or lark about. The people I saw worked very hard, ate together and clearly looked after their children very well. I noticed no tension between people, I never once saw a disagreement or row let alone a fight. My assumption about this was that the onslaught outside was enough to sap anyone's aggression; survival was hard enough without adding to your distress with petty bickering. But it wasn't exactly a joyous place to live.

Until the arrival of Cloud Eleven. Goodness me, that made a difference.

I stood silently for a moment looking around our small apartment and tried to have a feeling. I wanted a sentimental experience so I waited. I looked around at the sparse furnishings, the dull stone walls.

Nothing.

I didn't feel an attachment to this place in any way. I'd spent very little conscious time there, as I was mostly asleep in my comfortable wall pod. It wasn't stuffy, and the air-conditioning, if that's what it was, worked silently and effectively. It just didn't have any soul.

The private place that had stayed with me most since leaving 2011 had been my room at Goldacre Hall in Gardenia, that was special, and although my departure from there was so rapid and left me no time to get sentimental, it had come back to me regularly.

I had no emotional attachment to the Chicago Culvert, it simply wasn't that kind of place.

By the time I'd washed, changed into my flight suit, put the boots Noshi had given me in a small backpack and finally left the little sleeping quarters, all hell had broken loose.

Hundreds of people were rushing along the corridors. There was laughter, shouting, some people were skipping and jumping up and down, kids dashing around like mad. It was chaos, but a happy, party-time chaos.

'We go,' said Theda, as she walked through the dizzying crowds. 'They are lowering the elevators very soon.'

'Oh, blimey, the bloody elevators,' I said with a sigh.

'I think these ones are second gen,' said Theda with a smile. 'Bit different.'

I jostled in the crowds through the low dark corridors with

Theda and Noshi. I knew we were heading toward the reception hall where we'd first arrived.

At one corridor junction Noshi clasped my arm. I turned to look at him; he looked so beautiful it almost winded me.

'I will leave you now,' he said. 'I don't want to get upset in front of everyone at the reception hall. Please forgive me, Gavin.'

'Hey, it's okay. I understand,' I said, and we embraced again, but thankfully – I feel mean even saying this – we didn't kiss. 'I'll really miss you,' I said.

'Come, come,' urged Theda. I smiled sadly at Noshi and turned away. A few metres along the corridor I was engulfed by the mass of people around me but I glanced back for one last look. Noshi had gone. I would never see him or her again.

As we got nearer the reception hall we were joined by more and more people, again all races, ages and the air was filled with excited raised voices, shouts of greeting and whoops of joy. The arrival of Cloud Eleven was clearly a pretty big day in the culvert.

In the enormous reception hall the drably draped commissioners were standing in a serious-looking row to one side. All around them pandemonium, movement, colour, energy, enthusiasm and excitement, but they just stood silently watching.

Theda walked directly up to them and embraced Michiyo Nishimura, which looked a little alarming, partly because Theda was probably a metre taller that the diminutive scientist and partly because Michiyo didn't look like a huggy sort of person. It was fairly obvious she didn't enjoy the moment of intimacy. I took note and decided not to follow suit.

'Thank you, thank you for looking after us,' said Theda excitedly. 'I will never forget you.'

Michiyo smiled. 'We will never forget you also,' she said, then turned to me, 'or indeed you, Mister Meckler. However, you will, if all goes to plan, completely forget us. It has been a privilege and indeed an education to meet a man from the past. We are very grateful for all the information we have gathered from you while you've been here.'

Michiyo held out her hand and I shook it politely, trying not to squeeze too hard – her hand was minuscule in mine.

'I hope your return journey is safe and without undue trauma,' she said, and gave me a tiny bow.

That sounded a bit ominous but in the excitement of the moment I didn't really pay heed.

'Doctor Dorschel will accompany you on the start of your return trip,' said Michiyo. Brad was standing beside her, and I had already understood he was coming as he was the only member of the commissioners group to be dressed in the dull cream flight suit.

'That's good to know,' I said and I meant it. Brad had been one of the few people I'd met in this blighted dimension who had really tried to explain things to me.

'We need to get moving,' said Brad. He had a large case with him which looked like a solid box but covered with the same material as the flight suit and sporting the regulation pale blue pad on one side.

As he started to move off, the case raised up from the floor and followed him. I tried not to notice. I tried not to be interested in a floating case, I'd seen all kinds of things that floated just above ground level but it still caught my eye.

'Thank you for letting me stay,' I said to Michiyo as formally as I could. 'And good luck, I hope the weather gets better.'

Michiyo took hold of my hand and squeezed it without saying anything. She stared at me and I thought I saw something emotional happening. For me to notice something like that while all around me there was so much noise and movement means either she was very good at transmitting emotion or I had become a bit more receptive.

I nodded to the other commissioners, who nodded back to me politely, then I followed Brad and Theda towards the exit.

‘Got your wristband on?’ asked Theda. I held up my arm, there it was.

It was an amazing thing to witness the chaos and disorder in the main body of the hall transform itself into hundreds of well-disciplined and orderly queues of people waiting to exit into the open square. I joined the same queue as Brad and Theda and we edged forward quite quickly. As soon as I could see ahead of me I was slightly relieved, the elevator system on Cloud Eleven was noticeably different. I watched a row of people stand in a long line with their backs to the massive blue sheet, which I knew to be hanging from the cloud. At a certain moment they all leaned back and the sheet formed itself into a kind of long seating bench and then elevated the row of people out of sight with such speed it shocked my eyes. Whoosh, they were gone, soon to be replaced by another long line of people.

What was also different from my arrival was the fact that the individual blue elevator sheets seemed to be fairly stationary. I deduced from this that the still air I’d experienced when walking with Noshi meant the cloud was fairly static over the Chicago Culvert, but then how had it moved across the vast brown plains outside?

I didn’t know, all I knew was I was about to be sitting on a thin sheet of material that would lift me up into the biggest man-made cloud that had ever existed.

23

NTERING CLOUD ELEVEN?

I don't know where to start.

All the terms I have at my disposal – huge, colossal, enormous, gargantuan – they are all too frail, too weak and cannot begin to do justice.

By comparison to things I'd seen on my journeys up to that point, Cloud Eleven was just bigger. The space elevators in Gardenia, the mile-high buildings in Beijing? Commonplace and easily absorbed into a twenty-first-century mindset. The Squares of London, the buildings of Rio, just normal stuff, advanced, mysterious at first but eventually comprehensible.

Cloud Eleven was off every scale I have ever had at my disposal.

Where to start?

How about a 70 kilometre in diameter floating city, a brand new, squeaky clean, immaculate wonderland floating serenely above the ravaged earth?

How about a structure with a distance from the lowest part of the base to the observation tower at the top of close to four kilometres?

How about a floating city that could contain, feed and protect over a million people at any one time?

Or an enormous many-gusseted balloon that could maintain structural integrity from ground level up to an altitude of 12,000 metres?

How about a floating, self-supporting, energy-generating mega city that defied the eye and the senses with its exquisite beauty and size?

Or most intriguingly for me, a structure that used a material on the exterior that contained nanoscale particles known as Planck Mass Reflectors, or PMRs?

This was the first cloud to use this material. This was a new thing even in 2211 and clearly very few people knew much about it. From what I could understand, and I had the concept explained to me in great detail by Brad, a PMR is best described as a quantum gravity micro-engine.

Doesn't really help does it?

Clearly it wasn't an engine as anyone from 2011 would understand it, like a big diesel engine that powers vacuum pumps or wheels or hydraulic systems.

This engine was a material that needed no power, a material or engine that covered many thousands of square metres in area and from a distance looked like a cloud. Cloud Eleven looked more genuinely cloud-like than any of the other clouds I'd seen.

The little fellows embedded in the PMR material were so infinitesimally small that if, for instance, one of these high-energy particles was the size of a golf ball, then an atom would be the size of the visible universe.

That's about the only fact I could retain, the rest of it was fuzz-brain-inducing quantum physics, but what it meant was that Cloud Eleven, and all the other clouds being built at the time, would be capable of slow but controllable navigation. The cloud could rise and sink with less stress on the edifice of the cloud, using less energy and with greater control.

So the scale of the thing was impossible to comprehend. The number of people on-board? Bonkers. The weight of this lighter-than-air structure? Basic-laws-of-physics-defying. However, that wasn't the half of it. PMRs were embedded into the structure too, so the floor you walked on reduced your weight considerably. Apparently my normal weight of 81 kilograms was reduced to around 30. This didn't mean you felt lighter – well, not immediately, although I didn't seem to get as tired walking long distances as I did on the surface.

Finally, and for me the biggest relief, the luxury of the accommodation on Cloud Eleven?

Absolutely top-drawer posh.

On both Cloud Nine and Ten, the accommodation was adequate if a little rudimentary and cramped. On-board Cloud Eleven I had a suite. Well, not a regular suite, like in a twenty-first-century hotel, not a square room like you'd have in a building, but nonetheless, the elongated bubble Brad showed me into had a volume similar to a large high-end hotel suite.

I had my own kind of bathroom bubble at one side and best of all a huge circular window looking out over acres of the flowing flanks of Cloud Eleven and to the distant skies beyond.

I don't think I have ever felt safer on something that wasn't joined to the ground, this thing was so vast and its movement so imperceptible that it was always difficult to believe it was thousands of metres in the air.

After our initial arrival we had to wait quite a while in the truly vast reception atrium, but none of us minded as it was such a relief after the low stone ceilings of the Chicago Culvert. It struck me that whoever designed this massive floating city wanted to make a real effort to counteract the effects of being cramped underground in storm ditches, which is where most people spent most of their lives.

The faces of the people around us were happy and excited. They were alive, they were safe, they would not have to listen to the wind battering their culvert day after day.

In the sky, when you are floating, there is no wind.

Once the crowds had started to disperse, Brad led us along an incredibly wide and light tubular corridor and through an intriguing airlock that was entirely flexible. It was almost organic in the way it allowed our solid bodies to pass through but kept the elements at bay. I was so intrigued by the experience of squishing myself through this opening I had to do it numerous times to try and understand what was going on.

Imagine a taut white curtain with a split down the middle, not a big, obvious gap, in fact you only know there is a potential split there because you've watched someone else pass through it before you.

As you approach it you are essentially walking towards a blank white wall. You push yourself against it and it expands and allows you through. Not without a little effort; the tightness of the material was more like the skin of a drum, it looked like a sheet of solid white material but you could slither between its skintight wall.

Once I'd got over the weirdness of the air lock, I found myself along with a great many other people on a kind of flat, open area somewhat similar to where the Yuneec had been landed on Cloud Nine.

However, this was three times bigger and the walls of cloud structures rising up above and behind me were breathtaking and dizzying in their magnificent beauty.

'This must be the viewing platform,' said Brad. He was clearly excited about this, as no one from the Chicago Culvert had been on this cloud before. At last, I wasn't the only one stumbling about saying, 'Oh wow, look at that!' every three seconds.

'We should be able to get an aerial view of the culvert as we move off,' said Brad, leading the way to a distant gathering of people.

So try to picture this: you know you're on a cloud, you know that it's stable and safe, at least you hope it is, although it's brand new and has only been in the air a few days. You are on a vast, open, white kind of square surrounded by the truly awe-inspiring towers of cloud-like structures. The ground is soft underfoot but not bouncy, so walking isn't too difficult.

Before you is a wide vista, an opening in these cloud-like structures that gives you an uninterrupted view of the landscape and sky. Then as you approach the long row of people with their backs to you, you discover this is merely the back row of a vast, tiered viewing auditorium. This is like a rock venue on a scale that makes Glastonbury Festival look like a village fête, except people aren't looking at a band, they're looking at their world.

We made our way down one of the many gangways between the already jam-packed seating arrangement, row after row of people sitting quietly looking out over the vast plains of what had once been Illinois. Due to the dazzling setting sun on the distant horizon, most of them were wearing the slightly spooky-looking goggles.

I had mine on, so it wasn't like I wasn't used to them, but when you saw thousands of people wearing them it looked a little eerie, a bit like the black and white pictures of scientists watching the first atomic detonations.

We eventually found a space about halfway down the vast, slightly curved auditorium and took our seats. I had Brad on one side and Theda on the other.

'Pretty impressive, huh?' said Brad, once we'd settled.

'It's beyond anything,' I said, and then felt stupid. What a dumb thing to say, but then I wasn't really concentrating on being cool.

Brad smiled, which was unusual. He pointed ahead of us. 'The haze you can see to the left, that's Lake Michigan.'

'I was there today, I walked there with Noshi!' I exclaimed.

As was often the case with Brad and Theda, there was no response to this statement, they didn't do idle chit-chat. We sat in silence for a moment and I stared along with everyone else. I then focused my attention on a small dark patch of brown dirt that lined up with the edge of Cloud Eleven way down below me. By doing this I assumed I'd be able to judge our speed, and yet it wasn't moving. It seems the cloud was entirely static. I then realised I could feel a gentle wind around me.

'I can't tell if we're moving,' I said eventually.

'We are static at present,' said Brad. He then went on to explain to me about PMR material and Cloud Eleven's ability to maintain a static position above a culvert with local wind speeds of up to 15 kilometres per hour. He explained how the leading side of the structure, the one facing the wind, was inflated at a many times higher pressure than the rest of the cloud in order to maintain its integrity.

'We will start to move very soon,' said Brad, 'and then the culvert will be right in front of us.'

As usual, I wanted to know more, but I didn't even know how to frame questions into coherent sentences, the technology I was surrounded by was so extreme that I had no common point of reference.

After a few minutes I noticed the landscape below us start to shift. To be fair, what really made me notice was the rise in noise and excitement from the crowds surrounding me. The only way of telling we were moving was from the slowly shifting view in front of us and the fact that the shadows from the setting sun began to slowly slide across the seating banks to my left.

Then slowly the vast ramparts of the Chicago Culvert began to appear below us. Although they were not that far below us to start with, I could initially only see the distant edge of the black tile-clad mountain.

After a few minutes the entire complex came into view and this time it made much more sense seeing it from above than it had ever done when I'd been inside. It resembled a giant eye or maybe a fish, essentially two huge ramparts joining each other at a narrow junction at either end. In the centre, well below the upper surface of the outer abutments, there was a large and complex industrial array of what I took to be life support systems, energy gathering devices and presumably communication aerials, although I could be mistaken about those.

It wasn't like looking at a city, there were no streets or individual buildings, no towers or transportation systems visible, it looked like a super huge mega-factory surrounded by a ridiculously enormous wall.

'Quite a sight,' said Theda eventually. I nodded, then scanning around the crowds on the inflated terraces I could see people talking and pointing and commenting excitedly as we continued to rise high above the plain.

After about ten minutes, a low sound started to become audible above the chatting, shouts and hubbub around us. By this time we must have been at least a thousand metres above the surface; the culvert was still very much in evidence partly due to its size and partly due to the trajectory that Cloud Eleven was taking. We were travelling upwards gently and in an easterly direction and it was getting cold, really cold.

By the time we stood up and moved along with the slow crowds of people before us, half the seating banks had already been vacated. The low sound, it was a gentle repetitive tubular bell tune, was becoming slightly more insistent. As we climbed the many stairs back to the huge square above I found I was getting short of breath.

'We need to get back into the cloud,' said Brad. 'The air is getting thin and it will get very cold out here.'

By the time we'd finally managed to make it to the peculiar entrance I was freezing and wheezing. We had been climbing steadily all the time and I'd say we were maybe 3,000 metres up by the time we slid in through the bizarre white flange door. I could feel warm air rushing out as I pushed my body through the slit, but as soon as I got inside my ears popped quite badly. It was a very sudden increase in pressure and I was momentarily a bit deaf.

It's important to point out that all this time we were surrounded by thousands of people. It reminded me of either arriving at or leaving a huge public event like a concert or sporting match. Thousands of people were slowly milling around, vaguely moving in one direction along a massive tubular corridor. It was clear that Brad, Theda and I were not alone in not being sure quite which way to go. There were a lot of people around us talking very busily and pointing in various directions. I heard snippets of many languages, every variation of race and creed was present among Cloud Eleven's enormous passenger manifesto.

We rose up through the interior of the cloud by a similar seat-based elevator to the one that had lifted us on-board. I think we must have gone up a couple of hundred stories of the structure and emerged into a wonderland. It was like a food hall in a high-end mall in Asia, somewhere like Singapore, just a hundred times bigger.

Theda went off to procure food and I sat down at a vacant table in the middle of this huge space with Brad.

'What a place!' I said as we settled. 'I mean, this is just incredible, this is just so much better than living in a dark ditch.'

Brad stared at me with the slightest grin on his small face. 'Not bad, is it?' he said eventually. I then felt guilty because the dark ditch was actually his home and I remembered how proud Americans generally were of their hometowns. I decided to quickly change the subject.

'I can't begin to imagine how this works. I don't mean the cloud itself, that's completely beyond anything I'll ever understand, but the system. The kind of, well, the economic system that allows us to sit here, eat food, have a space to sleep, everything.'

'Well, you are registered,' said Brad flatly. He said it as if I should know that, as if I should have known all along. A very Squares of London experience.

'Am I?' I asked.

'Of course, otherwise, if you think about it, Gavin, you wouldn't be here.'

Theda returned carrying a large white bag. She plonked it on the table between us and sat down.

'I am starving,' she said. 'All that fresh air. It has given me a *Deutsch richtige appetit*.'

The big white bag contained a few small white bags. Bags which when lifted looked quite literally like balloons or condoms filled with liquid. However, as soon as I put one down on the table it reformed itself into a wide high-sided bowl. A solid bowl.

'Cool tech,' I said, grinning at my companions.

'Indeed,' said Brad. 'There are many new innovations which have been rolled out on Cloud Eleven.'

I watched as Brad and Theda picked implements resembling spoons from the big bag in the centre of the table. I did the same, scooping some of the creamy liquid from the bowl and gingerly putting it in my mouth. A liquid entered my mouth and immediately turned into a selection of solid objects. Delicious, crunchy solid objects – food. I couldn't guess what I was eating. Mildly curried shrimps with vegetables? Or it could have been a sweet chicken stew with noodles.

I chewed and swallowed.

'Wow,' I said, wiping my mouth with a small piece of material that had released itself from the swollen balloon of liquid as it turned into a bowl. 'That has to be just about the weirdest thing I have ever put in my mouth. What the hell was it?'

'Next gen transit sustenance,' said Brad. 'We have it in Chicago for emergencies but we don't eat it much. Some people actually prefer this stuff to freshly picked vegetables and fruit.'

'You understand that you decide what it is when you eat it, don't you?' said Theda while wolfing down the weird cream-coloured goo.

I looked at her chewing for a moment. 'So what are you eating?' I asked.

'Wiener schnitzel, sauerkraut, roast potatoes and fresh garden beans,' she said with a big grin. 'What about you, Brad?'

'Lasagne,' said Brad, as he held a creamy spoonful hovering in front of his mouth. 'Beef lasagne, not bad really. I've been dreaming about it for weeks.'

'How do you decide?' I asked, as incredulous as you might expect.

'Well, what have you been eating?' asked Theda.

'I don't know!' I said.

'It's kind of a good idea that you do know,' said Brad.

'It keeps changing!' I squeaked. 'One minute it's a kind of Thai noodle chicken thing, the next it's a mild prawn curry with rice.'

'Best to decide on one,' said Brad nonchalantly. 'But then again, whatever floats your boat.'

'I quite fancy what you've got, Theda,' I said. I hadn't eaten anything other than vegetarian meals for weeks so I leant forward to get a spoonful of Theda's weird cream that was really wiener schnitzel. She knocked my hand away impatiently.

'Eat your own!' she said. 'That is most unhygienic.'

'Sorry,' I replied. So I took another spoonful of my own cream stuff, shoved it in my mouth and sensed the texture of breaded veal. Not after a bit of chewing but pretty much as soon as I put it in my mouth.

'Oh my God,' I said through the mouthful of food, 'bloody extraordinary.'

'I agree,' said Theda. 'This is my first experience of this technology. I had heard people discuss it but I've never tried it before.'

'Let me tell you,' said Brad, leaning back in his chair. 'This stuff is way better than anything we've had in Chicago. They've really moved on.'

'The whole cloud is wonderful,' said Theda. 'Everything has moved on.'

Brad nodded.

'Okay, Theda, perhaps you can let me know this,' I said, holding up my wristband. 'Brad told me I'm registered. I don't know how anything works here. Like how we get this food. What transactions are needed to make it possible for me to be here, eat this, have a room of my own and everything?'

'You are enquiring about an economic model?' she said.

'Yes, what's the economic model? I know you had money in Munich, I certainly had loads in London, I was quite rich apparently.'

'Yes, you were very wealthy, but here there is no such system, more like embedded credit and debt. I think that's the best way to describe it. You worked in the garden in the Chicago Culvert. That would have helped toward your credit. You were also kind and considerate to others and that builds credit in your favour, plus as you were a guest you had an automatic balance increase. There is no way of keeping track of such credits or debits, the general wealth of the community is considered far more important, not individual wealth as you or I may be familiar with.'

I was eating through mouthfuls of meat, roast potatoes and beans as Theda spoke. It had occurred to me at one point to spit a bit into my hand to see if it looked any different but I decided that would be a bit rude, not to say potentially revolting.

'So there is no monetary system?' I said eventually.

'No, nothing like that.'

'So how is a machine such as this cloud produced? A project of this colossal scale requires enormous input, materials, manpower, R and D, everything.'

'As I believe you discovered in London,' said Brad eventually, 'the cost of many of the things you struggled with 200 years ago has reduced to near zero. Energy for instance. We produce more than we need, we can store it, move it and use it without much concern. The materials used to make this cloud were produced remotely and automatically using advanced printing techniques. I use the term "printing" as I believe you may understand that, I might say weaving or blending the base components on a nano scale. Do you understand that?'

'Well, yes, I get the overall notion. So what you're saying is there weren't, like, teams of engineers cutting out sheets and joining them together with glue to make this?'

'Precisely, it was essentially grown from base material in the most advanced culvert on the planet.'

'Beijing,' I guessed.

Brad nodded. 'They have the most advanced and biggest

fabrication systems. But what you have seen so far is merely the start. The support and control systems on Cloud Eleven far outstrip anything any of us have seen before.'

Before long I was completely stuffed. I hadn't had a feeling like that in months.

'That was probably the weirdest meal I've ever had,' I said, finishing the sentence with an enormous involuntary burp, which was a bit disgusting.

'Charming,' said Theda. She grinned at me.

'So, here's the plan,' said Brad, wiping his mouth with some kind of tissue. 'At some point we will dock with the other clouds. You will transfer to Cloud Eight, Theda. Gavin, you will transfer to Cloud Nine. It may then be some time before they can navigate to your target positions, but that is what they intend to do. There are a few technicians from Chicago currently on Cloud Ten. They've been carrying out experiments on similar power anomalies to the ones you experienced, so I will be communicating with them about their findings.'

'Experiments?' I asked.

'They've been sending probes through the cloud anomalies, probes that have the technology to send back data before they dissolve.'

'Dissolving probes!' Even with my jaded attitude to all the extreme technology that surrounded me, the idea of a dissolving probe piqued my interest.

'It is a very small object, a nano particle probe that travels through the cloud and as it drops on the other side it sends back data. It then dissolves into water vapour so as not to cause disturbance in the time fields.'

'Wow.' That's all I could say.

'So with information from these teams I will explain what's going to happen when you reach the anomaly. I will remain on-board Eleven as I've been invited to Beijing to consult on some new materials they are planning to use on Cloud Twelve.

 It's a shame you won't get to see that as it's clearly going to be a monster.'

'I am very sorry to miss the opportunity,' said Theda. She turned to me. 'Has Brad told you about Cloud Twenty? No, clearly he hasn't.' Of course she could tell that I had none of that information because of our kidonge connection, so I didn't even shake my head.

'Cloud Twenty is already being planned. It will be 300 kilometres long, 150 wide and house 11 million people in a permanent floating city. Before long there will be people alive who have never experienced living on the ground, they will be genuine cloud dwellers.'

I think my mouth was hanging open.

'Exciting times,' said Brad. He put a hand on my shoulder. 'I'll say my goodbyes now, Gavin. I wish you well on your travels and in good time I will check up on your history, see how you got on in life.'

'That's a spooky thought,' I said.

'I don't think the human mind will ever be able to adapt to meeting someone who has technically been dead for over 150 years, but it's been a fascinating experience meeting you.'

'Yeah, well, I'd like to say the same. I don't mean to be rude, it has been amazing meeting you and the incredibly resourceful people of the clouds, but I know I'm going to forget everything so it feels a bit pointless.'

'Gavin, what you have brought to our world, what you have shown us beyond question is that your journey has not been pointless. You have brought us a wealth of understanding denied to previous generations. Thank you.'

24

FTER SPENDING A FEW WEEKS IN THE CHICAGO Culvert, being on Cloud Eleven was not only a blessed relief, it was incredibly restful.

I had a very comfortable adaptable bed arrangement in my room that was perfectly positioned to take in the ridiculous splendour of the skies as we floated serenely above the storm-ravaged Earth.

I would wake up each morning and the transparent nanomaterial in the window would fade from blackout to super clear as my eyes became slowly accustomed to the brightness of the day.

It was impossible not to feel comforted, slightly smug and incredibly lucky in such truly fabulous surroundings.

It was during this period of calm that I started to half understand some of the resentment among the general populace toward the people of the past. It's not something anyone from 2011 could easily comprehend. If I thought about the people who had lived before me, the kings, statesmen, soldiers, workers, peasants, mothers and fathers who had lived and died before I was born, I don't think I had ever for one moment resented them.

In fact, quite the opposite was true. If I ever did think about them it was generally with some admiration.

Basically I'd always loved old technology. I was fascinated to see the crudity of construction and clearly I had the sort of brain that could look at a coupling on an early steam engine and work out not only how they came up with the idea but how they put the idea into practice. I suppose that's an engineer's brain.

I have a very happy early memory of walking around the Science Museum in London with my dad and brother when I was a young boy. I spent a long day staring in wonder at the incredible machines that had been built hundreds of years before my time. The beam engine pumps, the early steam cars and locomotives, rudimentary batteries and marine engines. Amazing big brass gauges and pipework all held an intense fascination for me.

I didn't resent the people who made them. What they had done back then had developed over generations so that I was lucky enough to grow up in a time of technological achievement and comfort that would have been impossible to imagine in the not-too-distant past.

I was always impressed with technological progress, with new machines, gadgets and inventions that made life richer, more fulfilled or easier.

That mindset had definitely changed in the world of the clouds.

The past was a dark place full of stupidity and destruction; the human race had been almost destroyed by the short-sighted ignorance of previous generations, including mine.

It all seemed a bit unfair. I wanted to tell them it wasn't all our fault, we didn't know any better, we didn't do it on purpose and there is no way we could have known what was going to happen.

It became clearer when Theda and I were sitting watching the sun go down from one of the 92 sun lounges dotted around the upper formations of Cloud Eleven.

'It's not my fault,' I said out of the blue. Theda had just been explaining the pressure variants on-board, how the pressure lower down the cloud structure was slightly higher than up where we were, which enabled the whole thing to maintain its shape. I mean, I was interested, but the blame thing was really on my mind.

'What have you done?' asked Theda.

'Nothing, that's just the point, it's not my fault that everything turned out so shitty for this world. It's ridiculous that the people here blame the past for their woes, it's not like we did it on purpose.'

'From what I understand the blame is very specific,' said Theda. 'They don't blame the people of 1811, or indeed 1911. However, by the time you left in 2011, there was plenty of understanding about what was taking place and yet it seems they did nothing.'

'It just doesn't make sense,' I said. 'We didn't have any hard evidence back in 2011, it was all speculation and a lot of people thought it was based on questionable science. It was all about what *might* happen. It was almost a belief system, a bit religious, that's what I didn't like about it. It was a bit like the voice of God: "You have sinned, you will be punished for burning fossil fuels." That's why I questioned climate change. And I've seen worlds where it didn't happen and those people didn't blame my era. Well, they might have been critical, but they didn't blame us.'

'I think you misunderstand,' said Theda. 'Think of it this way. If you had been walking down the street in 2011 and you were introduced to a military gentleman from say, around 1914, an English man, a military figure who was hell-bent on fighting a glorious war against my country. A man who took delight in all the military stupidity that war represented. How would you react to him?'

'Okay, I may have a couple of negative things to say,' I replied eventually, trying to imagine meeting someone like that in Chipping Norton on market day. For some reason that was the location that came to mind when Theda suggested it. A sunny Saturday in Chipping Norton, me and Beth going shopping and suddenly this smartly dressed man in military uniform with a silly moustache starting to hold forth about King and Country, the Bosch, the glory of war and the need for me to defend the British Empire. I'm sure I'd have something cutting to say, but knowing me, I'd think of it three hours later, when I was back at home putting stuff in the fridge.

'Okay,' said Theda. 'Now, imagine that the war Great Britain and Germany started didn't stop, ever. Imagine it was still going on when you were alive and all the young men you'd grown up with had been needlessly slaughtered in an endless war of attrition. You may feel more hostile.'

'Oh, right, okay, I suppose I get your drift.'

'People here, now, the people on this cloud, the few millions of people who manage to survive around the world, they are not constantly thinking that people from 200 years ago are all to blame. Of course not. But if they knew you were from 2011, then it might, as I understand it, cause considerable upset. Some people who have lost members of their families in chaotic weather accidents, people who know their forebears suffered greatly in brutal storms. Yes, there would be a lot of anger and despair aimed at you.'

It's important to point out that as Theda was saying this to me she was lying on her back, totally naked. As I recall it, the situation sounds odd, but at the time it all seemed very normal and humdrum. I was also naked and sprawled out on a big cushion beside her.

We were just topping up our cloud tans, it was all part of the daily routine.

After six days on-board Cloud Eleven, Theda told me we were approaching a big docking event. Clouds Six to Ten were converging over the Bay of Biscay and it was a very momentous event apparently.

I was intrigued to see how this could be achieved, but even this extraordinary airborne docking didn't hold quite the fascination it might have done at one time.

I was not overwhelmed by it; I'd grown used to life on the clouds and certainly preferred it to living in a culvert. Sure, the docking would be interesting but I was lost in a kind of mesmerised state. Whenever I looked out of a window or lay on a couch in the sun lounges I entered an almost zen-like state of calm, not something I could ever remember experiencing before. Maybe flying in mechanically powered, heavier-than-air machines had given me a taste for it, but flying a plane is quite complicated, requires a lot of concentration and planning, so going all zen-like and dreamy is probably not a good course of action, but on this big cloud it just became a way of life.

On my last morning on Cloud Eleven I had woken as usual. The amazing window that made up one side of my suite immediately turned from dark opaque to utterly invisible as soon as I started to move around. I was surrounded by embedded technology I'd become so used to that I no longer had any interest in discovering how it operated.

I had a shower and even that incredible system had become mundane. As soon as I'd had enough of being sprayed I just brushed a finger on a low set panel, the water stopped and I was instantly bathed in a powerful jet of warm air, which dried me in a few seconds.

I did some stretching, another thing I'd never done before I left 2011, but I'd found it highly beneficial to have a proper stretch in the morning. I wasn't doing yoga or anything. although I knew there were numerous yoga classes I could have attended.

I was just starting to ponder what to do with my day when Theda bustled into my silent reverie and, as I'd witnessed on a couple of occasions, she was excited and skittish. It is only worth mentioning because her mood was in complete contrast to her normal rather dour and serious Germanic demeanour.

'Come quickly, Gavin, we will be docking soon!'

'Really?' I said, without much interest.

'Gavin! Two of the biggest objects ever constructed by the human race are going to become one, we cannot miss this moment.'

'Great,' I said as enthusiastically as I could. I wasn't excited. I should have been, but by this point in my journey I didn't want anything to disturb my calm mental state.

Theda was pacing around the room, staring out of the window and jumping up and down.

'Also I have just been informed that there is a weather window making it possible for you to transfer to Cloud Nine and head for England.'

My reaction to this news was a little more enthusiastic.

'That soon?' I said.

'Yes, the weather patterns are indicating you could get back to Gardenia today,' said Theda. She walked up to me and hugged me. That was the first time we'd had any physical contact more than a handshake and I found it quite emotional.

That's correct, a feeling hit me and I was aware of it, still a slightly perturbing experience for me.

'I don't know if I want to go,' I said, as I continued to hold her, 'I love it on Cloud Eleven.'

Theda gently broke the embrace and smiled at me. 'I know it is a very amazing experience to be on-board,' she said. 'But we both need to go back home, we don't belong here.'

'I know we don't, but I don't want to forget all this. I don't understand why I won't be able to remember anything. I know Brad explained it.'

'It is a very complicated notion,' Theda conceded with a smile.

I stood in the middle of my suite feeling hollow, I was having all sorts of feelings all the time and I was very aware of them but that didn't really help. In fact in many ways having feelings but not being aware of them until much later has its advantages.

Eventually I said, 'Due to the madness of this whole experience, I'm prepared to accept that I'll forget all this. You, Brad, the Chicago Culvert, Noshi, the Squares of London, Gardenia, everything.'

Theda nodded slowly, 'You will, Gavin, it will be as if none of this happened. There won't even be traces of these events in your subconscious, it will all be completely erased. But remember there are benefits to this occurrence. Your complete lack of knowledge of everything you have experienced will make your return to your own time much less traumatic. If you knew this would happen to your world, you might go a little crazy, no?'

I shrugged. There was nothing I could do, the prospect of a return to Gardenia was enough to make me realise I'd go mad if I stayed in luxury on Cloud Eleven for the rest of my life. Besides, there was no way I could do that, I was sure to end up in some remote culvert growing carrots all day.

I started packing, which to be honest, didn't take long. My boots and a bag, plus the few bits of survival kit like my cool sunshade eye covers and a sachet of tooth regen-paste.

Yes, you heard right, there were no such thing as a dentist on the clouds; any decay just disappeared, this paste repaired any damage to your tooth enamel and neutralised damaging microbes from the gum line long before a cavity or gum disease could get a foothold.

I stood looking out at the majestic view from my stupendous windows for a moment, then sighed, turned and followed Theda out of my luxurious, peaceful Cloud Eleven suite for the last time.

25

IN TERMS OF SCALE ONLY ACTUAL GEOGRAPHY could match what I saw next. When I say geography I mean mountains, oceans, major land masses. I admit they are going to be bigger, but in terms of man-made objects there has, I am confident in saying, never been any single item bigger than Cloud Eleven.

You could suggest that mega-cities are man-made objects and some of those would indeed be bigger, but then Cloud Eleven was a very large floating city with literally millions of inhabitants.

It might not be as big as, say, Beijing or Los Angeles back in the day, but it wasn't far off. In terms of single connected objects it won the race, it was one enormous floating lump as opposed to a collection of millions of buildings scattered about on the ground.

While I was dreaming away in my suite, the cloud had been slowly reforming itself into a completely different configuration.

What I'd seen of it from the ground when I was stumbling across the dirt with Noshi was a structure that had looked very much like a cloud.

Now, from what I could gather by staring over people's shoulders at a viewing area, Cloud Eleven more resembled a massive swirling storm, a huge cloud formation with a 20 kilometre-diameter hole in the middle. What was rising to fill that mind-boggling cavern was Cloud Ten.

I soon learned from all the excitement around me that Cloud Ten would dock within Cloud Eleven, and according to one very knowledgeable woman standing next to me, in the not too distant future Cloud Twelve would be able to accommodate Cloud Eleven within its super-sized flanks.

The clouds were not only vast, they were able to reshape themselves. I was busy working it out with my crude twenty-first-century engineer's brain. I surmised that internal walls within the structure could separate in some elaborate way and reform themselves into a huge kind of doughnut shape, making a protected docking area in the middle.

I went through my, by this stage, very standard historical calibration trying to imagine what a sailor from the Napoleonic era would have made of HMS *Bulwark*, a British Naval assault support ship that can half-sink itself, allowing a large section of the interior to become a kind of dock. If you had only ever seen or sailed in wooden ships, if you only knew about tar, ballast, sails, ropes and rigging, the idea of a metal ship that could half sink and then raise itself at will would be preposterous and fanciful.

So I tried to accept that the notion of a lighter-than-air floating city that could reshape itself into a variety of storm clouds was, well, just one of those things.

The next two hours were spent either waiting in huge crowds in vast atriums or slowly shuffling forward as literally tens of thousands of people shifted from one cloud to another.

Theda and I made our way slowly onto Cloud Ten, although there was no narrow doorway, just huge open spaces with vast inner atriums that seemed to go on forever.

It was only the floor that indicated that we'd passed from one structure to the other. When these vast floating machines docked, their internal areas must have reached the same pressure. After this they retracted parts of the outer walls making two previously internal spaces become one.

Just as we passed the threshold my wrist buzzed gently, I assume Theda's did too as we both stopped.

'Brad!' she said. She looked at me with a very serious, concerned German expression.

I glanced around at the slow-moving crowd all around us.

 I couldn't spot him anywhere but after a moment or two he emerged from the throng.

'Glad I caught you,' he said. 'Kind of hard to keep track of people around here.'

'I did not think you were coming with us!' said Theda, the same thought had occurred to me.

'I wasn't planning to, but events have unfolded. We've had some less than good news about the, um, the possible arrival of slightly unwanted guests.'

Brad held my arm gently and we moved off to the side of the vast opening between the clouds. We found a quiet corner alongside a vast curtain of material that I took to be the folded back outer wall.

'The Original Five know about the weather anomalies,' said Brad quietly, looking at me carefully. 'It was bound to happen, we kind of forget about them most of the time as they tend to hang around the equator at low level, but one of their clouds is approaching our current location. It's not catastrophic, the news took a while to get through and the nearest cloud, I believe it's Three, is still a few hundred kilometres to the south. However, it's possible we're going to have to deal with a situation.'

'What situation?' I asked.

'Some disruption, the possibility of rapid replanning and for me, a lot of very complex negotiation.'

'Oh blimey,' I said.

The three of us moved off. Theda said nothing, in fact none of us spoke as we went deeper into Cloud Ten.

I couldn't help noticing it all seemed rather tatty. Using our wristbands for guidance we walked through Cloud Ten and eventually, after a few missed turns down identical tubular corridors, we found our way to the entrance of Cloud Nine.

That wasn't so hard to spot as the entrance to it looked so pokey and small. It was a surprise for me to think back to how impressed I had been with this tiny little structure, which was at this point totally engulfed within Cloud Eleven.

The crowds had thinned out by the time we arrived at the entrance; clearly not a lot of people needed to get on-board Nine.

'Here I leave you, Gavin,' said Theda as we stood in the near empty corridor.

Theda and I held each other for some time. She was effectively my great-number-of-times-great-granddaughter who lived in another dimension, who I would not only never see again but would also completely forget about.

'It's been immense,' I said.

'That is true. I hope your return home is without mishap.'

'You too, don't break any more legs and thank you, Theda, you are a truly amazing person.'

'That is kind, but then I have good genes,' she said with a smile. She possibly had a tear in her eye, I couldn't be sure.

At that she turned and walked away, leaving Brad and I standing in a totally empty corridor that led to the entrance to Cloud Nine. I had already started to miss her, not in a lover sort of way, more like how a brother might miss his older sister.

'Welcome back, Gavin,' said Kirubel as we passed over the threshold. He was standing just inside Cloud Nine looking very smart. 'You are looking very well, nice cloud tan.'

We shook hands and I felt the familiar and awkward bouncy floor beneath my feet.

'Thank you, Kirubel,' I said with a smile. I knew his name, I'd remembered it somehow and I was genuinely pleased to see him.

'This is Brad Dorschel, he's been helping me.'

'Hi, Brad, good to see you again,' said Kirubel. I glanced at Brad and he nodded and I felt a little foolish.

'I've travelled a great deal on good old Nine,' said Brad kindly. 'It's a fine old cloud.'

'As you can see we are almost empty,' said Kirubel. 'Only a few hundred passengers. They are all hoping to get to the Wycombe Culvert, which is, as you may know, close by to where we found you.'

'Wycombe?' I said, 'Oh, d'you mean High Wycombe?'

Kirubel smiled as we walked along an almost deserted reception lounge. 'It may have been high once, sadly it is now completely subterranean.'

That rushed journey through the various clouds was exactly the reverse of the experiences I'd had up to that point. I had gone from small and scruffy to huge and utilitarian to massive and luxurious.

Now I was back with small and scruffy. Everything about Cloud Nine was a bit tatty and worn out. I didn't notice when I'd first stumbled about on it, but the walls were a bit discoloured. I could see where repairs had been made to the material that made up the internal spaces and of course the elevators were crude.

We went up the elevator to the control room and this time I barely gave it a second thought.

'Doctor Bradley Dorschel, very nice to see you, old chap,' said Hector as soon as we'd made our way along the springy corridor. 'We're off on a bit of an adventure. And welcome back on-board, Mister Meckler, I see you've found your cloud legs!'

It was true. Somehow I had become used to walking on the springy flooring of the old cloud and I felt perfectly stable.

'Your drone is ready, it's stashed in the hold, we'll be setting off in moments, the wind is with us, Mister Meckler, we should make good time.'

He then turned and started conversing with Brad in a surprisingly quiet manner. I ascertained that this was a conversation that wasn't meant to include me so I moved away.

While they were talking I checked the view out of the surrounding windows, all I could see was white cloud material up close. Very close. I moved toward one of the windows and realised it wasn't just close, the material that made up Cloud

Eleven was actually touching the windows. Cloud Nine was tightly engulfed in the mother ship.

'Undocking complete,' said Kirubel. 'I'd hold onto something, Gavin, we are going to drop a little.'

At that point the light coming in through the windows changed rapidly and I felt the cloud drop just as Kirubel had warned. It dropped fast and I was grateful to be half-squatting and gripping a nearby handrail.

Within moments we had emerged from the belly of Cloud Eleven and started to move gently along the vast underside of the floating behemoth. It took a full hour to eventually emerge into open sky.

During that time I had clambered onto the seat that Hector had sat me on during my first visit to the control tower bubble. This gave me a good view of proceedings.

After another hour I could finally make out the full splendour of the floating city I had been residing in for the last few days. It was breathtaking in scale but it was also exquisitely beautiful. However it was constructed, it had to have been designed by people who really loved clouds.

The further away we got from this floating city, the more beautiful it appeared and I literally could not take my eyes off it. After a long, long time it still filled the horizon to our south, just a huge ball of white fluff resting in a peaceful blue sky.

Hector tapped me on the shoulder.

'We need to have a little chat, old chap,' he said. 'As you may have noticed, we have company on the starboard bow.'

I hadn't noticed anything but I looked in the direction Hector's enormous hairy finger was pointing in. In the distance I could see a little smudge, a kind of smear of grey stuff. I had no way of judging how far away it was or how large.

'Cloud Three,' said Hector quietly. 'Recently arrived from the equator where it normally resides, and judging by altitude and position a little worse for wear.'

'So that is one of the Original Five?' I asked.

'Indeed. It was, as the name suggests, the third ever habitable cloud machine. Very crude even by our standards and obviously many generations behind Cloud Eleven, but serviceable none-theless.'

'And is this a problem?'

'Indeed it is, dear chap,' said Hector. 'They are on your trail. Normally, you see,' Hector sat down beside me and patted my knee, 'normally we don't have much contact with the Original Five. They tend to be a moody bunch. Not dangerous, they're not pirates or warriors, they're just in a bit of a sulk and they really don't want you going back home on your own. They want one of their chaps to go with you.'

'I'm sorry?'

'I know, it's daft and it won't work, it's a one-way ticket, but apparently they are convinced if they can send an emissary back with you, someone who can shake things up a bit, well, they think things might not be as bad as they are. At least that's what some of them want, the bunch that are on that tatty old cloud.'

I looked back out of the window and noticed the grey smudge had drawn a little closer. It looked like a bag of rags floating in the air. I could sense now that it was a lot smaller than Cloud Nine, maybe only a few hundred metres long. It was long, low and fairly flat, it didn't have any of the splendour of the towering structures of the newer clouds and dangling from the bottom were ragged strips of material.

'What's all that stuff hanging down from it?' I asked Hector.

'Ahh yes, well, that's all that's left of the lower section. It's been badly damaged over the years. You see, when they come in close to the surface they don't have the ability to control their elevation very accurately, so occasionally I suppose they've been blown along the ground. That can really do damage to your undercarriage.'

At this point Brad joined us. 'Sorry, Gavin, there's not much we can do, what is taking place is my worst fear.'

I looked out at the scruffy floating rag sack again and couldn't see any reason to be alarmed. It was a tenth of the size of Cloud Nine and about as threatening-looking as a baby rabbit.

'They clearly knew more about our movements than we thought. They will be docking with us shortly, we could raise our elevation beyond their ability to reach us, Cloud Nine is capable of reaching 12,000 metres and they can only get up to about 9,000, but that really would be an act of aggression and we have no wish to antagonise the Original Five.'

I shrugged, the sudden appearance of this raggy old cloud didn't make much sense to me as I sat with Captain Hector, but that was all about to change.

26

I KNOW I DREAMT A GREAT DEAL WHEN I WAS ON Cloud Eleven. I dreamt about Beth and our little house in Kingham, I dreamt about the mining equipment I had been working on, I dreamt about long-haul flights, airports, shopping, cars, food in restaurants you had to pay for, trees, dogs, cows in fields.

In my waking hours I was only dimly aware of these dreams, and as a rule I'd always been totally unaware I'd been dreaming when I woke up. People assured me that I did dream, that it was a natural thing the brain did and loads of people had studied dreams and tried to make sense of them. The whole concept had never interested me, I couldn't see any use in worrying about dreams and I certainly didn't recall them, they didn't disturb me or make me wonder.

However, on the clouds it was all a little bit different.

I did remember little bits of my dreams as I woke up, just fleeting glimpses of what my soggy brain had been up to while I was sleeping.

I was a little bit annoyed that someone, somewhere, was recording my dreams, it made me anxious that I may have had dreams of a sexual nature, although I didn't recall any. I suppose it's likely, but the thing that did distress me was that dreams are often a bit mad. All sorts of weird stuff happens that doesn't make any sense, the bits of dreams I could recall were often about being embarrassed or socially awkward, of people taking offense at things I said or did, of me being lost and confused. I didn't relish the idea of some nerdy kid watching my dreams and having a chuckle about them.

This unusual state of affairs may have been due to the fact that the very nature of cloud travel was dreamlike. I became aware of the slightly different tone that everyone used on the clouds. It was as if they were barely awake and yet they and I seemed far more perceptive. I noticed things, tiny changes in the mood of another person, it was as if I was super-sensitive to my fellow cloud dwellers and this was not something I would ever have been accused of in my entire existence up to that point. I was always the one who was 'insensitive' and 'emotionally blocked' and 'incapable of empathy'. Well, according to Beth anyway.

This increased perception became more apparent when I met Ebrikke Karensdottir again. She was instantly recognisable as the attractive young woman who'd checked my vitals when I'd originally landed on Cloud Nine. As soon as I saw her I registered with some alarm that this was not just a normal woman, there was something very abnormal about her.

By the time I saw her the second time I knew she was not only a crew member from Cloud Three but she was the first person I'd met who was genuinely part human and part machine.

Okay, so you could argue that the kidonge was a mechanical enhancement, but what I was to learn about Ebrikke went far beyond that.

'I didn't want to tell you about Ebrikke because I wasn't sure how you'd react,' Brad said quietly. 'I didn't want to frighten you unnecessarily.'

I was sitting next to Brad in the Cloud Nine observation tower as we floated over the English Channel. Not that I could see anything; the cloud cover was unbroken. All I could see was a flat grey cloud layer and the tatty outline of Cloud Three below us, now alarmingly close.

'I was trying to protect you from her,' said Brad. I turned back to face him.

'Who?' I asked.

'Ebrikke. She is not entirely human, Gavin, it's important you understand that.'

'What, is she an alien?' I asked. She had looked entirely human to me when she gave me a drink after my arrival.

'Her body is entirely human, biological, organic. She was born of a mother and father just like you and me, but she's had the most extreme inclusion of non-biological material into her brain stem that has ever been attempted.'

'Eww,' I said, 'that sounds a bit gross.'

'It's not gross, Gavin,' said Brad staring at me, slightly confused. 'But it is something we have had to discuss at great length. We have procedures at our disposal, there is nothing remotely dangerous on a physical level, but the results we have seen in the past have been a little, well, I was going to say alarming but that would be to over-dramatise.'

'A little alarming. You mean people just go stark-raving doolally?'

'I don't know what that is.'

'They go mad, crazy, bonkers,' I said.

'Oh, I see. No, far from it, they become a real problem for mere mortals, that may be a better way of describing the results. We have had to introduce global legislation to contain the issues artificial intelligence brings up. Essentially anyone is allowed to have a 0.5 enhancement.'

'A 0.5 enhancement?'

'That means only a very small amount of the brain's total mass can be enhanced, 0.5 per cent of total brain mass.'

'So that's what Ebrikke has had done?' I asked, struggling to understand what all this meant.

'No, that would be fine and we wouldn't be dealing with this problem. Ebrikke has very publicly confronted the legislation and the general global agreement on brain enhancement. She has had over 50 per cent of her original brain mass replaced with non-biological systems.'

'Oh, right, I see,' I said, trying to imagine what that could possibly mean. 'That sounds like quite a lot.'

'Yes, it is an enormous amount. This has resulted in her being classified as a machine.'

'Wow, that's actually quite cool,' I said with a smile.

'That appeals to you?' asked Brad.

'I don't know, maybe. A lot of people have said I behave like a predictable machine. Well, one person.'

'One person?'

'Yes, my wife, but, well, that was a long time ago.'

Brad nodded. As was often the case I got the impression that what I'd just said to him was of such little importance it momentarily stumped him. He gave a big sigh and continued:

'You see, Ebrikke presents as a highly intelligent woman, effectively she is the most intelligent human being that has ever existed. She is the most extreme example we know of.'

'Well that doesn't sound so bad,' I said, even though I was grimacing.

'I am happy you have this attitude and it could essentially be a good thing. Indeed, Michiyo Nishimura had a small enhancement inserted in the Beijing Culvert by the same team who worked on Ebrikke.'

'Oh, right, well Michiyo seemed okay,' I said, 'she didn't seem like a robot.'

Brad smiled. 'No, we're not talking about robots, Gavin. But Michiyo's brain is 0.4 per cent enhanced, none of her original tissue was removed. Ebrikke's case is very different. A very large section of her human brain has been removed, she has sensory systems and memory enhancements even we only barely understand. She has the ability to, as it were, read another person's blood pressure and heart rate and her subconscious facial signal reading ability is beyond comprehension. She can't read your mind as such, not without physical contact, but she can get so much information about you merely by staring at your face.'

'Wow, that is incredible.'

'Yes, and somewhat unnerving. There are many people who

 are strongly opposed to this procedure and only very few people have had it done. Ebrikke has always been a bit of a renegade. She is supposedly the first person to be born on a cloud. As far as I know she has never once set foot on the surface. Her family was a little eccentric, they originated from the Reykjavik Culvert but fled after some difficult times. She is therefore one of the founding members of the Original Five clouds and has become something of a hero to them. She is very uncompromising, a little confrontational and completely determined.'

'Determined to do what?'

'We're docking!' said Kirubel. I glanced at Hector and Kirubel, they didn't seem overly pleased at this turn of events.

I looked out of the window to witness the dirty old ragbag that was Cloud Three eventually making contact with Cloud Nine and the comparison with old sailing ships was remarkable.

From my high vantage point in the observation tower I watched the small cloud pull alongside very slowly.

I saw what I guessed were men coming out of the cloud and throwing long ribbons onto the outer skin of Cloud Nine. These ribbons made firm contact with the material because they were soon pulled tight by unseen mechanisms and the two clouds become one.

Sort of.

One was huge, white, looked like a proper cloud and was rather beautiful. The other was a dirty grey colour, battered and tatty and looked like an old duvet cover from the 1970s that needed a good hose down.

'We'd better go and meet them, they can get very moody,' said Hector discreetly. 'Don't worry, they're not violent in a physical sense, just very demanding.'

I followed Brad and Hector down the blue lift, which was now second nature to me.

'Leave the talking to me,' said Brad as we entered the long cream tube of the docking area.

Two members of the Cloud Nine crew were standing by an opening in the outer wall of the space. It looked a bit like the entrance to a circus tent, with two sides of material being held apart by silent crew members.

As I got nearer I could see what looked to be a truly terrifying kind of inflated gangplank that traversed the narrow gap between the two clouds. It was a narrow gap but below was, I'm guessing, 500 metres of nothing and below that the English Channel.

Without wobble or hesitation a group of dirtily dressed individuals walked across this gangplank and into the tubular space. I could feel cold air rushing in through the opening and that gave their entrance a bit of added drama. I felt very cold.

After a few moments, a long line of individuals was stood staring at me. At a glance they looked like a bunch of Viking warriors in full fighting regalia, although to be accurate none of them had any obvious weapons. However, there was an air of menace coming from these people. Their dress code was different to anything I'd seen on the clouds. What they wore looked like old-fashioned space suits from Soviet-era space travel, dirty looking and very battered. They all showed signs of wear and much patient repair.

These rather terrifying-looking chaps stood to one side, allowing a much more diminutive figure to cross the fabric threshold. I recognised her at once. She was pretty stunning.

Whatever else she was with her half-inorganic brain, a shrinking violet she was not.

'Captain Hector, it is good to see you,' said Ebrikke Karensdottir.

Hector and Ebrikke shook hands. While she was looking at him it seemed the normally rotund and tightly packed form of the Captain deflated a little before my eyes.

Ebrikke then turned to Brad. 'Doctor Dorschel, it has been many storms.'

'Too many storms,' said Brad as he shook her delicate hand. 'It is good to see you again, Ebrikke, you are looking very well, as is your crew.'

'Our lives improve with each passing month,' she said, and almost smiled. The smile dropped when her eyes fell on me.

'Aha, the man of the hour,' she said. 'How are you, Mister Meckler?'

'I have just been explaining—' Brad stopped there because Ebrikke put her open hand toward his face. That's a fairly clear indication that you don't want someone to say anything more and it worked very effectively.

She stepped toward me, her rather gorgeous eyes staring without blinking into mine. I've never been good at the whole direct eye contact thing, but somehow I didn't mind with Ebrikke.

'Hello there,' I said as calmly as I could.

'Gavin Meckler from 1979,' she said. 'We meet again. I see from your cloud tan you have settled well in our world.'

'I have,' I said. 'It's been very—'

Again the hand went up, this time right in front of my face. I found it fairly annoying so I carried on talking.

'—interesting and I've learned…'

I couldn't say any more even though I wanted to. This woman had already rubbed me up the wrong way and I was feeling a little annoyed but I just couldn't continue talking.

'I know this,' she said. 'I know everything there is to know about you, which, to be fair, is not a great deal.'

She dropped her hand and I sensed a change in my entire body. It was mainly relief, almost as if she'd stopped me breathing and thinking for a moment.

We stood staring at each other and I was about to ask a question when she said, 'Of course, I don't have a kidonge.'

Had I never experienced the initial confusion of someone knowing what you were thinking this experience might have thrown me, but I was combat-hardened and determined not to allow her to have the upper hand.

'I knew that,' I shrugged. 'I knew that and I don't care. I also know all about you, Ebrikke Karensdottir, the woman with a half-inorganic brain. I'm not that impressed to be honest.'

'Funny,' said Ebrikke with a kind smile.

At this point Brad stepped forward and said rapidly, 'Gavin has maybe been slightly misinformed …'

'He has a kidonge,' repeated Ebrikke. 'Not interesting.'

'It's only interesting in that it can clearly communicate with whatever enhancements you have implanted in your head,' I said. 'I probably know more about you and your history than anyone else in this dimension.'

I knew this wasn't the case but for some reason I wasn't entirely clear about, winding this woman up and annoying her was very appealing.

'Doctor Dorschel, can you explain to Mister Meckler why his diminutive taunts are not very helpful.'

'I can do my best,' said Brad with a rather fake smile. He leant toward me and spoke rather rapidly. 'We now understand, Gavin, that there are four levels of consciousness on the planet.'

'Four levels of consciousness,' I repeated. It was meant to be a question but it didn't come out right, at which point I felt I had already lost a level of consciousness and had yet again revealed my caveman intelligence.

'Four levels,' said Brad. 'A lizard for example would be at level one, a monkey at level two, a person, a *Homo sapiens* from your era, Gavin, would be at level three.'

I nodded, then just blurted, 'Oh, wait a minute, you said there were four levels!'

'Indeed,' said Brad, 'most cloud dwellers, for example myself and Captain Hector, are both level four.'

'So you are more conscious than me?'

'Yes, that's correct, however, Ebrikke is level five.'

'Level five!' I said. Brad nodded.

'But you just told me there are four levels of consciousness.'

'There used to be. Ebrikke has developed higher reasoning and cognition due to her enhancements.'

'Okay,' I said quietly, and turned to look at the beautiful woman before me. 'I'm impressed,' I said, 'but I'm not going to pretend I understand what that means.'

'What that means, Mister Meckler, is that I know what is going to happen here today. All these interactions and your simple desire to set the agenda, control events and guide your destiny are nothing more than minor annoyances. Shall we proceed to the Yuneec?'

There was a moment's hesitation from Brad and Hector, which clearly annoyed the Nordic Goddess.

'Yes?' she snapped.

Hector coughed and said, 'Certainly, it's been brought out of storage and is currently in position on the rear patio.'

Ebrikke clicked her long fingers. The sound she produced was like a mini gunshot; it hurt my ears.

Her small entourage immediately turned and started walking toward the far end of the white tube.

Brad held my arm as we watched them lope off toward a circular hole in the far wall. Once they had disappeared I turned to Brad and Hector. Hector breathed out and relaxed.

'Oh dear me,' he said. 'I somehow always forget just how bloody terrifying that woman is.'

'The Yuneec!' I said as quietly as I could. 'You mean my plane! Why does she want to see my plane?'

'This is where it's going to get very difficult,' said Brad discreetly. 'Ebrikke is a fiercely intelligent and sensitive person, she's a level five, she can pick up minute variants in our behaviour and speech patterns. She knows what we're thinking, and remember she does this without a kidonge.'

'I'm sure you're right,' I said, feeling increasingly alarmed. 'But why does she want to see the Yuneec?'

'I believe she wishes to travel with you,' said Brad. 'We all know this is not possible, I have a feeling she knows it's not possible but, well, the crews of the Original Five are often very complicated to negotiate with.'

'Well I can help there,' I said proudly, 'because she's not coming.'

'It might not be as easy as that,' said Brad.

'No, seriously,' I said, 'it's as easy as that. I'm not having that computer-brained control freak in my Yuneec.'

'Please don't call her that, old chap,' pleaded Hector, 'it really isn't going to help inter-cloud relations. She is very difficult to dissuade, believe me, we've tried on many occasions in the past.'

'Can she fly a heavier-than-air machine?' I asked.

'Of course not,' said Brad, 'no one can.'

'There's your answer then,' I said, clapping my hands together as if brushing the dust off.

'But she can very easily convince you that it's a good idea to explain how to do it,' said Hector. 'She's convinced me to travel halfway around the world when I really didn't need to go before. The Tbilisi Culvert evacuation, I told you about it when you first arrived on Cloud Nine. That was at Ebrikke's suggestion.'

'Well, if I won't fly, she can't go. I've been away for so long I'm not in some kind of desperate rush to get back.'

'I wish it were that simple, Gavin,' said Brad, 'but your meteorological window is tight enough as it is. If you don't catch the predicted anomaly it could be months, even years before we can be here and make use of the situation again. To be honest, it really is now or never.'

27

HE YUNEEC LOOKED SO REASSURING THAT I almost burst into tears when I laid eyes on it.

It looked pristine and wonderful sitting on the inflated rear patio of Cloud Nine in the late afternoon sun. There was beautiful light brushing the wings and it stirred something in me I didn't expect.

I can only describe it as some kind of longing, the feeling of a light breeze on my skin as I walked toward the plane on Enstone Airfield on a summer morning. The knowledge of Beth, the sense of place, of belonging somewhere, of knowing people even if I had never wanted to talk to them.

Suddenly I wanted to talk to them, to find out how they were feeling. Not just other pilots at Enstone, but Beth, Kevin at the flying club, the lovely lady at the Kingham stores who was always nice to me even though I ignored her most of the time. My mum and dad, even my brother, Giles.

I wanted to know about them. I could not remember feeling that before, all I knew when I was back in 2011 was that people existed. I had to acknowledge their existence because they could have an impact on my life, but I never had any desire to know what was going on in their lives. As I stood staring at the Yuneec, I did want to know, even though they'd been dead for hundreds of years. I wanted to see them again and find out what was happening to them.

I must have been staring at the Yuneec for some time, because when I turned around Hector was standing next to me.

'We're just passing the coast of southern England,' he said under his breath. 'We're heading north at 50 kilometres an hour, ground speed.'

Standing in the perfectly still air on the patio deck of Cloud Nine did not give you any indication you were moving. It was quiet and still.

The patio deck had a transparent barrier around the edge which made looking down to the surface very easy. I had been eager to see England in post-storm 2211 but low-level cloud cover made seeing anything on the surface impossible.

Although we were floating at about a thousand metres above the ground we were also above the cloud cover, which seemed eerily smooth and uniform. In all my previous flying experience, I'd never seen anything like it. The uniform grey cloud cover looked like a recently painted concrete floor.

'Is that normal?' I said to Hector, nodding down in the direction of the low clouds.

He nodded. 'Sea mist. The sea is probably a bit warmer than it was back in your day. In still weather like this the mist is about 200 metres thick, it's probably quite cold down on the ground.'

The flat grey blanket stretched off as far as I could see. I was in a two-tone world, a flat grey sheet below and a crystal-clear blue dome above.

I turned to see Ebrikke and Brad busy in conversation.

'You see, the thing is,' said Hector moving me away from them and the rest of the Cloud Three crew, 'I think Brad has already told you Ebrikke is in a spot of bother.'

'He told me she has a computer brain and that she's a machine,' I answered.

'Yes, well, since the law has been passed, it's all got a bit difficult for her.'

'Oh, right, because she's had her brain mashed up she's on the run?'

Hector's face folded as he struggled to understand what I'd just said.

'I think so, old chap,' he said eventually. 'We've had a bit of trouble in the past with artificial brains, artificial intelligence and suchlike, that's why the law was passed. It's globally binding but obviously with renegade cloud dwellers it gets a bit difficult to enforce. So our lovely Ebrikke is now in rather a lot of trouble, hence her desire to use your Yuneec.'

'Bloody Nora,' I said.

'Who's that?'

'No, I mean, what a nightmare. This is going to get very ugly.'

'I sincerely hope not,' said Hector.

Suddenly there was that loud clicking noise again. I looked over at Brad and Ebrikke, she was looking at Hector with her spooky blue eyes.

'Hang on a moment,' said Hector. He patted me on the back, gave me a look that oozed resignation and walked toward them.

I tried to watch without making it too obvious. I wasn't worried, there was no way I was going to get in the plane with that annoying know-all woman even if she was gorgeous.

Hector stood near Ebrikke and rocked up and down on his toes, his hands behind his back. I suppose it was a sort of 'captain'-type stance but it wasn't very convincing.

It had crossed my mind to make a dash for the Yuneec and try and take off without telling anyone, but the rest of the crew from Cloud Three were standing around looking at the plane.

One of them, a tall African man, beckoned me over.

'This is electric powered?' he asked.

'Yes it is,' I replied.

'Did you change it?'

'No, that's how it was built,' I said. I was going to explain how it had been rebuilt in London but thought better of it.

'You mean you had electric planes back in 1979?'

'No, I was born in 1979. This plane was made in 2009, it was an early model.'

'So other machines you used, they burnt fuel?'

'Yes,' I said. I didn't want to elaborate. I had surmised that this crowd would make Greenpeace activists look like Republican tar sands extractors; they were a fairly hardcore bunch.

'Millions of machines,' he said.

'Yes,' I said.

Then he suddenly put on a kind of weird, nasal British accent and twisted his face into a pinched up expression. 'But we didn't know it would be a problem to burn all those hydrocarbons, we thought it would be okay. It's not our fault.'

I suppose I was offended because I supposed he was doing an impression of me. It was doubly chilling because I'd never said those things other than to Brad and Theda. It was even more distressing because his fellow crewmates all fell about laughing.

An older man moved forward and I started a little, only because his skin was as white as a sheet of paper.

'We didn't know it would have any effect. It's not our fault,' he said, in an even more extreme nasal accent. He added to this by doing a kind of knock-kneed walk which increased the laughter of his pals.

'Little bit immature for people of advanced intelligence maybe?' I suggested, when the noise of their laughter died down.

The looks I got for saying that were far from friendly. In all the bizarre places I ended up, other than the Weaver Woman, this was the only time I felt threatened by anyone. These people were very angry and it seemed it was all directed at me.

'Okay, chaps, you've had your fun, let's leave Mister Meckler alone,' said Hector who was suddenly standing beside me. I was very grateful for the support.

The African man bristled at this. 'Oh, we've got to be polite to your guest have we? The first time we have ever met a responsible one from the way back and we have to be fucking polite.'

'When you're on my cloud, sonny Jim, you have to be polite,' said Hector calmly. It had suddenly become a stand-off between these two. The tension was broken by yet another loud click in my left ear.

'Enough,' said Ebrikke, who was also now suddenly standing beside me.

The crew of Cloud Three stood back, clearly very intimidated by the diminutive figure standing beside me.

In various situations I'd encountered I'd felt confused, anxious or utterly out of my depth, but never more so than at that moment.

It was painfully obvious even to me that if a physical skirmish had taken place I wouldn't have lasted a second. 'No one is even considering the use of physical force,' Ebrikke said to me. I stared at her exquisite face. She was staring at me in that way again. I noticed something about her eyes, they were weird. Not altogether human.

'Glad to hear it,' I said.

'And no one is considering flying with you in the Yuneec.'

'Oh, right,' I said. I felt a wave of relief wash over me. At least I wasn't going to have to confront that particular notion. However, Ebrikke had moved so that she stood between me and the Yuneec.

'You like life on the clouds, don't you, Gavin?' she said.

'I do,' I replied. I didn't want to be rude but I also didn't want to say anything more. I could not fathom this woman out; she wasn't nasty to me, although it was clear she looked down on me as some kind of sub-species.

'But you want to get home to Beth, you want to get back to a time you understand, a simpler time where the world was still green and inhabitable.'

'Yes,' I said flatly, although I surprised myself by sensing where she was heading with her slightly chilling observations. She knew about Beth, she probably knew as much about me as anyone I'd met on my travels. I don't know how she knew, I suppose she could 'read my mind' or maybe she had managed to extract a copy of my mind when she put her gentle fingers on my temples when I'd arrived.

I could tell she was trying to talk me round to giving up, to not attempt to get home. She wanted something else but I wasn't sure what.

'But you know if you go back from here there might not be a Beth, there might not be a home and indeed, you might meet yourself, which would of course be fatal. You might find that another Gavin Meckler is following a completely different path in life, or you might never have existed because your father would not be your father, your mother may never have been born and the socio-political system you knew and understood may be so different you may feel just as lost there as you do here.'

I didn't say anything. This sounded very different to everything else I'd been told.

'Not quite what you'd expected to hear, is it?' she suggested.

'I suppose not,' I said carefully after some thought. I had to accept that up to that point I hadn't questioned the information Brad and Theda had fed to me. I had no more reason to believe them than I did to accept that Ebrikke was telling the truth.

'So now you are thinking, is it worth me going back? Will I just travel to yet another dimension in the same time sector, that's what you're thinking now isn't it, Mister Meckler? How will you know, how could you know, it is not possible for you to know. You can only do this journey on faith. You have no scientific understanding. It is just faith in the people you have met here that is driving you.'

Something was happening to me as she spoke. I was feeling weak and hopeless. What she said made total sense. I had listened to the people of the clouds and believed every word they'd said to me. Somehow Ebrikke had turned all their rock-solid predictions and advanced understanding of dimensions and string theory to silly mush.

Basically I felt like a fool, and when this had happened to me in the past, I became angry and tended to lash out. I don't mean I hit people but I could say cruel things.

At that moment as I stood facing Ebrikke I had nothing, no anger, no fear, merely resignation and acceptance.

'I operate at a higher brain function than you, I don't blame you for your frailty in this area and I know you will eventually co-operate with me.'

I looked at Brad and Hector, who were both busy studying their shoes.

I stood silently staring at Ebrikke for a while as I went through my response in my head. No doubt she could hear my dull brain clunking through a few mediocre thoughts but I didn't let that stop me. I searched for my anger. I knew I should feel angry, I really wanted to feel angry. I didn't want to accept that this woman with her fake brain really was that superior to me, or to any of the other people I'd met on the clouds.

I clenched my fists as tightly as I could and somehow got my pulse to race, I started to feel angry and that made me very happy.

'I can see that you intimidate the rest of the crew on Cloud Nine,' I said. 'I understand they need to maintain good relations with you and the rest of the Original Five, but I don't.'

I adopted a smile at that point. She didn't react.

'I don't care if you hate me or think I have the intellect of a slug, but I'm leaving and like you said, you're not coming with me.'

Then Ebrikke smiled. The smile was instant and yes, it was unnerving and my anger fled as soon as it had arrived.

She looked utterly beautiful when she smiled. Her teeth were so perfect; her skin had such a glorious sheen of health and her eyes sparkled more than any eyes I'd seen before.

'You are correct on all counts, Mister Meckler,' she said after a long pause. 'You, unlike the crew here, have nothing to lose. The new clouds are, as you suggest, intimidated by me and you do indeed have the insight of a mollusc.'

She stared at me for a while and I couldn't make myself look away, or sneer, or even come back with some witty and cutting reposts.

'You are also correct in the assumption that I am not going with you in the Yuneec. That would be pointless. However, more accurately, you are not coming with me.'

My silence became a prison. I could say nothing.

'I am going to control the Yuneec myself, alone.'

28

IT'S NOT SOMETHING I AM GOING TO EASILY FORget. I would surmise it took months if not years off my total life expectancy. The sight of the Yuneec flying into a monstrous cloud formation a few kilometres off the eastern side of Cloud Nine is a vision I cannot forget.

My Yuneec, finally gone.

My last possible chance of returning to my real life. It was devastating, like a judge putting on the black cap in a pre-1965 English courtroom.

To explain how Ebrikke had managed to talk me into not only letting her fly away in the Yuneec but also explain to her in great detail exactly how to fly the plane makes me feel so uncomfortable I don't wish to recall anything about it.

But recall it I must because it is the single most terrifying thing I have ever experienced. I'll go further. The ability this woman had could be the single most terrifying prospect the human race has had to deal with.

Forget the endless march of machines that take over the world and use our crude minds as an energy source. Forget the end of money, forget the end of fossil fuel or the Armageddon of the Anthropocene age.

The fact that one human being can take over the mind of another, make them do exactly what they want even though during the entire experience the victim is fully aware of the situation, fully aware, with their mind screaming at them to stop but with no ability to resist? It's terrifying.

Okay, so I've never been held at gunpoint by some state-sanctioned murderer or fundamentalist terrorist. I'd imagine that would be quite high on the fear list but I'd argue it wouldn't be as high as discovering you suddenly had fundamentalist religious beliefs that you could not resist.

I explained everything in clear detail to Ebrikke even as my reptilian brain kept turning my head to stare at the huge cloud formation we were approaching, a cloud formation I knew to be over the area where Didcot once stood.

I knew I had limited time to escape and yet there was nothing I could do about it. Not once did Ebrikke lay a hand on me or even threaten me in any way. I just had to do what she wanted.

The big squashy mattress under the Yuneec inflated and hummed a little and then lifted the plane high above the cloud. It moved forward at speed and then dropped away as the plane took flight, meandering violently at first before leveling out, gaining altitude and then diving at considerable speed into the vast grey cloud formation.

That was it. I was forever stranded.

I felt Hector's hand on my shoulder.

'I'm so sorry, old chap,' he said. 'I feel terrible about this. There was simply nothing we could do.'

I couldn't quite take my eyes off the area of cloud I'd just seen the Yuneec disappear into, I was brain-numb and still unable to take in what had just happened.

'It's all my fault,' said Brad, who stood on the other side of me. 'I should have been able to protect you. This is going to cause grave conflict between the cloud groups.'

I closed my eyes. I didn't want to allow the wave of anger and regret to overwhelm me, I could feel it building and I knew I would drown if I allowed the thoughts to burst out.

I felt some movement under my feet and opened my eyes to see Kirubel, Hector's delightful African crewman, running toward us across the quilted expanse of the rear patio.

'Heavier-than-air machine!' he shouted. 'We've just picked up a signal?'

The last phrase was a question – he clearly didn't understand what this information meant either. His arrival also alerted me to the close presence of the Cloud Three crew who were clearly alarmed at this information.

'Where?' asked Hector.

'Twenty-three clicks west, the other side of the anomaly.'

Hector and Brad looked at each other.

'Surely not,' said Hector.

'I don't think it can be a mistake,' said Kirubel, 'there's nothing else on Earth that would give a signal like that.'

'Release life drones and lock coordinates,' said Captain Hector with gusto. He didn't say it to anyone in particular, he just shouted.

At that point a flock of maybe two dozen white doughnuts left the underside of Cloud Nine and made their way toward the anomaly. They were followed by the slightly slower flying mattress from which Ebrikke and the Yuneec had just been launched.

Everyone on the patio moved to the clear barrier and looked toward the tower of cloud that was by this point slightly behind us. It remained in place while everything else, every cloud including the one I was on, kept moving slowly north.

'There!' shouted Kirubel. 'Look, to the south!'

There was a shout from the motley gathering on the patio, some shouts of despair – those were from the crew of Cloud Three – and some shouts of utter joy, mainly from Hector right beside me.

'She blew it!' shouted Hector at the top of his voice. 'She's not so damn clever after all! She just flew straight through the cloud!'

He laughed richly, pointing at the miserable-looking group of Cloud Three bullyboys. 'Superwoman is a dunce!' he bellowed between guffaws.

'But wait . . .' I said as my limited grasp of events started to emerge. 'Doesn't that mean the time shift thing, the anomaly or whatever it is, doesn't that mean it's not working?'

'I don't think she flew straight through the anomaly,' said Kirubel. 'We lost the signal completely for a millisecond.'

Brad turned to look at Kirubel. 'Not a signal glitch?'

'No, temporal anomaly, clearly registered and logged.'

Brad nodded and turned to me. 'We may have reason to be optimistic, Mister Meckler.'

I then witnessed something I'd already experienced but hadn't understood. The white doughnuts surrounded the Yuneec as it approached us. The white mattress rose slowly beneath it and guided it gently toward us.

It was only as it was literally a few metres above the patio that it became clear there was no one inside.

As soon as it landed, the big Cloud Three lads rushed up and opened the door. They hung their heads and simply walked away saying nothing. That was the last time I saw them.

I walked up to the Yuneec, which looked at first glance to be mechanically sound. I peered into the cockpit and noticed something tucked in the pilot's door pocket. I used to keep maps there as a backup in case the satnav failed. I knew it had been empty when Ebrikke took off.

I walked to the other side of the Yuneec, opened the door and pulled out the small sheet of paper. It was ruled A4, like I used to have at school. It was a letter written in large capitals as if it had been scrawled by a ten-year-old. It read:

MISTER MECKLER, I TOLD YOU I WAS TAKING THE PLANE, I DECIDED NOT TO TELL YOU I WAS SENDING IT BACK IN CASE CIRCUMSTANCES MADE THAT IMPOSSIBLE. IF YOU ARE READING THIS, MY PLAN HAS WORKED AS I EXPECTED. I HAVE TRAVELLED INTO THE FUTURE. I WON'T FURTHER CONFUSE YOUR SIMPLE MIND BY EXPLAINING WHERE, WHAT PERIOD

OR WHAT IT IS LIKE, ONLY THAT THE CHANGES I HAVE MADE TO MY CEREBAL CORTEXT ARE CONSIDERED NORMAL HERE. I AM FINALLY WITH MY OWN KIND AND THAT IS PARTLY DUE TO YOU. I THANK YOU FOR THIS. THERE IS A HOMING BEACON PLUGGED INTO THE DRONE'S NAVIGATION COMPUTER. YOU MIGHT WANT TO GET SOMEONE COMPETENT TO REMOVE IT AS ALL THAT WILL HAPPEN NOW IS THE PLANE WILL ALWAYS RETURN TO CLOUD NINE.

I HOPE YOUR TRAVELS ARE SAFE.
EBRIKKE KARENSDOTTIR

I passed the note to Brad.

'Wow, she is some lady,' he said after a mere glance. 'I guess she isn't coming back.'

'Kirubel, check out the control locker. Ebrikke's put a homing system on the drone. We need to get Gavin in the air.'

Kirubel popped open what I had known to be the small cargo hold behind the cockpit. Inside was a collection of white packets that looked like bags of milk all tangled up in white ribbons. I knew it wasn't milk or ribbons but I didn't know what it was. Kirubel pulled the entire collection of objects out and held it up.

'Not hard to find,' he said, removing one of the packet things. They all looked the same to me. 'Ready to go.'

I then received a hearty slap on the back from Hector. 'I never thought you'd be that useful,' he said. 'But you've just helped us get shot of one of the most terrifying women on the planet. Good job, sir!'

I was unable to respond. The sequence of events was at once so emotionally wrenching and rapidly unfolding that it took all my strength not to once again go completely doolally.

I climbed into the cockpit and the Yuneec's systems started up. Brad and Hector were by the door.

'Everything okay?' Brad asked. I nodded.

'Feeling confident?' asked Hector. I shook my head.

Kirubel appeared between them and handed me a white backpack.

'All your possessions are in there, Mister Meckler, washed and vacuum packed. You will be fine, sir, you are a very brave man.'

I shrugged. I didn't feel brave.

'Thank you,' I said finally. I stowed the bag behind the seats and pulled the elasticated mesh over it to hold it in place. One of the few remaining parts of the original plane. Holding it made me feel just fractionally safer.

I took a deep breath and turned to face them and once again said, 'Thank you, you have been very kind, good luck on your travels. Oh yes, and in calmer times.'

Brad nodded, smiling broadly. He closed the door and everyone around the Yuneec stood back a little. I felt the whole plane rise slowly as the large inflated drone took the weight.

I looked around the faces gathered around the plane. A few members of the crew, a woman with a young child, Hector, Kirubel and Brad. I hadn't got to know any of them very well, although I suppose Brad had been the one who'd followed my every move. He waved to me just before he went out of sight. I think I waved back just too late and I felt bad I hadn't thanked him more.

I could only hear a low rush of pumped air and cursed myself for never really finding out how these floating cushions worked.

Within a few moments I was high above Cloud Nine and turning toward the anomaly, which was now many kilometres away. I assumed it was very late to make this transition but I had to give it a go.

All I knew was I really didn't want to end up somewhere even more weird than the cloud world. I wanted to go home and this seemed to be my only chance.

When the Yuneec was well clear of Cloud Nine I started up

 the motor with the touchscreen control that Pete and his team had fitted in London. The big floppy blades started to spin and soon disappeared into a blur of high-speed rotation. I could feel us gather momentum and before long I felt I had control of the Yuneec, the control stick felt heavier and the plane started to do what I expected.

I knew from talking to Brad and Theda that I needed to get up high and dive into the anomalous cloud at a fairly steep angle.

With the new power system at my fingertips this wasn't a problem, I climbed to 8,000 metres and did a stall turn toward the lower section of the swirling grey cloud that by this stage filled my screen of vision.

The speed increased with stomach-churning force and I hit the outer edge of the cloud so fast that the shocking change in light made me scream.

I felt ridiculous. I'd done this before, I'd entered this damn cloud three times previously and survived, but this time I was terrified. I knew something was going to be on the other side of the cloud and on three previous occasions it had been completely at odds with what I was expecting.

This time I was expecting nothing.

29

OF ALL THE THINGS I HADN'T EXPECTED, I WOULD suggest rain was fairly high up the list.

Deep space, a million-mile-long alien battle cruiser, or a burning fireball of doom hurtling toward me; maybe armoured hyper-intelligent dinosaurs who mistook me for an insect and sent out their huge metal tongues to eat me...

Any of those were to be expected, but heavy rain? For some reason that made me start swearing uncontrollably.

I suppose the other thing that brought about a certain amount of alarm was the rapidly approaching trees. I hesitate to think how long it took my muscle memory to kick in and pull back the flight stick. It was a very close call but thankfully I was soon levelled out and scanning the ground for clues.

I was flying over planet Earth, that much I was confident of. I was flying through heavy rain, which reduced my visibility rather drastically and I was desperate to find somewhere to land.

All I could see was trees. I was flying above dense woodland but it wasn't the same as when I flew over Gardenia. The trees were a different colour, browns, reds and ochres seemed to make up the endless soaked landscape.

I banked as hard as I could and kept an eye on the ground. Just more trees as far as I could see, which I have to point out, wasn't very far.

Then something caught my eye, a shape in the distance, a building. I reduced my altitude and speed a little. I didn't want to zoom past whatever it was only to lose sight of it again in the sea of trees.

I shouted for joy. I knew that roof! It was Goldacre Hall!

I banked hard again and flew fast and low over the small

collection of buildings. There was the barn, the gardens and yet it looked very different. Sort of muddy and brown.

On my third pass I spotted figures out in the orchard. They seemed to be making their way to the Bow field, which I had managed to miss due to the fact that it was just a brown patch surrounded by trees.

I passed over it a couple more times, trying to judge the wind speed and direction, but it was pretty hopeless. The rain was pummelling the windscreen so hard it was almost impossible to see anything.

I banked around and passed over the field maybe six more times trying desperately to work out which way to attempt to land, but I could now see figures trudging across the small patch of open ground below me. It was clearly very sticky and muddy; hitting that quagmire with the Yuneec's fairly frail undercarriage would be disastrous. Before long I knew I could not attempt a conventional landing.

After a moment's reflection on my predicament, I decided to make use of the incredible power that the Yuneec had been vested with.

I turned and flew over the Bow field until it was just about in the centre of the open space and then wrenched the stick back and applied full power with the thumb slider on the control yoke.

The engine made a noise for the first time, a high-pitched scream as I started to climb at a ridiculous speed. The frame of the Yuneec vibrated rather violently and a thought crossed my mind for an instant: I might just tear this battered machine to bits.

After a couple of seconds I backed off the power as steadily as I could and felt the vertical speed drop.

I knew this was going to be next to impossible but in the conditions I was flying with I had no choice. I was going to have to make what equated to a helicopter landing, tail first into the mud.

As the speed dropped and I felt the Yuneec start to tip forward I increased power and pulled it up again. I continued to do this about a dozen times until I found a point where the whole plane was essentially hanging from the rotors but remaining motionless in the air.

Due to the thumb slide control this wasn't as hard as it may sound, a tiny increase or decrease was fairly easy to control.

Once I had this balance I glanced around frantically behind me, which was of course directly below me. I was in a vertical climb position and pinned into the back of the seat.

This was pretty terrifying but after going through the horror of the unknown in the cloud where I felt I had no control, in this situation I was very much in control. If I screwed up it would be my fault.

This manoeuvre would be impossible using the technology and control systems of the twenty-first century, but since my very brief flying experience over the Squares of London I knew the Yuneec had the power to do it.

Of course, the immense torque put out by the motor meant the whole plane started contra-spinning in the air with ever-increasing speed. This made judging my distance above the field, which I hoped was below me, very difficult. The landscape was spinning around me as I slowly descended. This made me feel dizzy and nauseous but I had to keep checking to try and judge how high I was.

I was glancing out of the window in a kind of strange controlled panic. I was so busy trying to control the Yuneec that every fibre of my mind and body was fully engaged. Somehow the ridiculous level of concentration needed meant I didn't go into a blind, and at that point fatal, panic.

I may have been spinning just above the ground for a few seconds before I felt the tail make contact with the ground. It was thankfully gentle and I pulled up a little as soon as I felt it. By now all I could see from the side windows was a blur of vegetation, flying muddy water and bits of twig as the incredible wash from the propellers sent everything around the plane flying in a whirlwind of debris.

The tail making contact with the earth meant the spinning slowed very rapidly. All I had to do from that point on was bring the plane to rest in an upright position.

Not easy. I made at least five attempts to reduce engine speed only to feel the plane start to drop backwards, meaning it would have come to rest upside down. Either that or it would lurch to one side, meaning the wings would make contact before the wheels. Each time I had to gently increase power just enough to pull the Yuneec onto a horizontal plane before reducing power again.

Finally I felt the nose dip in the way I wanted. I reduced power a little until I could sense some slow forward movement.

The relief was immense, as the nose came down and the entire plane regained its normal position on the ground. I jolted forward a bit as the wheels slid along the soft mud. I pushed the thumb slider all the way down to kill the engine and within a few seconds the enormous noise of motor, wind, vibration and heart-thumping concentration ceased. All I could hear was rain on the wings and fuselage.

Moments later this noise was joined by applause. There were bedraggled people approaching from every direction and clapping as they did so. Many of them were covered in specks of mud that was slowly washed away by the torrential rain.

I opened the door and smiled at them. The occupants of Goldacre Hall, a group of people I never thought I'd see again, indeed, a group of people that for a long time I assumed had never even existed, stood around me covered in dirt.

30

‘ELL I NEVER DID,’ SAID A VERY OLD MAN WITH A huge hood over his mud-spattered head. ‘I never expected to see you again, Gavin. Welcome back, dear boy.’

Although I could barely make out his face under all the mud, I knew the voice. It was William, the man who’d flown over Gardenia with me in the Yuneec.

‘William, mate,’ I said and grabbed him, hugging his frail wet body tightly. ‘Oh blimey, it’s good to see you,’ I blurted. ‘I really didn’t think I was going to make it.’

‘Is that sort of manoeuvre standard? It was blowing mud and muck to the four corners of the universe. I’ve never seen such a mess or heard such a hullabaloo.’

‘Yeah, sorry about that. I knew I couldn’t land conventionally, you know, like we did when you flew with me. I wasn’t sure where I’d end up landing like that though. Sorry about the mess.’

‘With this rain we can’t really make more mess, we can merely shift it around and you certainly did that,’ said William, wiping some of the mud off his cheek. ‘We all ran for our lives as the mud started flying.’

‘Yeah, sorry about that, must have looked a bit alarming.’

The soaked crowd around me were smiling but all of them looked genuinely surprised to see me. Unlike in London or more especially the land of clouds, they clearly didn’t expect to see me in Gardenia.

The rain was pelting down so heavily it was hard to actually hear anything.

'Let's get back inside and dry out,' said William. 'I'm quite exhausted from all the excitement.'

I closed the pilot's door on the Yuneec and sheltered under the wing, looking out at the sheets of torrential rain falling all around. My flight suit suddenly felt woefully inadequate; it was not only pouring with rain, it was also quite cold.

Someone stepped forward from the group and handed me a cape. I slung it around my shoulders and without a word we all set off back to the hall.

I glanced around at the Yuneec as we trudged through the sticky mud. It looked undamaged resting in the corner of the field and it was only as I could see the position I landed in that I realised I was frighteningly near some very large trees. It was pure fluke that I hadn't landed on them and once again ripped the Yuneec to shreds.

As we approached the front door of Goldacre Hall I could see a crowd of people had gathered in the entrance lobby and under the porch roof to greet me.

They were waving and cheering as we walked up the sodden path and the welcome I received when entering the Hall was nothing short of tumultuous. Well, as tumultuous as one multi-occupational household can muster.

After taking off the sopping cloak and removing my cloud boots I stood up, a big grin on my face. I was genuinely happy to be back in the least insane place I'd visited.

Along with William I entered the large dining area to yet another almost deafening cheer and round of applause. I know I was grinning like a fool but I also felt so welcome, so happy to be back in this charming place. I was shaking my head in disbelief at every face I recognised, but of course I was looking out for one particular person rather keenly.

William pulled back a seat for me and gestured for me to sit. 'If I remember correctly you will fall asleep in about an hour, so I'd better make sure you get something to eat.'

'How long have I been away?' I asked him as he sat opposite me on one of the long tables. A big crowd gathered around us immediately and it was obvious that everyone wanted to hear of my adventures. The noise of the crowd subsided, men holding children up to see stood at the back, older and more frail members of the Hall stood near the front.

'Well, you left in early July, it's now late November, so about four months I suppose.'

I shook my head. I hadn't kept any record of time since I'd left Gardenia but four months felt about right.

'Okay,' I nodded and noticed that someone had put a bowl of Gardenian food in front of me. 'Oh wow, proper food.'

'So where have you been?' asked William.

'And what was the food like?' asked someone in the gathering around us.

'And the weather?' said someone else.

'Were the people kind?'

'Did you go into space?'

'Did you go to Mars?'

The questions tumbled out, so many and so fast I couldn't hear them. I laughed.

'Let the poor man have something to eat!' said William. 'You look ravenous, I think you've lost weight.'

I started eating and of course, just as I expected, it was wonderful. The paste stuff on Cloud Eleven was close in flavour and texture, but at least this food looked the same in the bowl as it tasted in your mouth.'

'Cloud paste,' I said eventually, 'is truly amazing. It's like a cream-coloured paste but it changes into whatever you want when it's in your mouth. It's the weirdest experience I've ever had, but it does taste almost as good as this.'

That caused a great deal of discussion and lots of incredulous repeats of the term 'cloud paste'.

'I've been to two alternate dimensions, both of them really

 bloody difficult to deal with.'

'You've been through two folds!' said William. 'That is extraordinary.'

'Yes, the first was a big city, I mean so huge it took up the whole of Gardenia. It's right here where we are, don't even begin to ask me how any of this works but I've been there, seen it with my own eyes. I lived there and I didn't quite go mad.' I took another mouthful and after chewing for a moment I said, 'I got close on a couple of occasions though.'

I swallowed and saw a crowd of faces staring at me, all of them dumbfounded.

'Then today, I was living on a cloud.'

'A cloud!' came a chorus of disbelief.

'Yes, well, a huge lighter-than-air structure that looks like a cloud.'

'Heavens above,' said William.

I spent the rest of the evening in the dining area of Goldacre Hall answering questions about the Squares of London and the clouds of everywhere.

'You cannot begin to imagine how big those clouds were,' I explained. 'Bigger than anything I've ever seen made by people, they literally were the size of a storm, a floating city with millions of people living on them.'

'A floating city, how lovely,' said a very old woman standing beside me.

Everyone listened very intently, they didn't sneer or tell me I must be off my rocker, they took everything I said very seriously.

The main thing that stayed with me as my energy rapidly faded was the lack of surprise exhibited by everyone there. They clearly knew that my ridiculously fantastical tales were utterly plausible. They had no problem accepting the existence of alternate dimensions but they clearly didn't have the desire or the technical ability to cross through the anomaly or fold to get there.

As my eyelids began to get heavier and my speech started to slur, William suggested I rest. By this stage I was so flummoxed I'd have done anything; however, even in my advanced state of exhaustion I was disappointed to hear that someone else had taken over my room in the old barn. I was given a small attic room on the third floor of Goldacre Hall.

Once I'd followed William up the stairs and registered the wonderfully familiar smells of the old house I felt almost deliriously happy.

As soon as he showed me my room I turned and embraced him, thanked him and said that I may sleep for some time.

31

CAN'T HONESTLY EVEN REMEMBER CROSSING THE small room at the top of Goldacre Hall and collapsing on the delightfully cosy-looking built-in bed, but that's where I woke up.

My bleary eyes opened to see bright sunlight coming through the heavy curtains and covering the small dormer window. It was very quiet. Another thing I'd forgotten about Goldacre Hall was the incredible silence.

The clouds hadn't been noisy but there was a constant background hissing sound, a kind of aural awareness that I was in a pressurised vessel floating high in the atmosphere.

The noise in the culverts was constant and fairly frightening, like the thunder of a distant battle.

Although the Squares of London weren't as noisy as a twenty-first-century city, it was still a city full of buildings and people so there was background noise all the time.

Goldacre Hall was ridiculously peaceful and quiet. It was a few moments before my ears became accustomed to the low noise level and then I could just hear a song thrush outside the window somewhere.

I glanced over at something sitting in the middle of the floor. My bag, the one Kirubel had given me just before I left Cloud Nine and next to it a wooden box which looked a bit like a fruit box or something people ship tea in. Not polished and posh, just a rough timber box.

I was pretty sure it hadn't been there as I stumbled into bed the night before, but then again I had just cloud-jumped and I had been a waste of space soon after. Jet lag is nothing, it's cloud lag that really does your head in.

I got up and opened the box. It was full of my old stuff. My chinos, my shoes, socks, pants, my polo shirt, iPad, iPhone and wallet.

I wondered for a moment if Grace had brought them to me. Had she come into the room while I was sleeping, placed the box down carefully on the floor and discreetly withdrawn?

I could picture her doing that and I started to powerfully recall our time together. Then I sat up and decided that was probably a bad idea. I'd gone away in the middle of a storm, left her standing looking at me as I flew into the cloud. I had no right to be part of her life.

The items of clothing were neatly folded and placed inside the box. Placed on top of them in a very orderly fashion were my personal electronics.

I picked up the phone, still at 100 per cent charge but with no signal. I sat on the bed and looked at it. It still worked even though it was hundreds of years old.

I opened the camera app and took a picture of myself. Yes, I took a selfie.

I then started looking through pictures. I had a couple of thousand on the phone and even more in various albums on the iPad.

The ones on the phone were mainly of large earth-moving machinery, me standing in vast open caste coal pits and quarries in various parts of the world. Me standing next to massive bulldozers or by the 20-foot high wheel of a giant earth-moving truck in Australia.

My thumb flipped through the pictures without hesitation, muscle memory intact.

Suddenly there was one of Beth in our kitchen, with her friend Maeve from Ireland and Maeve's ridiculous Irish wolfhound that came to stay the weekend before I left. I could remember taking the picture, I had taken it something like seven months earlier, and yet it felt like years, decades ago. In fact it had been over two centuries.

Beth looked wonderful, smiling at the camera, and the light coming through the side window in the kitchen lit her face beautifully.

I looked at that picture for a long time. Getting back to Kingham in 2011 seemed like the most ridiculous notion I could have. It was painfully obvious I was only able to hop sideways through the various dimensions in 2211. Surely I was never going to be able to get back.

I opened the bag and extracted my body suit from London and my favourite boots that Noshi had given me. I showered in the tiny smooth grey cubicle built into the small room and got dressed.

I walked down the stairs and it was only then I noticed a distinct change in the weather. The sun was bright and the sky was clear, although I could tell the temperature outside was a great deal colder than when I'd left Gardenia back in the summer.

An old lady ran up the stairs past me. She had to be in her nineties but she bounded up the stairs without a second thought.

'Welcome back, Gavin,' she said as she whooshed past me.

'Thank you,' I shouted behind me but she'd already disappeared.

At the foot of the stairs a young boy was waiting. I didn't recognise him at first.

'Grace says if you want some nice tea she's at Oak House,' he said.

'Henry?' I said.

'Yes, that's me.'

It was Grace's son. In all the head-spinning pandemonium I'd been through I'd completely forgotten about Henry.

'How are you, Henry?'

'I'm very well thank you, Gavin, are you coming for tea and breakfast?'

I smiled. 'Yes, I would love to.'

So I followed Henry out of the front door and into the cold air of an English, or I suppose Gardenian, November morning. This experience was bizarre on so many multiples of layers. For a start I knew where to go. I knew Oak House and of course I knew Grace. I felt bad that I'd forgotten about Henry and I also felt a little bit uncomfortable about the fact that I really hadn't forgotten about Grace.

The hedges either side of the path to Oak House were covered in brown leaves, some of the trees were already bare and the narrow path was covered in fallen leaves.

We walked along in silence. Henry didn't want to talk, that much I could register.

I was, of course, full of questions about his mum but I contained them and we walked along in peace.

As we approached the familiar structure of Oak House I started to feel tense. Here I was about to meet the mother of my first child. Even with my confused relationship with time I knew she wouldn't have given birth to our child yet, but I had no idea what to expect.

Henry approached the beautiful door that looked like wood but wasn't and walked straight inside.

I paused in the porch, bent down and pressed the release button on the back of my boots. They flopped out around my foot and I stepped inside.

The sweet little kitchen was the first interior I'd seen when I arrived in Gardenia. It looked the same but the smell was delightful: roasted nuts, freshly baked bread and delightful warmth.

Grace was standing by the kitchen counter wearing a floor-length red dress. The material was tight around her stomach that revealed, without question or mystery, the fact that she was very pregnant.

'Hello, Gavin,' she said with a kind smile. 'I didn't expect you to come back.'

I smiled at her. She looked utterly stunning, there was something about the bloom of colour in her face that made her almost impossibly radiant.

'Hello, Grace,' I said. 'I never expected to be back. But here I am.'

'And for how long will you stay?' she asked, the faintest smile playing on her beautiful lips.

'Until the next anomaly, I am now equipped with a greater understanding and better technology to navigate through time,' I said, trying to sound calm and all-knowing. In truth I had barely grasped any of the concepts Theda and Brad had spent so many hours trying to explain.

'Do you know when the next anomaly is?' asked Grace.

'I'm not sure right now, I'd have to check my instruments but it should be quite soon.'

'And where will you go?'

'Back home,' I said, 'back to 2011, where I belong.'

'Back to your wife,' she stated and turned away from me.

'Well, yes, that's where I belong. I'm a bit of a fish out of water here,' I said, hoping she would look back at me.

'And are you well?' she asked without looking.

'Yeah, fine, pretty good actually. I've only just woken.'

'I know,' she said and then walked toward me and gave me a soft kiss on the cheek. 'It's nice to see you.'

She returned to the kitchen counter, picked up a large steel pot and put it on the table along with some steel mugs.

'I have just made some breakfast baps and Henry has made the most delicious strawberry jam, would you care to join us?'

'I grew the strawberries myself,' said Henry, putting a large steel container on the table. 'I collected 26 kilos of them so I produced really a lot of jam. Everyone loves my jam.'

'Sounds excellent,' I said and sat down at the table. I stood up again immediately and said, 'Can I do anything to help?'

I think I must have done this because an inner alarm went off; I had sat down in the expectation of being waited on by a pregnant woman. As soon as I stood up I realised that however potentially thoughtful and empathetic this original thought might have been, the result could easily be misinterpreted.

I then became aware of just how tense and uncomfortable I felt being in the same dimension, geographical zone, indeed the same kitchen, as a woman I had made pregnant but who didn't seem the least bit concerned about my role in her condition.

'Please sit,' said Grace kindly. 'It's no trouble, we have had a late start today and we're having breakfast anyway. Hallam and Mitchell will be joining us soon.'

I nodded and sat down. The awkwardness of being in Oak House came back to me at that moment. The fact that I never truly understood what was going on or who was related to whom made me feel tense.

Grace sat opposite me, next to Henry. They were both looking at me the whole time. There was a period when I would have found that extremely uncomfortable, but by the time I arrived back in Gardenia I realised how much I'd changed. I was intrigued by their rather peculiar manners but I wasn't upset or uncomfortable. I stared back.

I took a sip of the sweet black tea Grace had given me and I was transported back to the first moment I realised I had flown through time. I could almost sense the very frightened and confused man I was back then, battling to make sense of a world gone insane. Now I felt a lot older and wiser, and more importantly, calmer inside.

'So, how are you, Grace?' I asked after a long silence.

'I'm very well,' she said.

'And when is your baby due?'

I had gone over this question in my mind a few times to make sure I structured it in the right way. Not 'our baby' or even 'the baby' but very specifically 'your baby'.

'In February next year,' she said. 'Henry is very excited about having a baby sister.'

'I am,' said Henry flatly.

I was a little confused by his response. At first I couldn't judge the tone. Was he genuinely happy about it or was he saying what was expected of him and actually he was dreading it? I watched him spread strawberry jam on a warm lump of bread. He was happy about it, I could sense it from the relaxed movements of his hands.

'That's great,' I said.

'Thank you,' said Grace staring right into my eyes. I knew she was thanking me for the baby. A few mildly comical quips came to mind immediately but I didn't say any of them.

'One of the things I've learned since I've been away is that when I get back home, back to 2011, I won't be able to remember anything that has happened to me.'

'You won't be able to remember?'

'No, nothing. It's to do with the human brain, and electricity and the way the power surges affect your synapses. I'm not going to pretend I understood all I was told but so far everything my friends in the other dimensions explained to me has turned out to be true. I was told to dive at 48 degrees through the anomaly and I would come out in Gardenia. That is exactly what I did and here I am. To get back to Kingham in 2011 I have to climb at 42 degrees as I enter the anomaly, but when I pass through the cloud back to 2011 every experience I'll have had will be sort of burned out of my brain.'

'That's very sad,' said Grace.

'Does that mean you won't remember me?' asked Henry.

'I'm afraid it does, Henry,' I said. 'You see, where I come from, or more specifically when I come from, you don't exist yet, so remembering you is defying some of the very basic laws of physics. At least that's what I understand.'

'I see, but do you want to remember what you've seen and where you've been?' asked Grace.

'Well I've kind of got used to the idea of forgetting, but now you ask, yes, I'd love to.'

‘Can you record everything and take the information with you?’

I sat in silence for a moment. This idea had never crossed my mind and I felt rather stupid.

‘I don’t know.’

‘Surely if you can survive the journey, if your drone can survive, then maybe something else can survive, a record of your experiences?’

‘Well, yeah, I suppose so,’ I said. ‘It might work, it’s worth a try.’

‘You could write it in letters on paper and make a book,’ said Henry. ‘I’m doing a history project and making an old-fashioned book at the moment, I could show you how to make letters with a marker and paper.’

‘I think Gavin knows how to do that already, Henry,’ said Grace kindly.

‘Do you?’ asked Henry. He seemed very doubtful that someone as thick and old-fashioned as me would be able to complete such a task.

‘Yes I do. When I was a child everyone had to learn how to write by hand as much as use a keyboard.’

‘A keyboard?’

‘Letter press,’ said Grace. Henry looked at her and nodded his understanding.

‘If you just recorded everything you have seen, maybe writing on paper is the safest way to transport it. Then you could at least have a record. You never know, reading it might help you recall things, or even people that you came to know.’

I took a bite from my freshly baked bap piled up with Henry’s strawberry jam. I stared at Grace and thought about it as I chewed. When Grace said ‘people that I came to know’, I knew that she was referring to herself. She wanted me to remember her and I found that quite reassuring.

‘I don’t have anything to write on, or to write with,’ I said.

'Andrew showed me how to make paper for my old-fashioned book,' said Henry. 'I'm sure he'd show you.'

'Andrew?'

'I'll introduce you,' said Henry confidently. 'He's a very old man who lives at Goldacre most of the time. I'm sure you've seen him.'

'Okay then, that's a project. I'm going to write it all down,' I said.

At that point the door opened and Hallam and Mitchell walked in. From their demeanour they had already heard I'd arrived.

'Gavin Meckler, well I never did!' said Hallam. 'How wonderful that you're back. I've been hearing so many stories, everyone in the gardens is full of news about you.'

'Oh dear,' I said, in mock embarrassment. 'I hope you're not bored already.'

Mitchell shook my hand very warmly. 'It's wonderful to see you, Gavin, you look very well, although a little thin.'

I noticed that the moment Mitchell let go of my hand Grace reached out and took his; she then stood by him holding on to it. It wasn't a big statement, but it was unmistakable; she was with Mitchell and I wasn't part of her life.

Of course that is how it should have been, but I cannot lie and say I didn't feel pangs. To have met a woman like Grace was enough of an honour; to make love to her night after night and make her pregnant was up to that point the most wonderful thing that had ever happened to me.

I realise that doesn't say much about my feelings for Beth, in fact it makes me sound like a right rogue, but it is one of the most wonderful things, not 'the' most wonderful. I just mean it's right up there in a cluster at the top.

My time in Oak House was intense. We talked for hours. Okay, they asked questions and I talked. I told them about London and Rio, and the massive ships and the Weaver Women,

I told them about the clouds and the culverts and the incredible scientific understanding of the people in other dimensions and even the far future.

My parting from the lovely old kitchen was brief and informal. I knew I'd see them all again before my return home, but I also knew that I would never have quite the same experience I'd had as I followed Henry through the rain to the front door.

I had been so full of expectation and eagerness to see Grace again, I had seen her and she was more wonderful than I remembered, but also even more distant. I was a potential problem for her and I really didn't want to be that.

My return journey to Goldacre Hall was therefore much more subdued and calm. I was not meant to be with Grace, I did not belong. It wasn't hard to understand, she wanted another child and for whatever reason Mitchell was unable to fulfil that role. However things were arranged in Gardenia, it was obviously perfectly acceptable for her to use me as a surrogate father and I had to accept the role. I mean it wasn't as if I'd been digging ditches in the mud or slaughtering pigs. Making a baby with Grace had been a fairly amazing job.

32

HE MORE TIME I SPENT WITH HENRY, THE MORE I realised the kids of Gardenia were almost ridiculously mature. He seemed to know everything.

'I'm glad you're my new sister's father,' Henry said calmly as we walked through the slightly lighter rain. The ground underfoot was very soggy and I was glad to be wearing the wonder boots that Noshi had given me.

'Oh, right. I'm very happy about that, too,' I said, having no idea if that was the appropriate response.

'Grace told me you were to be the father when you first arrived in the summer.'

'Oh, right, yes, of course,' I said.

So that could only mean long before anything had happened between myself and Grace, she had already made the decision. She wanted a baby and I was a visiting male with no connections in her world. It made me understand my position and let go of some of the mildly sentimental feelings I'd been harbouring.

Thankfully Henry was walking just ahead of me, because I know my wretched eyebrows would have given away my astonishment. They were up and down like a Geiger counter on a windy day in Chernobyl.

We arrived at Goldacre Hall and Henry walked straight in. I followed him through this very familiar building until he turned through a door I was certain I'd never noticed previously.

In a room that ran along the south side of the house with floor to ceiling windows along one side, I realised I'd only ever seen it from the outside. I knew at once where we were as regards the floor plan of the house, I had walked past the outside on many occasions, I remembered seeing curtains drawn across the windows during the summer. I now assumed this was to protect all the books from strong sunlight.

With the curtains drawn back it was light and a rather wonderful space. On the opposite side to the windows were thousands of books on shelves going all the way up to the ceiling. There was a ladder mechanism at the far end of the room and high up on the ladder a quite ludicrously old man was putting books back on the shelves.

'Gavin wants to make some paper,' said Henry very seriously. 'He's going to write a book with letters so he can remember everything before the increased electrical activity in the anomaly removes all the synapses containing his experiences with us and in the general multiverse.'

I was looking at Henry as he spoke, barely able to believe what my ears were hearing. He was a little kid who'd taken all that in.

We waited in silence for old Andrew to descend. It could have been ten minutes, he moved so slowly.

'Sorry for the delay,' he croaked when he got to the floor. 'Doesn't do to rush things at my age. I'm 129, you know.'

I smiled at him. He moved to a long table that ran down the centre of the room, leaned on it and caught his breath.

'So, you want to make some paper. Well, it takes time. I don't know how long you have, Gavin. I might suggest you use one of the paper books I've already made.'

He pulled out a drawer in the side of the long table, which revealed numerous beautiful books that looked as if they were bound in leather.

'I made these 50 or so years back, these are the last few remaining. It would be an honour if you'd take one of these on your travels.'

He picked one of the books up and handed it to me. It was heavy but as soon as I touched it I understood the cover was not leather but rather a form of carbon material that looked a little like animal skin.

'Oh wow,' I said. 'I'm not sure I can take this from you. It's the most beautiful book I've ever seen.'

It took him a few seconds to lift his arm and pat me on the shoulder. 'I'm 129 years old. I can barely see, it takes me an hour to get up in the morning, I don't really have any need for it, and look,' he said, pointing to the remaining books in the large drawer, 'I've got plenty. You take it, Gavin, oh, and here.'

Again I had to wait some time for him to slowly turn and open a much smaller drawer in the big table. Inside this was a dark blue velvet bag. I watched as he very slowly extracted a black stick from the bag and handed it to me.

'You'll know what this is.'

I inspected it, a perfectly smooth black stick with rounded ends.

'It's a pen,' he said, 'to make marks on paper. It is good for about three million letters so you should be able to write your book with that.'

'Thank you,' I said.

So for the next three weeks I spent the mornings working with Hallam and Mitchell in the gardens and the afternoons writing my memoirs.

It has been hard work preparing all the vegetable beds for winter, cutting back hedges and moving boxes of produce in one or other of the store barns.

I also worked in the kitchen with William and found preparing food for a hundred people to be so much easier than cooking for two.

I had William to talk to and that made things a great deal easier to cope with. His understanding of the human mind, of the way we think and react, was a great help to me.

However, the most peaceful and rewarding time was spent alone in my little room at the top of the house.

It took me a while to get used to the activity of writing in longhand. My handwriting was appalling at first and I really had to concentrate to make my hand form the letters correctly.

However, after a few days the process became more relaxed and I scrawled these many pages.

This was helped in part by the extraordinary pen that Andrew had given me; the way it glided across the beautiful paper made the experience easier and pushed me to try and write my words more carefully. The line it created was very satisfying and I wrote more slowly but far more carefully because of it.

The process slowed down my thoughts, allowing me to concentrate and pull the memories out one by one, recalling them all in vivid detail.

No question here, this part of my journey was the most peaceful and contemplative of any part of my wanderings. The hours I spent in the little room of a house not yet built outside a town that once existed was very fulfilling. I had no idea if I would get back to 2011, to Beth and my real life.

Being alone in the little room but knowing I was surrounded by the kindest, most accepting people I had ever met was very conducive to my writing. I knew that if I ever got stuck on a part of my increasingly densely written book I could go down to the kitchen and talk to someone.

If I never got back, if indeed I ended up staying in Gardenia until I died, I would be perfectly happy.

But that evening, just before I had finished cleaning up in the kitchen, William returned from a meeting of the elders to say that the weather forecast was indicating that there may be an anomaly before the month was out.

It was now 15th November, 2211. The next few weeks could be my last in Gardenia.

33

EEING DIDCOT POWER STATION BELOW ME WAS at the same time nothing unusual and slightly alarming. In the few seconds I'd experienced being lost in the cloud I somehow managed to turn 180 degrees and come out the way I went in.

I'd experienced no sense of turning. I know I hadn't guided the Yuneec in a turn and I knew enough about basic aeronautics to know that completing a 180 degree turn with zero visibility in a matter of seconds was not remotely possible.

Therefore seeing Didcot Power Station made no sense and caused me to express my mental turmoil in a long list of expletives.

I was screaming questions at myself. How could this possibly happen? I knew, I was certain beyond any doubt, that I had flown past Didcot going south and now I was flying past it again heading north.

I knew nothing had happened as far as the sky above Didcot in 2011 was concerned. I had been in the thick cloud for a few seconds, the only disconcerting thing was the turn around and the machine I was flying in.

I had been flying along quite happily in a 2010 Yuneec E430. I somehow got sucked up into a bizarre and frightening cloud formation and I came out a second or two later, heading in a different direction in a completely different machine.

I screamed in shock when I glanced down at the controls. Everything was different. It was better, there's no doubt about that, but it was impossibly different.

Although at that moment I had absolutely no recall of anything other than flying, cloud, turning 180 degrees, a new machine and lots of screaming, I knew something had happened. I had a headache, my neck felt stiff, my eyes were incredibly tired and I felt a bit sick.

I was in a proper panic but this was tempered by the fact that I was in an incredible aeroplane.

Breathing rapidly and shouting, 'Oh fuck, oh fuck,' repeatedly, I banked the plane around to get a better look at what I'd just flown out of. As the cloud formation came into view it started to drift apart. It sort of broke up into smaller bits of cloud and long strands of mist until the overall formation of this cloud tower had all but dispersed.

Although the pitch, yaw and direction of the controls were effectively the same, the throttle control had gone. Instead, as I soon discovered, I was controlling the power with a smooth slider control under my thumb.

How did I know to do that? And how on earth did this thing accelerate so incredibly powerfully? As I pushed the slider gently upward I started to climb at what felt like fighter jet speed.

Up until a few seconds earlier, I had been flying what was virtually an experimental light aircraft with limited speed and range.

Now I was in some incredible machine that could have competed in the Red Bull aerobatic competition and possibly won. I had never flown anything so powerful. Before I knew it, I was, according to the incredibly detailed display on the dash in front of me, at 22,000 feet and climbing fast.

I should have passed out. The Yuneec wasn't pressurised and yet I felt no change in cabin pressure. I noticed the little window in the pilot's door had changed; there was no longer a slide back section. It was a pressurised cabin and clearly the altitude this machine could reach was beyond belief.

Thankfully at that moment my senses came back to me and I levelled out and started to descend as calmly as I could. I had entered commercial airspace and was going to get into a lot of trouble.

Twenty-two thousand feet in a single-engined, battery-powered plane is barking mad. It could not happen.

Once I'd dropped to 10,000 feet, I flicked something with my right thumb. A small light appeared on the dash, a symbol of two human hands waving.

I didn't know what it meant, but guessing, I gingerly and briefly let go of the controls. The Yuneec stayed true, flying level and fast at 10,000 feet, due south.

I screamed again as I glanced to my left to see a wooden box carefully strapped into the passenger seat.

That hadn't been there before. I went through the same deep breathing routine to try and calm down. Having a panic attack while in control of an aircraft flying over a densely populated area is frowned upon by aviation authorities worldwide. I leaned over and saw that the box was full of things: books, clothes that looked weird and on the far side, my iPad.

I reached over and pulled it out. It looked the same; at least the iPad hadn't changed into something weird. I pressed the top button to see if it had any charge. It came on at once and had a full battery. I felt my face flicker. There was some dull recall but it made my head hurt. I knew the battery shouldn't be at 100 per cent, I was certain it hadn't been full when I'd taken off.

I opened the satnav app and after a couple of moments as the iPad searched for a signal it located me over Blewbury, just south of Didcot.

I dithered again as I realised the mount I put my iPad on had disappeared.

Another scream and torrent of expletives.

In fact so much of what had been in the Yuneec cockpit only moments before that point had completely disappeared.

I was wearing the same clothes, but when I glanced down and saw my feet I almost jumped out of the cockpit door. I was wearing orange and blue boots that looked like no shoes I'd ever seen and I knew I hadn't been wearing them moments before.

Before what?

Something had happened while I was in the weird cloud but I had no clue as to what. My iPad was charged to 100 per cent, I was in a totally different plane that was incredibly powerful and I was wearing blue and orange boots I'd never seen before.

I checked the satnav again and I was already over Compton – I was travelling at a previously impossible speed.

My hands started searching for my comms headphones. I needed to contact air traffic control, I needed help.

No comms headphones, as my eyes darted around the cockpit. There was no air-to-ground radio, no nothing. This time the panic was palpable, my whole body was shaking uncontrollably.

This was worse than any nightmare I'd ever had. I was in some bizarre machine that I didn't understand and yet moments earlier I'd been flying it as if it was second nature.

Phone.

If I got low enough I could get a signal and call someone.

I craned my head around looking for somewhere relatively safe to fly low. I reduced speed as much as I dared and descended over a busy road. By this stage I had no idea where I was and cared even less about it. I needed help and fast.

My hand scrabbled around in the wooden box and finally found my phone. It was charged up and searching for a signal.

Ping. Five bars! Excellent.

With one hand I scrolled through my enormous address book. I needed Ed.

I pressed call and waited, switched to speakerphone and heard it ringing.

'Yay, Gav, wassaaaaaap!'

Ed had generally annoyed me since I'd met him two years earlier, but his jolly response made me almost scream with joy.

'Ed, really need your help, mate,' I said.

'Name it, old chap,' he replied, his speech just slightly slurred.

'I'm flying the Yuneec, except it isn't the Yuneec. Something very fucking bizarre has just happened. I can't explain. Where are you?'

'I'm in the Falkland Arms, mate, having a lunchtime pint. You should drop in.'

'I can't,' I shouted. 'I'm not sure I can land.'

'Where are you?' he asked, his tone finally changed to something resembling concern.

'Just south of Didcot, I don't know, I've got no air-to-ground. I'm stuffed. I need you to guide me back to Enstone.'

'Wait, you're calling me from your plane? You're in the air!'

'Only just in the air,' I shouted. I dropped the phone into my lap at that point as I had to gain altitude rather rapidly as I was approaching some power lines.

Once I was over them I picked up the phone. 'I'm flying at about 50 feet at the moment so I get a signal, there's no time to explain. Get in that bloody kite of yours and head south, keep your phone on you.'

'What?' said Kevin. 'But I'm —'

'Kev, this is life or death, mate, I'll make it up to you.'

The line went dead. I don't know if Kevin hung up or I lost signal. I checked the phone and knew it was the latter.

I climbed and turned hard, heading north as fast as I could. That action gave me a bit of a shock. The Yuneec was anything but a performance plane. Whatever it was I was sitting in pulled a tighter turn and accelerated at such a powerful rate I almost blacked out. Within a breath I was travelling at over 400 miles an hour, in an electric plane, at a thousand feet.

I backed off, sliding my thumb down the control pad on the flight controls, too fast, too high and I didn't know where I was going.

I knew I was breaking all kinds of regulations by flying without being in contact with any ground control stations. I had no choice but I kept low, never going above 2,000 feet. I decided that was too high, there may be other planes at that height trying to contact me and my failure to respond might cause alarm. I dropped down as low as I dared to 200 feet.

Flying at that altitude requires a lot of concentration. Pylons, power lines, communications towers, buildings, even trees on hilltops all start to look alarmingly close.

I glanced down and saw that I was already travelling over the red rooftops of Abingdon, although I was in a state of profound confusion mixed with terror. Something happened as I looked down and saw green open space surrounded by trees and houses.

I knew it was probably just the playing field of a school, but I felt I recognised it. Maybe not the actual place, but something about the open space surrounded by buildings made me feel peculiar.

I ignored the feeling, I had plenty of things to feel peculiar about. My shoes for one thing. Where the hell had they come from?

I wriggled my toes inside them just to make sure I still had toes. I did have toes, but that didn't give me much relief.

Something caught my eye on my left-hand side. An airfield. Of course! Abingdon airfield. Maybe I could land there. I knew it was used as a test track for cars and you could go there on weekends and have a track day experience for a few hundred quid.

I banked over to have a closer look. It would be so easy to land, a great big World War II runway with no trees or power lines anywhere near it. But what would I do when I landed? I wouldn't know how to explain myself, I wouldn't have permission.

I circled the airfield a couple of times, all the while scanning the sky for other light aircraft. At this height I needed to keep a constant eye out for gliders, light planes and microlights.

I levelled out and continued heading north. I decided to skirt around Oxford to the west, I didn't want to attract attention by flying low over heavily built-up areas.

I kept glancing at the incredible display the Yuneec had suddenly developed; there were so many indicators glowing at me but I didn't know what they meant. I was looking for something that might give me an indication of the state of charge left in the batteries. I know I hadn't been worried about it when I went into the cloud, but I couldn't remember exactly what it was. One thing was certain, this sudden and dramatic increase in the capacity of the motor must be draining the hell out of them.

I needed Ed and I needed him fast. I picked up my phone. Thirty-five minutes had passed since I spoke to him. I tried to calculate how long it would take him to get from the Falkland Arms in Great Tew to Enstone Airfield, take the wraps off his microlight, get in the air and head toward me.

The answer was simple: longer than 35 minutes.

34

WAS FLYING VERY LOW OVER WATER THAT I knew from previous flights to be the collection of old flooded gravel pits between Stanton Harcourt and Standlake, just west of the city of Oxford.

Finally my phone buzzed. It was a text from Ed.

'Just north of oxfd. Wher U?'

I knew this was the first text I'd ever received from a man flying a microlight, but I still don't know how he managed to send it.

I started to scan around the fields and lakes below. I had to put the Yuneec down somewhere we could both land.

I gained altitude with alarming speed and circled around above the village of Standlake. I knew the area vaguely as I'd been to a pub called the Rose Revived that was on the river at Newbridge. Something about seeing the river meander through the fields seemed bizarrely familiar but I couldn't work out why.

Of course it was familiar, it was England. I'd flown over this area a dozen times before, but this felt different. My eyes went a bit fuzzy and I rubbed them with the back of my hand. I couldn't understand why I felt so tired.

Alongside the river a little way upstream of Newbridge was a flat area of pasture; short grass, no power lines and it looked fairly smooth and solid.

I dropped down and flew low overhead.

There was a string of high-voltage power lines running across the fields and lakes in the distance, but if you approached the field from the south-east they weren't a problem.

The other advantage was the lack of houses, farms or people anywhere near the field.

One more circuit and I slowed right down and brought the Yuneec in to land.

It was very easy, the land was flat and there were no cows in the field. The reason I suspected there normally were cows was the preponderance of cowpats that I splatted through as I came to a halt.

I pulled the thumb slide power controller all the way down and as the propeller span down I got yet another eye-popping shock.

The propellers weren't solid. The last few turns revealed that they were made of something floppy. As the rotation slowed they looked a bit like wet towels. They eventually flopped down and simply hung from the central hub.

'Jesus Lord Almighty,' I think I said.

My mouth hung open as I sat motionless. I had just been in the air, travelling at previously unimagined speed, being pulled along by floppy blades.

I rested my head back and stared in disbelief at the rather nice padding on the roof of the cockpit. That looked different too but by this time I was losing my mind.

I felt incredibly tired all of a sudden. I shook myself, got out of the Yuneec and looked at it from a distance. Other than the splats of cow poo thrown up by the landing wheels it looked pretty much the same. I checked my phone, I had one bar of signal left so I sent a text back to Ed with a description of my position complete with some map coordinates I got off my iPad.

'Field, near Thames, South of Standlake 51 degrees 42'38.7 North, 1 degree 26'31.7 West.'

I stood motionless in the field. I could hear a sheep baa-ing, I could hear birds and in the distance traffic rumbling along the A415. Everything seemed normal and yet I was totally confused. I'd been flying to a meeting in Basingstoke and now I was standing in a field by the Thames in Oxfordshire.

I walked back to the Yuneec after a few moments and leant

into the cockpit to get a look inside the box that had somehow appeared while I was flying in the cloud.

It was carefully strapped into the passenger seat – someone had strapped it in, and I was bloody sure it wasn't me.

It contained some weird-looking rags. I pulled them up to see it was a ridiculously lightweight kind of body stocking. I'd never seen anything like it in my life. I could see it but it had no weight, it felt as if I was holding up light, there was nothing to it and yet I could see it.

Next I extracted a pair of very cool goggles and a weird backpack that contained a large old-fashioned leather-bound book.

I pulled the book out of the bag and opened it. It was crammed full of really small and neat handwriting. My handwriting.

As my eyes stared at the densely filled pages, I felt my legs give way and I was suddenly sitting on the grass next to a cowpat feeling decidedly worse for wear.

How had this book appeared and where had it appeared from? And when, for goodness' sake, had I written it?

I don't know how much time had passed, I can't really remember, but something pulled me out of my shock-induced stupor. I remembered the damn meeting in Basingstoke and my whole body shook as if I'd just heard a gun go off close by. I checked my phone again. I was already late, there was no way I could get there in time.

I sent a text to Mike Rogers at Tempus Engineering who was hosting the get-together.

'Very sorry, Mike, severe technical difficulties have made my arrival impossible. Will call soonest. Apologies to all.'

As soon as I'd sent the text the phone buzzed.

'I C U.'

It was from Ed. I scanned the horizon and couldn't see anything, the sky was relatively clear although there was a low-lying haze. Then I heard the unmistakable sound of a Verner Scarlett mini 3, the engine on Ed's microlight. Moments later I saw him teetering about in the sky. Microlights had never appealed to me, a bit too much like riding a bike. Okay on a sunny day if you're not too high, freezing cold and wet at any other time.

A minute later he landed at the far end of the field and taxied toward me, stopping just by the wing of the Yuneec.

Once the engine stopped he climbed out and took off his helmet.

His grin was enormous.

'What the living fuck is going on?' he asked. 'This is mad. It was a bloody million-to-one chance I'd be around, I was meant to be in Mayfair today but everything was cancelled last night.'

Ed was a consultant. I never knew what that meant, I certainly never saw him doing consulting. I'd seen him play the guitar, which he did quite well, but he never claimed to be a musician. I knew he was mates with Alex James, the man who makes cheese at a local farm who used to be in a band called Blur, but that was the full extent of my knowledge. I also knew he didn't really need to work, not for money. Ed never needed money.

'Okay, this is mad, right. Prepare for your brain to melt,' I said as we walked toward the Yuneec.

'Does it look any different to you?'

'What?'

'The Yuneec. It looks the same, right?'

Ed didn't say anything, he just looked a bit worried.

'Check out the flight controls.'

He looked into the cockpit, he stayed silent a moment longer then turned slowly to me.

'What the living fuck has happened?' he said eventually. 'When did you do this?'

'I didn't do anything.'

'What d'you mean? This is totally different, where are the dials, where's, well, everything?'

'I don't know!' I squealed.

'It's just flat glass, how the fuck d'you know where you are?'

'Watch,' I said. I put my hand on the flat black dash and immediately the whole thing lit up, coordinates, speed, altitude, pitch, yaw, engine speed, G reading, everything.

Ed walked backwards away from the cockpit. He banged his head on the wing strut and stood rubbing it.

'Get the fuck out of here, Gavin, what the fuck?'

I walked toward Ed and stared right into his eyes. Even as I was doing it I knew I would have found this impossible before I'd flown into the cloud.

'Listen, and listen really carefully,' I said. 'I don't know what's happened, I really want you to understand that this is as fucked up for me as it is for you. I take off this morning, I'm flying to Blackbushe, I see this weird cloud over Didcot, I start to skirt around it, I end up in it, I fly out of it a few seconds later facing the way I came. I didn't turn, I didn't do anything and the bloody Yuneec is totally changed, it flies like a Spitfire, it's so fast I can barely control it, I look on the passenger seat and there's a box full of weird stuff strapped next to me and I'm wearing freaky boots. You tell me.'

Ed looked down at my feet.

'The fuck,' was all he could say.

'Ed, listen, seriously, I don't know what the hell is going on,' I said. 'All I know is I have no radio and I don't want to get in to trouble with the CAA. I want to get back to Enstone, get this thing in a hangar, go home and lie down for about a month.'

'The fuck,' said Ed, almost to himself. 'This is seriously fucked up.'

'I know, but that really isn't helping,' I pleaded. 'Will you fly with me back to Enstone, will you shadow me and explain to ground control?'

Ed was just staring at me with bloodshot eyes.

'Tell them my radio's packed up. You'll have to fly behind me and inform Enstone control that I'm coming into land. But don't make too big a deal out of it or they'll all come snooping.'

Ed didn't respond for a moment.

'Ed, did you hear me?' I asked quietly.

He nodded, still looking at the Yuneec. 'Yeah, yeah, have you seen the lump?'

I followed his gaze and saw that indeed the underside of the Yuneec had changed shape. There was a perfectly smooth extra lump beneath the cockpit. It looked so much part of the plane and I'd been in such a state with the book discovery that I hadn't noticed it.

'What is it?' he asked.

'No idea. I don't know what's going on. I can't find a battery gauge, it just flies.' Then I remembered the floppy propeller blades.

'I'll tell you why I didn't notice the lump, look at this.'

I grabbed the shoulder of Ed's flight jacket and pulled him to the front of the plane.

Three strips of soft material hung down from the prop hub. I lifted one up, it was heavy but somehow I was expecting that. Once again I felt my vision fade and come back. I thought I was going to faint.

'Have you ever seen anything like it?'

'The fuck,' said Ed.

'They work, they work really well. The power this thing has is off the scale, Ed, seriously, it's really powerful now.'

'What are those?' he asked.

'I don't know, I didn't notice anything different about them until I killed the motor.'

Ed reached forward and gingerly touched one of the dangling propellers. 'What's it made of?' he asked eventually.

'Don't know. The whole thing is a freakish mystery,' I said. 'That's why I want to hide it at the back of your hangar at Enstone. Come on, let's get in the air before some irate farmer arrives to see what's going on.'

Once again I grabbed Ed's jacket and started pulling him toward his microlight.

I encouraged him to climb into the pilot's seat by pushing him. I handed him his helmet that was lying on the grass where he'd dropped it.

'I'll spin it over, ready?' I asked.

Eventually Ed nodded and I walked to the rear of the craft, grabbed the wooden propeller and gave it as big a turn as I could manage. The engine fired up right away and I closed my eyes until I got out of the wash.

I hand-gestured for him to turn and take off the way he'd landed, the power lines were too close the other way and I didn't think Ed was firing on all cylinders. He seemed to be more bamboozled about the Yuneec than I was and my head was spinning.

I climbed into the cockpit and strapped in, shoved everything back in the box beside me, put my hand on the flat black dash and watched as everything pinged to life.

I then applied my thumb to the power control and the floppy blades started to spin up, very quickly returning to their fully extended shape.

I hard-turned the Yuneec at about quarter power, which was already too much. The plane lurched forward with such force I nearly lost control. I could see the field before me and I watched Ed take to the air, and the sight was a great relief. I half expected to see him still sat in the grounded microlight with his mouth hanging open.

As soon as I was lined up I pushed the power upwards, probably no more than half but due to the incredible power of the motor and the ever extending sweep of the flexible propellers I rocketed forward with neck-breaking rapidity.

Before I was halfway prepared, I was airborne and rapidly catching up with Ed. I backed off on the power slightly, going well to his right so as not to cause too much of a shock.

We both banked to the right and turned to face north, then I opened up a bit and overtook him with such ease it was ridiculous. In the Yuneec that I'd flown into the cloud I'd have been hard-pressed to fly faster than Ed, in this Yuneec it was hard to fly slowly enough.

I slowed down again and dropped to my right. Once I'd levelled up with Ed I pulled in as close as I could.

We were still only at about 500 feet and I wanted to fly higher, I didn't want people seeing us from the ground. I could see Ed looking over toward me as I flew beside him. I motioned to him as best I could, pointing upwards. I then climbed steeply to 3,000 feet and levelled out, looking around to see where he was.

I couldn't see him and I knew this was dangerous; he could be behind me or below me so I had to take care. I continued to fly at around 70 miles an hour, straight and true, due north.

About five minutes later I noticed Ed pull up alongside me. I could see him talking into his headset. I guessed he was talking to a tower control of some nearby airfield.

I glanced down at the Oxfordshire countryside below. We were just crossing the A40 to the east of Witney and I could see the parkland of Blenheim Palace in the distance. At least we were heading in the right direction.

A few minutes later and I could make out the main runway at Enstone. A huge wave of relief overcame me. I kept looking around for other aircraft, which was now dangerous as any number of planes could be climbing out of the airfield and because I had no radio I had no idea where they might be. I could only hope that Ed's communication with Enstone ground control had warned them I was flying blind.

I slowly started to descend as we got closer. I was hoping all along that Ed was well behind me, it was very basic CAA rules that the plane with radio contact should remain behind the craft with no comms, keeping it in sight at all times. It made sense for the plane with the radio, it made life very hard for someone with no clue as to what was going on.

I peered out to my right to make sure Ed wasn't around. I couldn't see him and the sky seemed clear. I then banked hard to the right and climbed. Within a heartbeat I was at over 3,000 feet and I could see Ed's microlight flying toward the runway.

I turned again and circled around him. I was dizzy with excitement and kind of lost the plot, the joy of the power and manoeuvrability of the Yuneec made it almost impossible not to show off.

I levelled off just behind him and watched him glide down to the runway. I then turned again with the intention of getting into position to come into land. However, it seemed like a second or two later I could see Chipping Norton on my right – that was a good four or five miles away. I glanced down at the dash; I was doing 370 miles per hour.

I slowed, turned and started my descent. By the time I reached the runway I could see Ed waiting on the side, standing next to his microlight with a phone in his hands. As I landed and slowed I realised he'd been filming my descent on his Nexus S.

Once I had slowed to a crawl, I made my way to Ed's hangar on the far side of the airfield, thankfully as far away from the flying club building as it was possible to get.

I was hoping there weren't going to be too many people hanging around.

I passed a neat row of stationary aircraft parked on the side of the taxiway and turned into the big hangar.

No one.

I slid the power controller to off, waited for a few seconds for the motor to stop spinning and breathed out.

I was back.

35

SAT IN THE CORNER OF THE HANGAR FOR some time. In fact I think I may have dozed off.

Someone kicked my foot.

'Gav, wake up, mate.' It was Ed.

I looked up groggily. 'What is it?'

'What's going on?' he asked. His microlight was nowhere to be seen, he was standing in front of me wearing a T-shirt and jeans. 'Why are you sleeping?'

'I don't know,' I mumbled, my mouth feeling like it was full of dead stuff.

Ed rubbed his hands over his face. 'Look, this is all too weird. We've got to get the freak Yuneec under wraps, mate.'

'I know.' I groaned as I slowly got back on my feet.

Ed walked to the back of the large hangar and started hauling a huge sheet of dusty material toward the Yuneec.

'Loads of people are going to turn up for a fly after lunch, you know that.'

I yawned and stumbled toward him.

'I feel like I've got jet lag,' I said.

'Gimme a hand you fuckwit,' said Ed, and he started to unfurl the large sheet of cloth. 'If people see that prop, well, I just don't want to be around. What the fuck have you done to this plane?'

'I haven't done anything.'

'Mate, that thing,' said Ed pointing toward the Yuneec, 'that thing flies like a Spitfire. It's so fucking fast, it used to be the most puny little toy, now it's a fucking fighter jet. How did you do it?'

I grabbed the opposite end of the large sheet and started to drag it over the Yuneec.

'I didn't do anything. I flew into a weird low-level cloud, came out again and it was all different.'

'Yeah, right,' said Ed. 'Bloody aliens did it.'

'Yes,' I nodded, 'that's right, aliens did it, Ed, that's really helpful.'

With a bit of a struggle we covered the Yuneec and before long it looked like all the other planes in the hanger, covered in sheets and parked up.

'I just spent half an hour in the control tower with old Ron trying to explain,' said Ed when we'd wrapped the Yuneec as best we could. 'He saw your aerobatics when we were coming in to land. I managed to bluff over it, it's just as well Ron is a bit thick, but he wants to know what happened to your radio.'

'I want to know what happened to it. It's not in the plane. Everything's changed. I've just flown something like 150 miles at speeds I could never have hoped to achieve before and for whatever reason the batteries are still good. Well, I think they're good, there's no charge port and no battery level monitor. It just flies. What am I supposed to think?'

'You look like shit, too,' said Ed.

'Thanks,' I replied, rubbing my face to try and wake up. 'I'm supposed to be at a meeting in Basingstoke. Everything's gone tits up.'

I lifted part of the cover and leant into the cockpit, pulled the odd assortment of things out of the wooden box in the Yuneec cockpit and walked out of the hangar.

The sun was bright outside, I could hear the distant buzz of light aircraft engines, everything was normal and yet it felt weird. The noise hurt my ears.

I followed Ed across the grass to where his microlight was parked. Next to it was his battered old Land Rover. I had never discovered, and I still don't know what Ed actually does for a living. Beth says he's a trustafarian, whatever that is. He has a lovely house outside Oddington, he has his microlight, his old Landy and a few classic cars he keeps in a barn.

'Get in, I'll take you home,' said Ed as he started up the rattling old diesel engine. The noise of the thing made my ears actually hurt.

I climbed in the passenger seat and strapped myself in. Ed doesn't drive his Land Rover like a farmer, he drives it like a man who wants to die young.

I found the noise quite distressing and uncomfortable. I'd been in it before but when he started it up that time the noise really grated against my eardrums.

We drove the few miles from Enstone Airfield to Kingham, through the middle of Chipping Norton, which was busy with a farmers' market. Of course, the farmers' market was on.

I didn't say anything on the journey and neither did Ed, there was nothing to say.

I thanked him profusely when he dropped me outside the house and he roared off down the road leaving a haze of dirty grey smoke behind him.

As the noise died down I turned and faced our house. It looked weird and yet it hadn't been more than a couple of hours since I left.

I found my key among the stuff in the box and let myself in.

'Beth?' I called when I closed the front door behind me. Nothing. My voice seemed to echo around the small interior.

I had a piss, washed my face, went upstairs and looked in at my office. It was all just the same as when I'd left. I pondered for a moment, I could switch everything on and check my e-mails, but I was sure my eyes wouldn't stay open.

A few moments later I must have collapsed on the bed because when I woke up, I discovered it was the following day.

After stumbling about in a state of profound confusion I ascertained that Beth had been in the house, she'd slept in the spare bed but I hadn't heard a thing.

I had a shower, got some clean clothes on and went down to the kitchen. It was very tidy, which was a relief. Beth had a tendency to 'leave it for later' when she went to work that had grated with me in the past. This time I was almost disappointed that it wasn't messier.

I made myself a cup of tea, sat at the kitchen table and looked out onto our small garden and the long wall of the barn conversion.

Everything was normal and yet I felt utterly confused. I knew we'd had a row, I'd left, flown to Basingstoke, get lost in a cloud, came out and something very weird had taken place.

It was only as I sat with my cup of tea in the deep silence of our little house that I realised something must have happened, something which contradicted everything I believed in, everything I understood.

Machines don't simply reinvent themselves when they fly through clouds, they just don't. Ask anyone. It doesn't happen. And yet it had happened and I knew it had happened, the proof was currently tucked away under a tarpaulin in Ed's hanger at Enstone Airfield.

I was feeling tense, my heart started racing even though I was sitting down doing nothing. Something had happened to me but I didn't know what it was.

I checked the date on my phone. Monday 16th May, 2011. I shook my head as I looked at the date. It was correct, of course it was Monday 16th, I'd left the house on the morning of Sunday 15th, flown off, gone through the cloud, come back, fallen asleep and now it was the 16th.

I suddenly remembered the box. I couldn't remember where I'd put it, the magic wooden box that just materialised in the plane when I was in the cloud.

I wandered about the house with my cup of tea looking for it. It was only a two-bedroomed house so it didn't take long.

After not finding it anywhere obvious I went up to the small top room that we used as my office and there it was, sitting on the floor next to my desk.

I sat in my chair and looked down into it. Everything had been in it: my phone, iPad, shoes and the very strange-looking lightweight body stocking thing.

I lifted everything out and spread it around the floor. Just inexplicable, how did all this stuff get into the box? How did the box get into the Yuneec? As I was reaching for the weird boots I noticed something else in the box I hadn't seen before. Resting on the bottom was a small square of some kind of material. A handkerchief-sized square of creamy material that looked decidedly odd. Not plastic, not silk and yet it was slightly reflective. I tried to pick it up but it was so incredibly fine it just wafted away from my fingers when I put my hand near it.

I put one finger in my mouth to wet it and tried to use that to pick it up. When the damp tip of my finger got near it I thought my eyes were deceiving me. The material moved away from my finger as if it were frightened, it moved as if I was trying to push two negative poles of a magnet together.

Eventually, after drying my finger and using both hands to kind of grasp the material into a ball, I lifted it out of the box. I could only register that I had lifted it with my eyes, I couldn't feel the material with my hands. It was so fine I couldn't feel anything on my skin.

I stared at this bizarre material for a long time. I felt it was telling me something but I didn't know what.

Then my eyes fell on the book. It was lying on the floor beside me. Then I looked at the weird boots. For some reason that's still beyond me. I looked at the piece of material, then the book, then the boots and then back at the piece of material.

I think I may have been waiting for some kind of memory to be stirred by the presence of these objects. Nothing.

I picked up the book and opened it.

It was my writing. My handwriting is fairly poor which I know isn't unusual, everyone uses keyboards and no one writes by hand anymore. Well, I don't. The first few pages were very laboriously written with loads of mistakes but after about ten pages, whoever wrote it, and I can only assume it was me, got a lot better at it.

For the remainder of that day I did nothing except drink tea, urinate and read. I read the whole thing from cover to cover, constantly amazed, constantly rubbing my head trying to remember any of the events that I'd written down so carefully.

If this was some kind of hoax or practical joke it made no sense. Why would anyone go to such absurd lengths to make me, a humble engineer and scientifically minded sceptic, believe that time travel was remotely possible and that we lived in a pan-dimensional multiverse?

String theory. I beg your bloody pardon.

However, I was so engrossed I completely lost track of time and before I knew it I heard the front door open. I checked my phone, it was 5.30 in the evening.

I put the book into the bottom drawer of the filing cabinet I kept in the built-in cupboard in the top room, covered it with the weird boots I'd found myself wearing and covered that with the strange body suit.

Then I went downstairs to face the music.

Thankfully, the music was more gentle folk than thrash metal.

'Hey,' I said.

'Hello, Gavin,' replied Beth. She smiled at me. 'Sorry…'

I held up my hand to silence her, it was a gentle movement that surprised her as much as it surprised me. I looked her in the eye and it was only as I was doing so I realised how rarely I'd done this before.

'Please don't apologise. I was being a prick. I'm the one who should say sorry.'

'Oh,' said Beth, clearly taken aback by what I was saying,

 which made me surprised. To be honest, it wasn't that hard to connect with her but I'd always found it near impossible in the past.

'You're back early,' she said.

'I cancelled the meeting. I don't want to go to any more meetings.'

'Blimey, what's happened?' said Beth, not taking her eyes off me but dumping her bag on the floor near the front door. This bag dump routine used to make me quite tense. Beth was very often in the position of not knowing where her bag, phone, laptop, phone charger, keys, purse, hairbrush, glasses or any number of other vital support items were at any given time.

Now I barely noticed that the bag was right in front of the door ready to trip up the unwary visitor.

'I don't know,' I said as I followed her into the kitchen. The same kitchen where we'd had a huge row the day before, and yet the memory of that row seemed so distant.

I put it down to some kind of bug. I never normally sleep that much, and reading the book I'd clearly written hadn't helped my equilibrium.

Instead of standing by the kitchen door ready for a quick exit as I often did during moments of tension, I walked right into the kitchen and sat at the table.

'I just feel different. I don't want to work as manically as I have been. I want to take a bit of time, smell the roses.'

'Smell the roses,' Beth repeated slowly, her face lighting up with a big grin. I know I grinned back. I couldn't help it. It had been quite a while since anything I said had made Beth grin.

'Yes. I want to stand in a garden and sniff roses.'

'Gavin, you've never been in a garden, you don't know what a garden is,' she said. It was true and she was laughing as she said it, but it wasn't a cruel laugh, it was a charmed but incredulous laugh.

'I know, but I think I want to try doing things like gardening, and I'm sorry about yesterday morning,' I said. 'I was a prick.'

'No, you were your normal annoying self, but I was being a nightmare. I'm sorry too.'

I was glad I was sitting because, for all my many failings in our relationship, I always apologised and Beth never did. Well, she never did before this moment.

'I want to change things,' I said eventually. 'I want to live differently.'

'Oh dear,' said Beth. She grinned again. 'You've not had a religious experience have you?'

'No, no, nothing like that, I just want to see if I can connect with people. I know I've been difficult to live with. I know I tend to see things in a mechanical way, but, well, I had a bit of a scare in the Yuneec.'

Beth's grin disappeared. 'What happened?'

'No, nothing, nothing, I'm fine, the Yuneec's fine, I just, well, I got lost in some low-level cloud and, it's very confusing, when I managed to get out of the cloud, well, I felt different.'

Beth sat down at the small kitchen table opposite me. She tidied some bits of paper that were scattered across the table and then put her hand on mine.

'What happened?' she said flatly.

'Honestly, nothing. I wasn't in danger. I don't know how to explain it. Afterwards I just understood things a lot better. It made me tired, which is why I slept for something like 14 hours last night.'

'I know, I couldn't believe it when I got back. I came and checked, and you were out for the count. Are you feeling ill?'

'No, I'm feeling rather good actually. Hungry, but fine.'

Beth continued to look at me with a slightly concerned expression.

'You look different,' she said, 'you look older.'

That made me worry. For some reason hearing her say that made what I'd read in the book seem more credible. I had decided that there was no way I could tell anyone, even Beth, about what the book implied had happened. I knew people would think I was barking mad and also, I had no memory of any of it. Reading the descriptions of the places I went to and the people I met did not jolt a single memory. I had absolutely no recall of anything.

'I feel a bit different. It's very weird,' I said, 'but I think it's best if we don't tell anyone. I don't want to have to explain to people because it sounds like I've gone a bit loopy. I flew into a cloud and came out and I was different. It doesn't sound good does it?'

'Well, it sounds mad. I mean you are a bit…'

'I'm a little bit on the autistic side, I know,' I said.

Beth grinned again. 'Wow. You've never, ever said that before.'

'Haven't I?'

'No.'

'D'you think I'm a little bit autistic then?'

'Well…' Beth sighed deeply and pulled her chin back, which wasn't her best look. 'I suppose some people would say you were on the mild end of the autistic spectrum.'

'There you go,' I said, sitting back and grinning at her.

She let go of my hand and stood up.

'I haven't been shopping, I don't suppose…'

'I haven't set foot outside the house all day,' I said.

'D'you want to go and get something to eat?'

'Yes,' I said.

'Wait. You, Gavin, are prepared to go out, to go to a pub or a restaurant and eat, with me?'

'Yeah, I'd love to,' I said.

'Wow, you really have changed,' said Beth. She walked out of the kitchen shaking her head and singing. Beth only sings when she's in a very good mood.

36

T'S NOW EXACTLY A YEAR TO THE DAY SINCE MY flight through the cloud and a few things have changed in our lives.

Beth says I've changed beyond all recognition but I think she's changed quite a bit, too.

However, the biggest change is the one sleeping next to me at the moment. My three-month-old daughter.

She's called Grace.

After I had repeatedly read the book I accept I must have written somewhere, somehow, it seemed an appropriate name and thankfully Beth didn't disagree.

Grace was born in the John Radcliffe Hospital in Oxford on March 3rd, without question the happiest day of my life.

I hold her for hours just listening to her breathe. She is beyond miraculous.

I've never had any interest in babies or other people's children. I don't think I hated kids, I just wasn't interested in them.

That's changed; I'm obsessed with Grace.

I regularly think about what the world will be like when she's an old woman, what her children's lives will be like, and her grandchildren, and her great-grandchildren who I could potentially have met if what I recorded in the book has any truth.

Every day I slip her into the backpack carrier I bought and take her for walks through the village. If there's one thing I've already learned about parenting it's all about routine. Grace loves her routine.

As we walk I think about the way I described Kingham, or the complete lack of Kingham in Gardenia, the fact that it probably ends up as a Garden Square in London, or a blasted flatland of bare rocks in the world of the cloud cities.

I want the world to be better for her, not worse. I want to do what I can to bring that about. Sometimes this makes me worry that I'm becoming a bit of a hippy but if that's the case it's a small price to pay.

The other big change is where we live.

We moved house, although we only moved about 50 metres. We sold our little house and bought the barn conversion that our old garden backed onto.

I kept it as a surprise for Beth. I heard it was being sold, made an offer and boom, that's where we live.

I like it, Beth absolutely loves it and we are fairly broke. I managed to cash in some of my pension, I sold my shares in Tempus Engineering, which thankfully raised more than I expected and we have a modest mortgage.

After a long hassle with the Oxfordshire planning authorities we were allowed to install solar panels on racks in the garden. Because the building is listed we couldn't put them on the roof but they are quite discreet, tucked away from neighbours unless you are actually in the garden.

Beth changed jobs, which came out of the blue for me but she told me she'd been thinking about it for a long time.

She left Kingham School and started teaching at a comprehensive in Bourton-on-the-Water. She tells me she loves it but it sounds like a tough job to me.

Along with this change of career has been a change in our Sundays. Beth no longer goes to church. I have to say it always struck me as a bit odd that she went because she never mentioned anything religious on a day-to-day basis. It turns out it was expected of all the staff at the private school she used to teach at.

We now go for walks on Sunday and I cook dinner. I love cooking. I've even started a vegetable patch in the garden. All

Beth does is stare at me dumbfounded as she watches me weed around my very orderly rows of carrots.

As for my so-called career, I've effectively taken a year off since the cloud incident. I've done quite a bit of work on the house; apart from the solar panels it's been mainly insulation in the barn and replacing the windows. Triple glazed and super-tight seals. I love our windows.

I am going to start work again soon, consultancy work for large-scale wind and solar energy companies. It will involve a bit of travel but nothing like I was doing before.

I can't say if my change of direction is as a result of reading my own book and contemplating what it's clearly telling me, or if the events really did happen and that's what changed my outlook.

And the Yuneec has been an endless worry.

I haven't flown it since I got back from the cloud.

For a few weeks after the cloud day, I spent weekends with Ed taking it to pieces. Some of the fittings on it were baffling. I eventually had to go to a toolmaker in Milton Keynes and hand-make a tool to undo some of the holding bolts on the motor mounts.

Ed is really the only person who knows anything about my adventure and so far he's been very discreet. He's also let me store some of the Yuneec components in his barn.

When Ed and I investigated the motor one night we were both a bit frightened by it. It's essentially a doughnut-shaped alloy casing full of a peculiar mauve liquid. There are no obvious magnets or commutators, no solid axles or gear systems.

It's just a pot of liquid. There are no power inlets or outlets and yet we know from seeing it in action this small device has incredible power.

We also removed what I can only assume was a battery pack, although again this turned out to be a small, pillow-sized container full of a yellow viscous liquid.

I have kept a small sample of each liquid in two jam jars and one day, maybe in a few years' time, I'll take them to a materials science professor I know who teaches at Imperial College London.

I'd love to know what it's made of. The only thing holding me back is that I don't want to be asked where it came from. I simply don't know.

Grace is going to wake up soon, and I've got to get the lasagne I made out of the oven ready for when Beth gets home.

Subscribers

Dear Reader,

The book you are holding came about in a rather different way to most others. It was funded directly by readers through a new website: **Unbound**.

Unbound is the creation of three writers. We started the company because we believed there had to be a better deal for both writers and readers. On the Unbound website, authors share the ideas for the books they want to write directly with readers. If enough of you support the book by pledging for it in advance, we produce a beautifully bound special subscribers' edition and distribute a regular edition and e-book wherever books are sold, in shops and online.

This new way of publishing is actually a very old idea (Samuel Johnson funded his dictionary this way). We're just using the internet to build each writer a network of patrons. Here, at the back of this book, you'll find the names of all the people who made it happen.

Publishing in this way means readers are no longer just passive consumers of the books they buy, and authors are free to write the books they really want. They get a much fairer return too – half the profits their books generate, rather than a tiny percentage of the cover price.

If you're not yet a subscriber, we hope that you'll want to join our publishing revolution and have your name listed in one of our books in the future. To get you started, here is a £5 discount on your first pledge. Just visit unbound.com, make your pledge and type **newsfrom8** in the promo code box when you check out.

Thank you for your support,

Dan, Justin and John
Founders, Unbound

Jay Abbott
John Abraham
Geoff Adams
Mark Adamson
Eric Aitala
Ellis Alden
Fran Anderson
Tyler Anderson
Steve Angell
Brian Appel
Paul Arman
Helen Armfield
Marc Armsby
Fred Armstrong
Simon Arthur
Darren Ashby
Stuart Ashen
Kathryn Ashworth
Hassan Aslam
Michael Atkins
Nick Baber
Kevin Bachus
Thomas Baekdal
Karen Baines
Rob Baird
Ken Baker
John Baldwin
Mark Baldwin
Graham & Caroline Ball
Arthur Banks
David Barfoot
Stuart Barkworth
Tom Barnard
Simon Barry
Michelle Bartholomew
Dan Bayliss
Andrew Beale
Matthew Beale
Neil Beasley
Gerald Beattie
Pete Beck
Warren Beckett
Lucy Bedding, Alan Brooks & Pam Brooks-Bedding
Phil Beddoe
John Beisley
Adrian Belcher
Steve Bell
Jo Bellamy
Amanda Benson
Calum Benson
Andy Bentley
Shawna Bergen
Ben Best
Allison Betts
Tim Biller
Keary Birch
Alistair Bisatt
Wendi Blair

Philip Blom
Nathan Bloomfield
Christof Bojanowski
Bill Bonwitt
Becki Boot
Duncan Booth
Phil, Nat, Sarah & Katie Boot
David Boston
Karl Bovenizer
Doug Bowers
Noah, Nicci & Simon Bradley
Paul Bradbury
Roger Braithwaite
Christian Bray
Robin Bray
Jon Brazelton
Vicky Breading
Jon Breen
Greig Brierley
Daniel Brook
Scott, Sophie & Finlay Brown
PJ Bryant
Robert Bryden
Paul Bucknell
Geoff Bullock
Mark Bulpitt
Matthew Bunce
Daniel Burne
Ali & Tony Burns
Jason Burrows
Chris Busby
Marcus Butcher
Jason Butterworth
Clare Cambridge
David Callander
Paul Carlyle
Susan Casey
Tony Castley
Fay Capstick
Alexis Carpenter
Barry Carpenter
Stacey Cassie
Dominic Cave
Chris Chadwick
Rohan Chadwick
Rick Challener
David Callier
Darren Chandler
Martin Chapman
Phil Chapman
Michael Chapple
Benjamin Chiad
John-F. Chmiel
Neil Christie
Paul Churchley
Meagan Cihlar
Ross Clark
Garrett Coakley
Mark Cockshoot
Nicholas Cohn
Sean Colbath
Daniel Cole
Stevyn Colgan
Timothy Collinson
Melusine Colwell
Michael Comerford
Dave 'sircompo' Compton
Brian Condron
Neil Cooper
Ryan Conway
Andrew Corney
Paul Crouch
Lewis Curley
David Dallamore
Richard & Jane Dallaway
Peter Dalling
Lisa Dalton
Mark Daly
Gerald Daniels
Josephine Daniels
Mick Dann
Ian Davenport
Dave 'dod' Davies
Colin Davis
Ian Davis
Adrian Davison
Jonathan Davison
Alex Daw
Tony Dawber
Darren Dawson
Matt Dean
Ryan Dehmer
Laura Delderfield
Andy Devanney
Si Dew
Miranda Dickinson
John P van Dieken
Thijs van Dijk

David Kinzett
Keith Douglas
Roger Downing
Lawrence T. Doyle
Simon Drinkwater
Will Dron
Jonathan Dubrule
Christopher Dudman
Keith Dunbar
Roger Dunce
Justin Dykes
Cariad Eccleston
Terence & Elizabeth Eden
Gordon Edwards
Roger Edwards
Christophe Egret
Thor-Dale Elsson
Chris Emerson
Charlotte Endersby
Jamas Enright
Derek Erb
Charlotte Evans
Bill Evetts
Per Fagrell
Di Farence
Laura Franks
Alan Freeman
John Frewin
Rafael Fritz
Anthony Froissant
Glynn Field
Paul Fisher
Anna Eve Figueroa
Bård Fjukstad
Sharon Forman
Paul Forster
James Fowkes
Ian Frank
Stephen Frost
Graeme Fullerton
James Fursse
Ina Gallo
Gareth Gamble
James Gander
Simon Garland
Chris Garnham
Gordon Garb
Saman Gerami
Stuart Gilbert
Ben Gillam
Melanie Groom
Kevin Groombridge
Paul Gregory
James Godfrey
Paul Golder
Nikki Gordon-Bloomfield
Michael Gough
Jean Graham
Neil Graham
Ian Grey
Arthur Green
Mike Griffiths
Stuart Gunn
Simon Hackett
Lance Haig
Rachel Hales
Thomas Haley
Andy Hall
Chris Hallam
Alex Hansford
Pete Harbord
Neill Harper
Peter Harrigan
Paul Harris
Susan Harris
Vron Harris
Bryan Harrison
Joy Harrison
Kris James Harrison
Richard Harrison
Stacy Harrison
A. F. Harrold
Dave Hawkins
Darren Hawkshaw
Christopher Haywood
Jeff Hazel
Elizabeth Henwood
Stuart, Katherine & Isabelle Higgins
Adam Hinton
Karen Holtorp
Mark Honeyborne
Chris Hopkins
Christine Hopkins
Rod Howitt
Matthew Hudson
Brian Hughes
Jack Hughes
Owen Hughes
William Hughes

Jordan A. Hulme
Gary Hummerston
Luci Humphreys
Andrew Hunter
Neil Hunter
Ian and Tracy
Deb Ikin
imsradio.net
Martyn Ingram
Tom Ingram
Richard Isherwood
Lee Israel
Glyn Jackson
Steve Jalim
Fiona James
Paul James
Risto Järvinen
Trish Johns
Adam Johnson
Dan Johnson
Dean Johnson
Ian Johnson
Erin Jones
Heather Jones
Jessica Jones
Matthew Jones
Peter Jones
Simon Jones
Stephen Jones
Steve Jones
Ola Jonsson
Richard Judd
Jasmine Kaul
Andrew Kavanagh
Martin Kelly
Tom Kelsall
Scott Kennedy
Hilary Kemp
John Kent
Mark Keogan
Phil Kernick
Alex Kerridge
Philip Kerridge
M Keys
Matthew Kidd
Andy Kiernan
Dan Kieran
Brian Klosterman
Emily Joanne Kneeshaw
Jon Knight
Peter Knight
Alexis Kokolski
Karim Kronfli
Thomas Kyvik
Chris Lamyman
Stephen Landry
Tony Larks
Mats Larsen
Zoe Laughlin
Paul Richard Lauff
@lauracowen
Jennifer Lawson
Gareth Layzell
Jimmy Leach
Kate Leask
Andy Lewis
Ian Lewis
Monika Lewis
Wendy Lewis
John Lindsay
Mark Lis
Sharon Lloyd
John & Christine Lomax
Andre Louis
David A Luckhurst
Russ Levett
John A Lynam
Daniel Lynch
Alistair Mackie
Terry Mackown
Matthew Mouse
Maclellan
John Macmenemey
Simon Macneall
Cait MacPhee
Ewan Mac Mahon
Kerry Maidment-Grocke
Kevin Mahy
Alice Maltby
Sarah Markall
Charlie Marriott
Gary Marriott
Brian Marshall
Karen Marshall
Mandy Marshall
Mike Mason
Karen Masson
Tim Martin
Gordon McCague
Rod McDonald
Beth McGeachy-Blay
Nick McGill

Dustin McGivern
Paul McHugh
Ben McKenzie
Nicola McKissick
Bernard McLaughlin
Iain McSpuddles
Ian McWilliam
Neil Melville-Kenney
Tamsin Middleton
Miggi
Daryl Millar
Nick Milligan
Richard & Tracy Mills
Laurie Mistretta
Michael Mitchell
Scott Mitchell
John Mitchinson
Deena Mobbs
Danny Molyneux
Kian Momtahan
Jim Mooney
David Morgan
David Morton
David Moss
Chris Mountain
Paul Mullett
Craig Naples
Chris Neale
Kerry Neale
Jaime Nelson
John New
Simon Newson
John Nichol
Al Nicholson
Colin Nicholson
Chris Nicolson
Martin Nooteboom
Bethany, Grace & Morgan Norcutt
Paul (from the dwarf) Oakley
Adrian Oates
Stuart O'Connor
Erwin Oosterhoorn
Tyler Opsal
Amy O'Reilly
Benjamin Osaka
Stuart Owen
Lawrence Owens
Louise Paddock
John Page
Sal Page
Michael Palmer
Ernest Panychevskyy
Yianni Papas
Lesley Parker
Kevin Parker
Richard Parker
Mark Parkinson
David Parry
Kevin Pascoe
James Craig Paterson
Aaron Patterson
Terra Patton
Andrew Paul
Shaun Payne
Dave Pearson
Bella Pender
Kev Penny
Clifford Perry
Dan Peters
Mark Phelan
Chris (furrie) Phillips
Laurie Phillips
Eric Phillipson
Steve Pike
Mark Pitcher
Brian Pitkethley
Mike Pooler
Justin Pollard
Edward Pollitt
Darren Powell
David Powell
Chris Price
Christopher Pridham
Adam Priestley
Lawrence Pretty
James Pritchard
Donald Proud
Fiona Pugh
Andrew Pullan
Adam J Purcell
Huan Quayle
Dawn Raison
Mark Randall
Hans Rasmussen
Stuart Rawlings
Colette Reap
Simon Reap
Nichola Redworth
Julia Rees
Ian Reeves

James Reid
Craig Reilly
Paul Renold
Claire Reynolds
Andy Rice
Christopher Richardson
Jamie Richardson
@RickMGoldie
Andrew Riddell
Ewen Roberts
Ian Roberts
Andrew Robinson
Andy Robinson
Stevie Robinson
Paul Robinson-Farenden
Anne Rock
Kenn W. Roessler
Gareth Rogers
John-Paul Rogers
Chloe Rowley-Morris
Allan P. Russell
Alan Rust
Petre Rodan
Mike Roest
Charles Ross
Craig Ross
Darren Ross
Lynn Rowlands
Claire Rudkins
David Rutt
Jamie De Rycke
Paul Sadler
Lynne Salisbury
Tim Saltmarsh
Adrian Samm
Christoph Sander
Darren Sant
Jonathan Sartin
Steven Saunderson
Neil Sayer
Carol Sayles
Hugh Scantlebury
Donna Scattini
Claire Scott
Tony Scott
David Seeley
Pat 'Samhain' Seery & Kerrie 'Caflas' Gray
Chris Senior & Lem
Jonathan Sharpe
Sue Sharpe
Jo Sharples
Tony Sheehan
Darran Shepherd
Karl Sherratt
Jennifer Shipp
Andrew Shugg
Jon Shute
Sam Sibbert
Darren Sillett
Andy Sillwood
Alexander Sims
James Sinclair
Vicki Sivess
Keith Sleight
Lauren & James Smith
Mathew Smith
Trevor Smith
Nat Snell
Nicholas Soucek
Mark Sourbutts
Chris Spath
Ben Spencer
Rich Spencer
Mat Stace
Caroline Stammers
Andy Stanford-Clark
Richard Stephens
Adrian Stewart
Alex Stewart
Peter Strapp
Mark Sundaram
Charlie Styr
Lindsay Swann
Trina Talma
Andrew Taylor
Andrew Taylor
Greg Fenby Taylor
John Taylor & Wayne Woodward
Mark Taylor
Miles Taylor
Mark Taylor-Hankins
Chris & Michelle Thomas
Jo Thomas
Lynda Thomas
Rebecca Thomas
Maddox David Thomas
Mark Thomas
Andrew Thompson
Scott Thomson
Stephen Tilley

Catherine Tily
Barry Tipper
James Tombs
Paul Tompsett
Craig Tonks
Julia Tratt
Ole Traumüller
David Tubby
Martyn Tupper
Twisty
Pete Tyler
Unascertained Unacertained
Mark Vent
P Verbinnen
Kathy Vickers
Robert Vincent
Chris Wade
Steve Wadsworth
Jody Walker
Nathan Walker
Steve Walker
Stewart Walker
Antony Wallace
Nick Walpole
Katherine Walton-Elliott
Rachel Ward
Paul Warren
Emma Watkins
David Watt
James Watts
Matt Webb
Naomi Webb
Glenn Wehmeyer
Tom West
Alan White
Matt White
Matthew Whittaker
Carol Whitton
Jason Wickham
Rob Widdowson
Hank van der Wijngaart
Tom Wilkinson
Craig Williams
Andy Willy
Matt Wilmshurst
Donna Wilshere
Martin Wink
Graham Wise
Carl Withers
W Mark Witherspoon, Dr. Les Witherspoon ND, Aryeh, Amber, Chaya, Yitzi, Eli
Ian Wolf
Chris Wood
Kevin Wood
Rupert Wood
Alan Wright
Colin & Rachel Wright
John Wright
John R Wright
Simon Wright
Tim Wright
Paul Wyatt
Ian Yates
Kym Yeap

A note about the type

THE BODY TEXT OF THIS BOOK IS SET IN LTC Cloister, designed by Morris Fuller Benton (1872–1948). Benton was chief designer at the American Type Foundry from 1900–1937 and was America's most prolific modern type designer, responsible for Century Schoolbook, Franklin Gothic and the revivals of Bodoni and Garamond. Cloister is a roman face based on the work of the fifteenth-century French engraver and type designer Nicholas Jenson (1420–1480), who was based in Venice and had been a pupil of Gutenberg. Jenson is credited as the inventor of roman type. Previously, books had been set in the gothic 'blackletter' style. Jenson's elegant type was much admired by William Morris (1834–1896), the founder of the arts and crafts movement. Chapter headings are set in Morris Troy, an adaptation of William Morris's semi-Gothic Troy type designed for use in his Kelmscott Press books. The Kelmscott Press's great project was the production of a hand-printed edition of Chaucer's *Canterbury Tales*, which contained 87 illustrations by Edward Burne-Jones. A masterpiece of book design, it is the embodiment of Morris's theory that work should be collaborative and the results both beautiful and useful. Burne-Jones called it 'a pocket cathedral'. The ornamented initial letters are also adapted from Morris's designs for his Kelmscott Press editions.